Multiples of Six

By Andy Rane

www.andyrane.com

Acknowledgments

Behind every writer is a group of people who have helped, coaxed, poked, prodded, redirected, and motivated them along the road toward completion. This book is dedicated to the folks in my life who have been there for me in one way or another: my wife, Kelly, for letting me escape to write; my mother, Kathleen, for encouraging me to follow my talent and instilling in me the understanding that everything happens for a reason; my buddies, Joe, Matt, and Brian, for their regular inquiry of "Finish that novel yet?"; and finally, my father, David, for teaching me the difference between wrong, right, and just plain bullshit.

The following people were instrumental as readers, commenters, and editors: Laura Klein, Laurene Graham, Mollie Friedman, Jo-Ann West, Glenn Wieland, Carolyn Nicholas, Craig Nicholas, and Kelly Mulraney. Your help and input brought this story to a whole new level. Thank you.

Chapter 1

Agnes Richardson knew as soon as she saw the curtain out of place that she wasn't alone. Years of living in fear had attuned her to the slightest details of her house. She knew where everything was supposed to be. She didn't have animals because she knew the constant variables they would present. That was why she knew that her curtain had not been ruffled before she left for the store. She hated that she knew that. She hated that she had lived in a silent fear for twenty-four years. And, a part of her was actually happy to finally see something amiss. It would be a release. She was finally going to pay the price for taking part. She spoke out loud.

"You don't have to hide. I'd prefer to see you."

The response came from her bedroom.

"Agnes Richardson?"

The voice was a man's.

"Why ask when you know the answer?"

"I wanted to see if you'd lie."

"Why bother. I'm dead either way," she said, then added "Right?" She heard him chuckle.

"There it is. That faint hope beyond hope. You know you're dead, and yet you cling to that last thread. That chance that somehow I'll change my mind, or that maybe fate has had a last minute change of heart. Hope all you want, Agnes. See what good it does."

The voice was closer, but she still could not see the speaker. She assumed that he could see her clearly.

1

"Hope is all I've had over the years."

"Oh…boo…hoo. It's too late to shed tears about the past now, Agnes. Too fucking late! All you've had. Good God, woman. By the looks of it, you've had it pretty damn easy over the years."

The man walked out of her bedroom as he said this and she dropped the bag of groceries she had been holding. He walked right up to her, the gun held loosely in his hand. Everything about him told her she was looking at an elderly person. A lanky, almost gaunt man, he wore something she expected to see in a Florida retirement community; a straw fedora with a red plaid band sat atop a crop of thinning white hair. He wore a collared white shirt and white slacks that didn't quite reach his ankles. The tight white socks only helped to emphasize the white boat shoes he wore. All this was topped off with a lightweight cherry red sport coat. The only things that defied his age were his bouncy step and something about his eyes. The insanity was clear, even through the strong prescription glasses and the apparent beginnings of a cataract in his left eye. He stood before her, slightly hunched, staring into her eyes. Then he smiled, a crooked-mouthed, toothy smile with what appeared to be perfect false teeth. Her mouth dropped open.

"Oh, yes. See…that's the kind of response I was looking for. Yes…let it sink in, Agnes. Because, you do recognize me now, don't you?"

Agnes could do nothing but raise a trembling hand to her mouth and nod slowly. His voice rose in a crescendo as he spoke.

"Do you see this? Do you see this mockery of a man before you? Do you see what your precious doctors created, Agnes? I've had arthritis since I was six. My teeth started falling out the first time at 8 months, the second time at thirteen years. Thirteen years old and wearing dentures! My hair turned white by the time I was sixteen. Not exactly a big turn on for the girls, let me tell you."

He wiped away the spittle that had trickled out over his bottom lip.

"I..."

"You couldn't possibly have anything to say about this, Agnes, so save your breath. Do you see what you helped to create? Do you see the precious life you helped to create? Have you enjoyed your life? It doesn't look half bad. Judging by the extra pounds, life has been ok for the last twenty-four years. Me, not so much. And, after all these years, it's time someone paid for what was done. Someone's idea of a science project created me, molded me into what I am today...and now the Frankenstein is loose! Bring on the torches and pitchforks! But, the townsfolk won't arrive in time for you, Agnes. No...I'm afraid they won't arrive in time to rescue you. But don't worry...you won't have died in vain. You'll be the shot they all hear. And, when they run...I'll be there."

Agnes bowed her head and sobbed lightly.

3

"Look at me, Agnes."

She shook her head. He grabbed her chin and forced it up with alarming ease.

"Look at me! Look at me and know that your life…your simple, everyday life has been a lie. Do you have a god, Agnes? Agnes? Stay with me here. Do… you… have… a…god?"

She nodded.

"Did you ever ask your god for forgiveness? Did you ever cry out in the middle of the night, hoping to your god that your actions were for the best? Well, there's that hope word again. Maybe you didn't pray hard enough. Oh, wait, yeah, I know you didn't pray hard enough. Or, maybe I wouldn't be standing here right now."

"I had a family to take care of."

He struck out at her with the gun, knocking her to the ground. He raged over her, his eyes rolling madly.

"At any cost? How dare you say something like that? Do you hear how insane that response is? If they had a job flipping the switch at a puppy burning mill, would you have taken that instead? Good God, woman!"

"I didn't know…that…this…I didn't know you…"

"Oh, save it, Agnes! It's too late to play the innocent card. It's not worth anything," he said. He stepped back from her, straightened up, adjusted his collar, tidied his jacket and continued in a calm voice.

"Besides, I'm not the jury. I wouldn't be here if you were innocent. You wouldn't have run away and adopted a new name if you were innocent. You knew what they were doing. You read the reports that came across the good doctor's desk. You signed every goddamn one of them. But, I digress."

The man relaxed and stood before her, the gun hanging limply in his hand at his side. He was breathing heavily, as if the exertion of shouting had tapped his reserves more than he'd expected.

"If it's worth anything to you...I'm sorry. I was too ignorant and afraid to do anything back then," she said looking at him. She looked away and wiped the blood from the corner of her lip.

"It might be the only apology I hear, Agnes, so yes...it is worth something."

He reached into the inside pocket of his jacket and pulled out a metal tube and began fitting it to the end of the gun. She had seen enough movies to know a silencer when she saw it. He wasted no time and she quickly looked out the window at the blue of the Texas sky before it all went black.

Chapter 2

The clock on his mother's dresser said it was 6:37 AM. James Masterson knew better. He knew that the clock had never been set back from daylight savings since the last time his mother had used the room almost two years ago. Now, as it beamed its lie into the darkness of that December morning, it stood as an incorrect anomaly; an incorrect clock in a room where time no longer mattered.

Leaning against the doorway, James glanced around the room. From the time she had been unable to use it, James had entered it little without her permission. He made sure to dust the woodwork per her request on a biweekly basis. He'd retrieved clothes when she requested them. Two weeks ago, she'd asked him to get her the necklace his father had given her on her birthday before he had passed away. It consisted of a small silver feather with a turquoise stone at one end. She died that night in the hospital bed that had been erected in the living room of their house; the cancer finally wearing away the last of her constitution. Even now, as he stood in the doorway, he felt like he was intruding.

After his mother's death, James had been overcome with the guilt of feeling relieved. It had sickened him to the point of exhaustion. But his girlfriend, Nicole, insisted that it was all part of the process of grieving. It was natural to feel relief. He had taken on a lot of responsibility at the age of twenty-two and there was nothing wrong with the way he was feeling now.

James made his way down the hall and peered in at her still form in his bed. She had only stayed with him these last two nights. Although she hadn't said it, he got the feeling that she didn't want him to feel like she was pressuring him to move in. And though that was exactly what he wanted her to do, he just couldn't bring himself to admit that he loved having her there. Knowing she was there made the silence of the house more tolerable. But, strangely, her words of reassurance had done little to comfort him. And, though he was able to fall asleep better at night, he still found himself staring at the ceiling by two or three in the morning, his mind racing and his body unable to relax back into unconsciousness, despite his exhaustion.

Nicole had suggested anti-anxiety pills. Something to take the edge off; let him sleep through the night. James wasn't a fan of drugs he didn't absolutely need. He'd seen enough of what the drugs had done to his mother...and they were meant to cure her. But, Nicole knew all about *head cases* like him. She worked with them every day. Wanted to work with them for the rest of her life and put that psych degree to good use. James often told her that she only stuck with him because he'd make a good test subject someday. She invariably shrugged and said, "That's not the *only* reason," then laughed and kissed him.

He made his way down the stairs, glancing at the photos adorning the wall: his father and mother smiling in the peak of health, thankfully oblivious of any future pain; little James on his father's shoulders in the back yard, mere feet from where the man would someday collapse and die from a massive heart attack at the age of fifty-two, two weeks after James' high school graduation.

He walked to the kitchen and mechanically prepared a cup of tea, not really even knowing if he really wanted one. James found himself standing with a spoonful of sugar hovering over the cup, unable to remember if he had already added it to the tea or not. He glanced into the cup, sloshing the hot liquid around, then decided to err on the side of caution and dumped it in; too sweet, he could handle.

As an only child, adopted shortly after he was born, James could hardly remember a time that didn't include at least one of them. Now that they were gone, he wondered if the house would ever feel complete again.

Uncle Ted, his father's brother, was the only "blood" relation left. A hulk of a man, he had commanded respect with his sheer presence. Ted had spent a few days with James after the funeral to make sure everything was in order. The will had been straightforward; James got everything. Ted hugged him the day he left. It was quick and left James feeling more lonely than ever. "Take care, boyo," he had said, then left without looking back. "Call if you need something. Otherwise, I'll give you a call at Christmas."

James found himself at the bottom of the stairs looking up into the darkness, cup of tea in hand. He wanted to go up and crawl back into bed with Nicole, but a feeling of guilt held him in place. He ran his hand along the wood at the end of the worn handrail. It was worn. He could remember thinking, as a teenager, that someone should replace it, or refinish it. Now he was that someone. No one else would replace it; it was his alone.

He made his way back into the kitchen. The back door window was coated in a thin layer of frost. The warped wood groaned and the hinges sounded ancient as he pulled it open. He pushed at the storm door and stepped out onto the porch. The air was crisp, and there was little to disturb the peace. He watched his breath float out into the morning. The light from the coming sun was chasing the stars away and just starting to tint the sky a pale blue in the East. He leaned back into the door and turned out the kitchen light, allowing his eyes adjust to the darkness.

There had been many a winter day when James would wake up, come downstairs and find one or both of his parents on the back porch, sipping tea and talking, or just taking in some morning air. He would join them, but only briefly before being shooed back into the warmth of the house. Even now, he fought the urge to return to the warmth of the kitchen. This morning, the cold felt good, even cleansing. He needed that.

He was just able to make out a squirrel darting out from under the oak and running across the back yard to the maple when three things seemed to happen at once. Someone spoke over his left shoulder, something cold and metallic was pressed against his left temple, and he was fairly certain his heart skipped a beat.

"I…" James began.

"Shut up, just shut up, and keep your hands on the railing where I can see them," came a man's nervous voice from next to him.

He emphasized each word with a push of whatever it was against his temple. It had to be a gun, James thought. He thought he could see a metal shaft in what little light there was.

"James Masterson?" The man said.

"Yes," James said.

"James Devon Masterson?"

"Yes," he said.

"Jeee…sus. Jesus Christ. He didn't say…you…this if fucked up. Fucked up!" He had been whispering, up until the last two words. The words carried through the back yard. Not that anyone would hear. The neighbors were too far away to notice, and the lot backed to woods.

So, this was it, James thought. He would die on his back porch. At his home…where his parents had died. His mother in her rented hospital bed. His father in the garden, clutching his chest on that sweltering August day. He would leave Nicole as his parents had left him. Except James would die having done nothing more in life than existed. He had graduated high school and college in unspectacular fashion. He'd managed to get a job that he had kept for two years. He was vanilla. He had simply been. His grave marker could read "James Masterson was." He managed to chuckle at this thought.

"I've got a…gun…to your head and you're laughing?"

"Are you going to kill me?"

"I might ask you the same thing," the man said, and James might have heard a hint of doubt had he not been focusing so hard on the barrel pressed against his head.

"I don't get it," James said.

"Neither do I," the man said. "You…shouldn't be here. I mean, he told me that you were here, but not this you…I mean, not a you that *looks* like you. You shouldn't…can't…exist." The metal scraped his temple and James flinched.

"I don't understand what you mean," James said, then added, "Any chance I could get you to remove the gun from my head?"

"Can't. You might turn around and eat me or something, man. You're like my worst nightmare."

"Are you high?"

"No, man. No way. You're real."

"Are you sure? Maybe you should just walk away. Maybe if you kill me, it'll turn out to be your mom or something."

"Fuck you, dude. You got a lot of balls sayin' shit like that with a gun to your head."

"What do I have to lose?" The hand steadied and resumed its pressure against his temple.

"What's your birthday?" the man said.

"What is this…?"

"Just answer the question, dude," the man said and poked James' temple with the gun.

"September eleventh, nineteen eighty-two."

"You're lying. You're fuckin' lying!"

"Friend, why would I lie, and what the hell does that...?"

"Shut up. Just shut up...I gotta think about this," he said and pulled the gun away from James head. The sinking feeling in his chest subsided a little. James kept his head forward but could see that the man was gazing at him, peering around him like James was some sort of oddity. True dawn was still hours away and what little light there was, was coming up on the wrong side of the house. The best he could judge was that the man was about his height with a cap on and smelled a bit like a wet dog. He shivered.

"Are you alone?" the man asked.

"No."

"Who?"

"My girl is upstairs, sleeping."

"Why didn't you lie?"

"What good would that do me now? Besides, you would have killed me if that's what you came to do."

"I still could."

"I know," James said, and his head turned ever so slightly.

"Don't! Not yet...don't turn yet."

"Ok, I won't!" James said, waving his hands.

"Tell me your name again. I need to hear you say it."

"My name is James Devon Masterson."

13

"And, you're twenty-four years old."

"And, I'm twenty-four years old."

"And, you were born on February eleventh, nineteen eighty-two."

"And, I was born on February twelfth, nineteen eighty-two."

"Now listen to me and try for a moment to understand why I feel the need to keep this gun on you."

"Ok."

"My name is Kevin Powers and I was sent here by a man…a doctor who told me I would find…someone. A member of my family. I'm twenty-four years old as well and born in February of eighty-two. Now turn around."

James turned around and looked into the darkness that was the face shadowed beneath the cap. The man was his height, maybe a few pounds less, with a familiar roll to his shoulders. His eyes adjusted and it was like looking in a funhouse mirror. There was his nose, his high cheekbones, the narrow chin, thin lips, only this face was covered in a thin mustache and goatee. He held a short metal tube in his hand, tucking it into his jacket apologetically. The man removed his cap, and James' head swam. The sinking feeling shot through his stomach to his knees and he reached for the porch railing. Kevin leaned forward and grabbed his shoulder, squeezing it a little, as if to make sure that James was real.

"You see why I freaked out a bit? I came looking for a family member, maybe a long lost cousin. But…not you…not this…not like this."

"I…you…" James managed.

"Exactly," Kevin said, "Fucked up."

"Why the gun trick," James said, pointing to where Kevin had tucked away the tube.

"Oh…yeah…my bad…"

"My bad?" James asked.

"I--," Kevin began.

The storm door flew open and, before either one of them could react, a jumble-haired brunette had swung the biggest caste iron frying pan Kevin had ever seen at his head. He didn't react in time and the blow landed with a resounding "Gong!" square on his right temple. Kevin crumpled to the porch floor in a heap.

"Nicole! No!" James shouted too late.

"He had a gun! I heard you two talking. He said he could kill you."

"It wasn't a gun…he was lying!"

"I…oh, James…"

"Jesus, Nic…"

"Oh my God…did I kill him?"

"I hope not. I think he's my brother."

Chapter 3

The hotel room was cramped, but he'd lived in worse. For twenty-four years he had moved from room to room, never staying in one spot for more than two months at a time. The coat he wore was the same one he bought new in the winter of '83. It had been tan at the time; it was now a mottled gray. It was never far from him and most nights he slept with it on, just in case. If his old pair of shoes hadn't actually fallen off of his feet at one point, he might still be wearing those too. Instead, he'd been humiliated into diving into one of those clothing drop-offs in a desperate attempt at finding his size. His first attempt landed him a pair of Nike high tops, which looked just slightly ridiculous on a man wearing slacks, a sport coat, and a trench. It had garnered him a few wary looks from mothers with small children. But, after twenty-four years on the run, he'd gotten over his humiliations. After twenty-four years, Dr. Fred Taylor was too tired to care. He was done with the running. That was why he had sent his letters. That was why he threatened to do what he was doing. And, that was why they would probably kill him. He just didn't really care anymore.

He watched the screen of his laptop; the one luxury he had allowed himself over the years. Even that was looking tired now. The five-year-old computer had been trucked in and out of cars and hotel rooms in all kinds of weather. It had been left on for days at a time in his futile attempt at keeping an eye on his enemy. As if they might signal him via an ad on the internet or an email letting him know they were on their way. He understood his own potential for insanity, but the glowing screen was the only thing that brought him any comfort. He hated it and loved it all at once. He wouldn't know what to do without it. He had set up a simple program to search for certain terms every five minutes. He had developed a filter that provided him with only the most likely of hits so if James Masterson or Robert Paynter appeared anywhere, it would show him right away. It was the same for the other names on the list. That was why he flinched when the hit suddenly popped on the screen. He clicked on the link.

Police had found a woman in her fifties, Agnes Richardson, dead in her home. There were no immediate signs of forced entry, but the death had been ruled a homicide because of "her manner of death." Investigators were able to identify footprints that possibly belonged to the killer, but even canine units lost the trail. They were looking for anyone with information to come forward. Taylor knew there would be no one. They didn't mess around. The coroner had determined the time of death to be 2:33 PM on Friday, December 15, 2006. Taylor looked at the clock in the corner of the screen. It was Saturday, December 16th and the time was 8:32 PM. That meant the killer had over 29 hours on Taylor. If he was next, it might already be too late. Texas wasn't that far off for a determined individual.

He leaned back in his chair. The sound of the wood creaking made him turn quickly. He tried to shake off the fear that had squeezed his insides tight. He pressed the wire-frame

18

glasses back up to the bridge of his nose and eyed the window. He had unlocked it upon coming in. It would remain that way in case he had to make a quick exit. The second floor window looked out onto a patch of bushes below. At best, he would walk away bruised. At worst, he would break his hip and have a heart attack. Then he wouldn't really care if someone killed him. He chuckled in the silence of the room at his own madness. He was mad, but in acknowledging so, he allowed himself a little relief.

How else might someone explain this diminutive man, who sat fully dressed, long coat and all, in front of a laptop computer for most of the waking day? He left for certain meals, skipped others, and made damn sure that his schedule was never the same in a two-week period. He checked the parking lot every ten to twenty-minutes and never from the same spot at the window. He never answered the phone and always paid in cash. He had a dozen IDs he had crafted over the years. He cycled through them at each hotel, motel, boarding house, or hostel. He had several bank accounts, none of which were under his actual name.

Now, he turned off his laptop, folded the screen down, and packed it into the lone bag he carried with him. He wasn't going to run anymore. It was time to pay a visit to a boy he had not seen in twenty-four years. He had no idea what he was going to do, but his hand instinctively found the handle of the .44-caliber revolver in his pocket. He would think of something.

Chapter 4

James and Nicole sat together on the love seat in the living room looking at the man named Kevin as he lay quietly on the sofa. He was lucky to have only been knocked unconscious. Using the training that had been useless in saving his mother, James had checked his vitals and guessed that Kevin would be ok. They had an icepack propped on his head, as the cast iron pan had caused quite the bump.

"He might have a concussion, but I don't think his skull is fractured," James said.

"I can't believe you have a brother," Nicole replied.

"Me neither. It doesn't really make sense."

"An identical twin," she said.

"Yeah," said James.

"I wonder if he has the same screwy birth certificate."

James thought about this. His birth certificate, according to the powers that be, was fraudulent. His mother only told him the story after his father's death. The piece of paper had named a proper hospital and apparently nonexistent doctors. It had no indication of his birth parents. It was a flimsy piece of paper that represented nothing to anyone. No one at Morristown Memorial Hospital could deny the fact that the document appeared to have been produced there. But, no one there had ever heard of a doctor named Robert Paynter.

"He is my twin, isn't he," James wondered aloud.

"Are you kidding? He's you with a goatee, maybe a few pounds less. You look cute with facial hair," she said, cocking her head wistfully at Kevin.

"Facial hair makes me itch," James said folding his arms across his chest.

"He's even got your slouch," she said.

"I don't slouch…," James said, suddenly puffing his chest out and straightening his back, "much."

"Maybe we should try and wake him," Nicole said.

"You're right."

He pulled out the bag he had kept for his mother. The smelling salts were something he had never used until the day she died. He moved quickly to get the thought from his mind. He waved them under Kevin's nose, gingerly at first, then directly under each nostril. The reaction was delayed but intense.

"Get…get that shit…oohhh...get it away…oooahh" Kevin groaned.

"Take it easy. You're ok."

"Who…what the hell…ohh…why does my head…" He felt the ice pack with his fingers. "What the hell is this?"

"Ice."

"Ah…God…damn…why does my head feel like it's about to peel open?"

"That's my fault, I'm afraid," Nicole said, half hiding behind James. She waved at him weakly.

"Who said that?" Nicole stepped out from behind James to look down at Kevin.

"Aluminum bat?" Kevin asked.

"Frying pan,"

"Classic. Was the Acme wooden mallet not available? Spare anvil in the shop?"

"I am so sorry," she said.

"Oh, hey, no problem. I'm sure I've done more damage to my brain than you have."

Kevin sat up slowly on the sofa, clutching the ice pack to his head. His face contorted in pain.

"Why do you have smelling salts? You're not a doctor are you?"

James smiled humorlessly, then cleared his throat.

"My mother was very sick at the end. We had a lot of supplies around the house. Smelling salts were something I kept handy."

"*Was* sick?"

"She passed away a couple weeks ago."

"That really sucks. I'm…I'm sorry for saying. Sorry to hear that."

"She had cervical cancer for two years. None of the treatments worked and she was in a lot of pain. It's ok. She's not in pain anymore."

"She wasn't your…real mom, though, right? Was she? I mean, that would make…"

"No. I…was adopted."

"Good. I mean…well, yeah…good."

"Good?" Nicole asked.

Kevin readjusted his position on the sofa to get a better look at her.

"Well, yeah. See, my mom…my adopted mom left when I was a kid. Just me and my old man for the last twenty years or so. He never treated me wrong or anything, but we have our differences and it'd be a little shitty to find out that my real mom was just around the corner. Do you read that? Make sense?"

"I didn't mean anything by it," she said.

"No, I know you didn't, killer. But, this opens up a whole new can of worms. Yesterday, I was just a kid who got adopted by some people who didn't love one another. Today, I find out that maybe I just got the short end of the stick. I spent a lot of time blaming myself for the way things were. Eventually, you get beyond yourself and start looking for someone else to blame. You figure it couldn't just be your fault. Now I really know it wasn't my fault. Maybe just my environment. By the looks of it, this was a pretty comfy environment. Mom and Dad that loved one another and their little guy. I wonder how I didn't land here. Bad call on the coin toss I guess."

"You didn't have to watch your parents die, though," James said blank faced.

"Mmmm…yeah…I don't know. I might have traded that for some solid family years. Tough call. Too late to play the what-if game though. I'm sorry…I didn't mean to accuse you of anything…just makes you think. Y'know?"

"Yeah…yeah it does," James said.

"You grew up around here?" Nicole asked.

"South Jersey. Deptford."

"Think I've heard of it," James said.

Kevin sat forward, still clutching the icepack to his head. He groaned low and slow as he reached the full sitting position. He kept his eyes closed for a while.

"Got any aspirin…codeine?"

"No pain killers," James said.

"What? No, you don't have any?"

"No, you can't have any."

"Explain that one to me."

"You need to be able to feel what's going on. Gotta make sure there's no hemorrhaging, so nothing that'll thin your blood…at least for now. Maybe some Tylenol, but that's it. Here, look at me for a second."

James approached and gently leaned Kevin's head back, lifting the lid of his right eye. It was bizarre to be holding what amounted to his own face in his hands. He pulled out a little flashlight.

"For a non-doctor, you sure know a lot of shit….or else you're faking it well. What's with the light?"

"Just look at my finger."

James flashed the light into his eyes.

"Don't blink!"

"What the…"

James watched as the pupils failed to dilate properly for the light.

"You've definitely got a concussion…no surprise there. You may have headaches for the next couple of days. Dizziness. Nausea. You shouldn't drive."

"No car, so that shouldn't be a worry. Thanks, doc," Kevin said.

"I took classes in first aid as soon as my mom was diagnosed. I wanted to know as much as I could in case…I don't know…I just didn't want to be the one…responsible…for her death."

"Dude, no offense, but she had cancer," Kevin said.

"I know. It sounds stupid, but I wanted to make sure that… it wasn't me. That it wasn't something like a staph infection from a paper cut or choking on a grape or…I don't know…something stupid like that. I just couldn't have dealt with having anything to do with her death. So I learned how to take care of her as best I could."

"What about your dad?"

"He died…over six years ago now. Heart attack. Right in the back yard. I was at the beach with some friends."

"Jesus, James. We're a pair, huh?"

It was the first time James had seen anything resembling a smile on Kevin's face. It was half a smile at best. He stood slowly with James close by.

"Dude, it's ok. I'm not going to fall over," Kevin said.

"So you say," James said.

"As long as she doesn't plan on whacking me with that frying pan again, I should be fine."

Nicole backed out of the room, excusing herself to make coffee.

"How long was I out?" Kevin asked.

He walked around the small living room. There was a TV in a large wooden entertainment center that dominated the corner nearest the only window in the room. Multi-photo picture frames adorned every wall. He examined one closely. There were three pictures; each was of James as a little boy. In one, he was sitting in a canoe with an oar that dwarfed him, a life-jacket that swallowed him, and a New York Mets cap that covered his ears. A tan, well-built, shirtless man at the rear of the boat was splashing water with his oar. The next picture was of James and the same man, this time accompanied by a woman. They were at the Grand Canyon, all squinting at the sun and the unseen photographer. The third picture was of James with a hulk of a man who made smiling look like a serious event. The only thing that took away from this imposing figure was the shorts and sandals he wore. He towered over James and rested a firm hand on his shoulder. James was trying to stand as tall and proud as the man, but the crooked remains of a smile gave him away.

"My Uncle Ted," James said.

"Alive?"

"Oh yeah. They're too afraid to take him," James said, smiling.

"Looks it. Veteran?"

"Naw…carpenter. Helped my dad build the porch out back after the first one collapsed in a storm when I was a kid."

"He was your dad's brother?"

"Yeah."

"Close?" Kevin asked.

"Ted's lived up in Michigan for as long as I can remember. They weren't close in a way that was tangible, you know? It showed when he visited, and he was pretty tore up when my dad died. But, you had to know him. Anyone else might have thought he could've cared less," James said.

Kevin moved from picture frame to picture frame, glancing at the various photos.

"It's like a weird dream," he said. "I'm looking at pictures of me doing things I never did. Sorta like a phony picture you have taken at the fair."

Kevin stopped, and stared at one of the few photos without James in it. His Mom and Dad were sitting on a wooden bench somewhere, and whether posed or not, the camera had caught them ignoring everything else but one another. It was one of James' favorite pictures of them.

"They seem like good people," Kevin said, looking back at James.

"They are…were. My dad was a good friend. Mom too. They were good people."

Kevin groaned again as he sat back down on the sofa. He pressed the ice pack against his head, as if the pressure might make it feel better.

"Did she say she was going to make coffee?"

"Yeah, but you'll have to settle for decaf," James said.

"You're kidding me. Really?"

"Not the doctors decision on this one, though you should probably avoid the caffeine. I don't drink coffee. The only thing I've got in the house is decaf."

"Wow, a twenty-something that doesn't drink coffee," Kevin said.

"Yeah, I'm the freak of my office," James said.

"The office," Kevin said, a laugh behind the words. "You're a desk jockey?"

"Pretty much."

"A paper pusher."

"Sure. Any other clichés you want to throw my way?"

"Pencil pusher?"

"Thanks."

"Well, maybe your life isn't so golden after all, brother. I think I'd rather be beaten with a frying pan than be strapped to a desk for life," he said. A feigned cry of anguish came from the kitchen.

"I heard that! I said I was sorry. Jeez…" Nicole called from the kitchen, her voice fading to a mumble.

"I've thought of quitting," James said.

"Think harder. Nothing quite like sitting around making money for other people."

"That's usually how it works. Seems like all the good ideas are gone. What do you do?"

"Right now?" Kevin said, and a sheepish smile crossed his face, "I do nothing. Nada. Haven't had a steady job in the two years since college. All that bullshit and for what? I could probably work retail if I was desperate, but I'm not…yet."

"A leech of the system. Nice," James said.

"Not really…Dad's got some money. It's not like he does anything to spend it. Eats, sleeps, shits, goes to work, repeat. I've never collected unemployment if that's what you mean."

"I didn't mean anything by it," James said.

"No, it's no biggie," Kevin said. "What does your pencil pushing involve?"

"Editing," James said.

"Ooo…wow…you are the exciting one aren't you. A regular grammatistician," Kevin said.

"It's grammarian, actually," James said.

"Saw that one coming," Kevin said and smiled.

Nicole called from the kitchen again.

"Kevin? Milk or sugar in your coffee?"

"It's decaf? Lots of both," he said.

"So tell me more about this doctor who sent you," James said.

"He called me up out of the blue. I'd never heard of the guy before. Said he knew of someone I might want to get in touch with. Said it was important for me to contact you…today."

"Today? Why?" James interrupted.

"I have no clue. He wouldn't say. Said he had to keep the call short. Gave me your address and a rough description of the house, but…" Kevin finished by pointing at James and shrugging his shoulders.

"Nothing about the fact that I look just like you…give or take a pound or two and a weeks' worth of facial hair," James said.

"A weeks' worth? Took me three weeks to get this kind of coverage," Kevin said, rubbing his chin and frowning.

"Looks good to me," Nicole said with a smile. She handed Kevin the coffee and sat down next to James on the loveseat. "I've been trying to get James to grow some facial hair for years."

Kevin gestured for a moment of time as he sipped the coffee. He nodded approvingly and lifted the cup toward Nicole.

"Not too bad for decaf. Yeah, so he was like, you really need to see him and now. He said he would meet me here."

"He did?" James said, looking toward the door as if someone might knock.

"Yeah, he said it was important for him to meet with the two of us," Kevin said.

"That's just bizarre," Nicole said, sweeping a strand of hair out of her eyes and tucking it behind her ear.

"I'll say," James said. "What was his name again?"

"I never said," Kevin said. "He said his name was Paynter. Robert Paynter. James? Are you all right?"

"Paynter? You said Paynter," James said.

"Yeah, that's what it sounded like, you know," Kevin said, waving his hand in the air as if he were painting a wall.

"That name is on my birth certificate," James said.

"No shit," Kevin said.

"Yeah...and he's bogus...or at least I thought he was. The hospital never heard of him. Caused a mess when I went to get a license," James said.

"Can I see it? Your birth certificate?" Kevin asked.

James left the room and returned a moment later, a slightly disheveled, folded envelope in his hand. Kevin took it from him and cautiously opened it.

"Mom showed it to me when I was a kid. Wasn't till I got older that she let me in on the fact that it was a lie," James said.

It was Kevin's turn to look somewhat stunned. He handed the paper back to James, then produced a nearly identical page from the pocket of his coat. He handed it to James.

"It's the same paper. Same layout. Same imprinted seal. Same hospital name and different doctor. Fred Taylor" James said.

"Curiouser and curiouser," Nicole said, taking the paper from James.

"I'll say," Kevin said.

"Can't wait to meet this guy," James said.

Chapter 5

Special Agent John Norris drummed his fingers against the steering wheel. Normally, it was the traffic that brought about his ire. This time it was the one-sided conversation that was pouring out at him from the earpiece of his cell phone. No, conversation was the wrong word. Conversations were a give-and-take between two people. There was definitely no give on his part. He was taking a verbal beat down. The tirade that had been going on now for, he looked at the dashboard clock, seven straight minutes, required little input from Norris. He probably could have hung up. It was at this point that he tried to determine if he had just stopped listening or whether he could no longer actually hear what was being said. As if in response, the Deputy Director's voice reached a crescendo. Norris pulled the phone away from his ear and looked at it as if it might suddenly provide a moment of rationality. No such luck. He pressed the "end" button and tossed the phone onto the passenger seat.

It was a first-year move and he knew it. At the same time, he already knew everything the DD was telling him. He'd heard it before, unfortunately, and it wasn't like a refresher was going to do him any good. He was too old for that. There wasn't much more he could say. Norris knew he had fucked up. You just couldn't throw protocol to the wind anymore without having it fly back in your face. And, getting your partner, a half-cocked rookie fresh out of the academy, all shot up because a hunch went bad wasn't real great either. It wasn't the hunch that had been wrong though. It was his decision to follow up on it without backup. That, and accepting another rookie partner. They just can't teach you about the tension that bullets, fired to kill, create. They were both lucky to have escaped with their lives, and Norris was lucky to still have the badge in his pocket though he wasn't quite certain how long that would last.

Norris had defied retirement again when given the option. It was the third offer in five years. The kid would recover, but his field days were over. The left eye was done. He'd eventually recover forty percent of his vision if he was lucky. Norris had spoken with him in the hospital. The kid didn't blame Norris. Not now, at least. Norris had lost his New York post, and nearly his job. They even threatened to take his pension away, but Norris knew that was just smoke. Why they bothered with him anymore, he didn't know. But, when he posed the same question to himself, all that came were more questions. The fact was he didn't know why he still wanted to work. But, when it came down to it, he didn't know anything else. And now, he was stuck in traffic from a five-car pileup on the outbound George Washington Bridge, driving to his exile.

He had hoped that maybe they would just send him out West. Give him some time in California to mellow out. He could use a little sun. To his great dismay, the Cleveland office was in need of some "seasoned" field agents. It was the only option given him. He took it. He had nothing else.

The car in front of him moved up five feet. He didn't bother moving up. He watched as another ambulance struggled to make its way up the emergency lane. He took a long drag on the cigarette that was dwindling in his hand and squashed it in the tray. The dull pain in his chest returned and he rubbed it absent-mindedly. He coughed, bringing up a mouthful of phlegm. He cracked the door and spit it onto the roadway, looking up just in time to see the lady in the car next to him make a face and turn away. He shut the door and moved up the five vacant feet. Maybe he would finally see a doctor when he got to Cleveland. He doubted it though.

The phone on the passenger seat was vibrating. He glanced at it with the desire to not answer. Then he picked it up. It wasn't the call he was expecting.

"Norris," he wheezed.

"John, it's Dennis."

"Den. What can I do for you?"

"John, you hung up on the DD."

"Connection must've got lost."

"John, c'mon…"

"Hey, I've heard it all. Do I really need a kick in the ass on the way out the door?"

"He's fuming," Dennis said.

"Good. Gives him practice."

"John--"

"Den, he's an arrogant little prick. If he was a field agent…wait, let me correct myself, if he had *ever* been a field agent, he couldn't keep up with me. And, in my prime I'd have kicked his ass for saying some of the shit he just laid on me."

"Things don't work that way anymore," Dennis said.

"I know. It's a damn shame," Norris muttered.

"John, listen. You're going to have to talk to him eventually."

"No, I'm not his responsibility anymore. Why should I give him the pleasure? Tell him to go fuck himself."

Dennis sighed.

"He could make Cleveland hell for you."

"More so than it already will be? C'mon, Den, you know as well as I do that it's a Siberian banishment. They may as well have sent me to the Dubuque office. At least out there, I might get a radical militant group."

"There were no openings," Dennis said.

"I was kidding," Norris said.

"I wasn't," Dennis retorted.

"Nice."

"That's not the only reason I called."

"More good news...I can tell."

"It's about your number one. He's back in country."

Norris felt the old sensation of heat and fear rise up from his gut and he fought it back with anger, almost growling. He pulled the phone away from his face and wiped his brow. He felt light-headed and for a moment, he considered opening the door and stepping out. Then he remembered where he was.

"John?"

"I'm here. You're absolutely sure?" Norris asked.

"Would I tell you if I wasn't?"

"How?"

"Texas. Bill Hanlon came across a strange name/number combination at customs. When he couldn't find a match, he sent it my way. The camera shot is fuzzy at best, but I'd bet a bill on it."

"And Hanlon hasn't done anything?" Norris said.

"He wasn't sure, and I haven't told him yet. Figured I'd let you know first," Dennis said.

"And how are you so sure?"

"Two days later they found a woman killed in a small town in the middle of nowhere, Texas. Not quite his style, but definitely a hit. A bit too coincidental."

"So he didn't come back to sight see. What do you mean by not quite his style? You mean he didn't shoot her in the back and sneak away in his 'Cuda?"

"No…face-to-face. And, get this…he went back to the crime scene."

"You're sure it's him?"

"Well, that's the thing. He wasn't seen until he came back. Neighbor saw the car circling the block on Saturday morning. Coroner's report says she died Friday afternoon," Dennis said.

"That ain't like him. That ain't like him at all. She?"

"Well, that's the other thing. Interesting target. She had a file, but it appears to have been cleaned up. She had clearance at one time, but no record about what the clearance was for."

"Really," Norris said.

"Yep."

"So, someone has brought him back to clean up. Do you think that's it?"

"Do you really think he'd risk coming back for one woman in the middle of nowhere, Texas?" Dennis asked.

"For the right amount of money, maybe, but no…I don't think that's it. He's gotta have a list. He wouldn't come back for just one. There's no challenge in it. Ok, Den, get me what you can on the woman. Is the ballistics report in on the gun yet? He likes large caliber handguns…usually a .45 revolver. Or, if he's in a wistful mood--"

"John, you know you can't take this on."

"Why did you tell me then, Den?"

"I…I just thought you should know."

"Then get me what I need. He's not leaving country again. I don't care what it takes."

"John."

"Den…don't argue with me on this. I've been waiting twenty years. Twenty years and he's left his first print. I'm not letting this opportunity slip by. You get me her info and anyone who might be even remotely connected."

"I can't send that to the Cleveland office."

"That's why you'll send it to my secure email. Hell, text it to me if you have to."

"John…"

"Den, I'll convince them that it was all me. I threatened you with…I don't know. Some dirt on your sister."

"I don't have a sister, John."

"It won't come back to you, Den."

"I can't afford for it to, John. I only got a year left for a full pension."

"I know that."

"I wouldn't stick my neck out for anyone else like this," Dennis said.

"You know I wouldn't ask you. You know that. But, this…," Norris said.

"I know. I knew this was what would happen if I told you. I'm just saying it to make myself feel better."

"Do you feel better?" Norris asked.

"No. I feel like I just told the last dumbass knight where the dragon sleeps."

"Maybe so," Norris said.

"John, this'll kill you if you're not careful."

"I could be careful, and it might still kill me, Den. That's already written. If I can take him with me, maybe I can tag some undeserving worth to this bullshit life."

"John…"

"Den, just send me the info. Then go home and get some rest. Sleep well. I'll do the worrying. You do what you've always done. Keep an eye out when you can, but don't worry. Nobody will cry over this soldier anymore. There's no one left to care and…that's ok by me."

"She still cares, John," Dennis said.

"Not enough to matter," Norris said. His words hung heavily on the ends of the broken conversation.

"Goodbye, John," Dennis said.

Norris hung up the phone. He stared at the tail lights in front of him. The darkness was coming with the sunset and he wondered if he would see the other side of the bridge in the fading light of day. On the horizon, the clouds looked ominous. That made sense, he thought. He would face the storm soon enough. He just hoped he was facing the right direction when it finally came.

Chapter 6

"Dad's an accountant or finance guy…or something like that. A pencil pusher who crunches numbers," Kevin said. He was looking between James, who was seated across from him at the kitchen table, and Nicole, who stood at the stove, occasionally flipping some bacon and hash browns. The room was awash with the smells of breakfast. A pile of toast was already on the table, and the scrambled eggs were nearly ready. James stared at Kevin. There was something mesmerizing about watching yourself talk. He didn't think he would ever get over it. Identical twins that grew up together didn't have to look in a mirror to see how they looked when they talked or made faces. They had a sibling mirror. He looked into his sibling mirror with some concern. Did his nostrils flare that much when he talked? Now that he saw it, he couldn't *not see it* anymore. He rubbed his nose self-consciously.

"Will you stop!" Kevin said, breaking James out of his fugue. He had a broad smile across his face.

"What?" James said, pulling his hand away from his nose.

"You're giving me the creeps," Kevin said.

"What's he doing?" Nicole asked.

"He's eyeing me up…lustily," Kevin said, openly winking at Nicole, who turned to James with a mock look of shock.

"Even I don't get those kinds of looks…anymore," Nicole said, and turned back to her pan with an overly haughty huff.

"I am not…and you do too," James sputtered.

"I think there's a note of guilt in that response. What do you think, doctor?" Kevin said.

"Oh, definitely," Nicole said, expressionless. She brought the pan out to the table and began heaping piles of bacon and hash browns on their plates. "Narcissus all over again."

"Wow…good thing you're cute and can cook," James said.

"Uh-oh…you gonna let him get away with that?" Kevin asked.

"He gets away with nothing…even if I don't have a snappy comeback…he pays in other ways," Nicole said. She turned to place the pan back on the stove.

"Boy do I ever…" James mumbled through a mouthful of hash.

"What was that, honey?" Nicole said without turning.

"Nothing, dear," James said, wiping his mouth with a napkin. Kevin nearly choked on his orange juice. Nicole fixed her own plate and sat between the two.

"Hey, thanks for making breakfast. I thought people only ate like this at the diner or…Vermont or somewhere like that. It's really great," Kevin said.

"Why, thank you, Kevin. I see your father raised a gentleman," Nicole said, flashing James a quick smile.

"If such a thing exists anymore. Yeah, my dad taught me some manners," Kevin said.

"Yeah, I mean, walking up to a guy on his back porch and sticking a metal tube to his head and pretending it's a

42

gun…there's some damn fine manners," James said straight-faced before cracking a smile.

"Not gonna live that one down, am I," Kevin said.

"Well, if I can't live down the frying pan thing, then you shouldn't live down the metal thing," Nicole said. She stood and they watched her clear the table. She shooed their offers to help.

"So, when did this Paynter fellow--," James began.

"Doctor…Dr. Paynter," Kevin interrupted.

"Oh, my apologies…when did this Dr. Paynter fellow say he was going to arrive?"

"He didn't really," Kevin said.

"Huh…well, you'll stay, right? I mean…at least until he comes?" James asked.

"I…well, yeah…I guess so. Wouldn't really make sense for me to go back home now."

"Well, I'd like you to stay," James said. "Even if this guy turns out to be a nut bar. I mean…after he's gone. If you want to, that is. I mean, I've got this whole house to myself. Even with Nicole here, it wouldn't be too much. You'd have your pick of the two spare rooms."

"Really? I…don't know quite what to say…"

"I don't want to put you in an awkward position. I just thought it might be a nice change of scenery. Get out of the house. Get to know your brother. Don't answer now…just think about it."

"Alright…we'll see," Kevin said. "I don't know if we'll have that much time to play house though."

"What do you mean?" James asked.

"Well, the good doctor said I was to meet you then get you ready to go."

"Go? Where?"

"He wouldn't say. Told me there was something we needed to understand about who we were."

"Were…or are?" James said.

"He said 'were…I think,'" Kevin said.

"Interesting choice of words," Nicole said from over her shoulder. She stood at the sink, rinsing the last of the breakfast plates.

Kevin gingerly touched the lump that had formed on his head.

"I bet a warm shower would make that feel better," James said.

"That would be great," Kevin said.

"Bathroom is at the top of the stairs, first door on your right," James said.

Kevin stood, rubbing what little belly he had, and made a satisfied groan.

"Nicole, that was a fantastic breakfast. My compliments to the chef."

"If you want, leave your clothes outside the door. I'll take care of them," James said.

Kevin frowned then sniffed under each arm methodically. He winced.

"Good God, why didn't you tell me I smelled like a week old pair of underwear?"

"There was no gentle way to let you down," Nicole said.

"Ouch," James said.

"On that note…" Kevin said, and he turned and walked out of the kitchen.

James stood and he and Nicole watched as Kevin made his way down the hall and listened as made his way up the stairs. She wrapped an arm around his waist and pulled him close to her, pressing her head against his chest. When the water began to run for the shower, they both started to speak.

"You first," James said.

"I can't believe how much he looks like you, even with the weight difference. This could be a great opportunity for him. You could really help him out." She patted his chest.

"I could help him? What are you really saying?" he said.

"I just think the timing couldn't have been better. You've been miserable since your mom died."

"Well, that's not really fair, Nic. How was I supposed to be?"

"I don't mean it that way, James, it's just that…you've been *more* miserable since she died. It's been a really long two years. I'm sorry, but I thought that maybe…her death would bring you some sort of release…something that might snap you out of this funk you've been living in. I know it's only been a few weeks, but it's been really hard," she said.

"Well, I'm sorry *you've* had it so tough," James snapped, pulling away from her to sit down at the table.

"James, don't be like that," she said, pulling out the chair next to him and sitting down. "You know I love you. I just think this…I think Kevin could help bring you out of this. Distract you for a while."

"What if he doesn't want my help?"

"He does. He needs it just as badly as you do, but you're certainly of the same stuff. Neither one of you wants to admit just how important this all is. I can see that. By the sounds of it, he's had no true family presence in his life for some time. Now he meets you, the one thing he's probably craved for years, but learned to live without. God forbid either of you admit how happy you are to see one another. Silly boys and your pride."

"Don't analyze me, Nic. I know that's your thing, but please don't," he said without looking at her.

"I'm just saying, don't let this opportunity go. I think it'll be really good for you."

"And, if it isn't?" he said.

"What doesn't kill us only makes us stronger?" she said, a half smile on her lips.

"Ugh, my life's become cliché worthy. How depressing."

She slapped him on the shoulder and then wrapped her arms around his shoulders, kissing him on the neck and ear.

"I love you, ya big jerk," she said.

"Where are you going?" he said.

"I gotta change this shirt. Slopped oil all down the side."

"But," James began.

They heard the water stop upstairs, followed by Kevin's voice. James moved to the bottom of the stairs.

"Everything ok?" James called.

"Umm…so, I don't want to impose, but you wouldn't mind if I borrowed your razor, would you?" Kevin asked, opening the door just wide enough to stick his head out.

"Oh…no, I…uh…sure."

"Are you sure? I mean, I know how some people can be weird about stuff like that, and I don't want to go grossing you out or anything, but I figure while I'm at it, I may as well go the distance, y'know?"

"Go ahead. If you want, there's new toothbrushes in the towel closet. You're welcome to take one," James said.

"Oh, cool…yeah…alright. Cool…thanks…" He ducked his head back into the bathroom. James was left standing at the bottom of the stairs looking up. It was all too strange, he thought. He could almost hear a resemblance in voice. He'd have to let Uncle Ted know. Family was family in Ted's book, even if it wasn't blood.

He looked at some of the pictures that lined the stairway leading upstairs. Most of the pictures were of him but one of his favorites was of his mother, alone on a park bench with an apple in one hand and a book in the other. The apple had a bite out of it, and his mother had a look on her face that said,

"You're taking a picture of me with my mouth full?" She was young and very pretty. She had told him that the picture was taken about five years before he was born. It was in the same park that his father had proposed to her. They had returned there for their anniversary and picnicked in the park one afternoon. But, it had rained the night before and they were forced to have their picnic on a park bench, much to the delight of the pigeons. His father had called it one of his favorite pictures of James' mother, but it wasn't until after his death that he heard why. His mother explained that it was later that same week that they received word she would never be able to have a child of her own. They were both devastated by the news and Margaret had even contemplated divorcing William so he could find someone who would bear his children. He would hear nothing of it.

When Nicole tapped him on the arm, James nearly jumped.

"Are you with us?" she asked.

"For now," James said and smiled at her.

"What's that supposed to mean?" she said.

"Aw, nothing," James said. "I was just staring off at this picture of my mom."

"She had a great smile, James. She was always making me laugh."

"Yeah, she was good for that. She would have been mad at me for acting the way I have, Nic, but I just can't help it. I think about how much she went through and how I couldn't do anything to stop it and it just breaks me up inside. I'm just afraid I'll never be the same."

"It's been two weeks. You have to give it time. It'll pass," she said.

"That's what I'm afraid of. I feel like if I don't always feel this way, I'll somehow be disowning her, disregarding her memory. I didn't give up on her when she was alive. I guess I'm afraid of giving up on her now that she's dead."

"But, you just said it yourself, James. She wouldn't want you to mope around for the rest of your life. And, you're not giving up on her. She's moved on…it's time for you to do the same."

"I know, I just…I don't know."

"I tell you what, why don't we celebrate a little tonight."

"Celebrate?"

"Yeah! Hello? You just met your brother for the first time. Don't you think that's worth celebrating?"

James looked up the stairway. Yeah, I guess it is."

"I'll run out and get some steaks, a bottle of wine, a couple of beers, and we'll do it up right tonight."

"Sure, Nic. Are you sure you don't want me to go with you?"

"No, you take care of your brother. Talk with him. I'm sure you've got a lot to catch up on."

"Yeah, I guess you might be right."

"I'll be back before you know it," she said.

"Alright, I'd better take him a towel before he starts running around naked," James said.

"Yeah, and I don't need to see *exactly* how identical you are," Nicole said.

Chapter 7

The drive from Florida to New Jersey, the Opa-locka area to be precise, can range anywhere from 20 to 24 hours depending on your penchant for highway driving and the weight of your foot. Some people like to avoid the straightforward approach of Interstate 95 for the wistfulness of Route 1 up the coast, but Dr. Robert Paynter wasn't in a wistful mood. He pushed the 2004 Chrysler 300M's relatively weak six-cylinder engine to the limit. He had driven through the night before, only taking a couple of one hour naps, in hopes of reaching the Garden State late that evening. He hoped to find them there, still safe, but time was not on his side.

There had been the possibility of flying. He hadn't dismissed the thought. It would have been quicker. But, if they were watching closely, and he had to believe they were, it was not a mistake he could afford. All the years of living successfully under a fake name were coming to a close. Larry Reed had lived the quiet life, but now it was time for him to go. So, Dr. Robert Paynter walked into his home, packed his things, and booked a ticket for Larry Reed to Seattle, Washington, round trip, to return on Wednesday of the following week. The flight would cost him a fortune with so late a booking, but it had to be done. That afternoon he wrote a note to his neighbor, left his key in an envelope on her doorstep. He hesitated a moment at her door. His only real regret was leaving behind his cat, Queenie. He'd miss that damn cat. Paynter got in his car and left for the airport. But, instead of driving south into Miami, where the plane would depart in approximately two and a half hours, he drove north to route 75 and eventually out of the state near Jacksonville some five and a half hours later. He knew that the lack of a passenger who had booked a flight that afternoon would cause some alarm, but that was ok. As far as he was concerned, Larry Reed had met a tragic end in a marsh somewhere back in Florida, never to be seen again. And, the resurrected Dr. Robert Paynter had never booked a flight to Seattle in his life.

The roads had been quite clear up the southern half of the east coast. Late at night, it was limited to tractor-trailers and a few desperate individuals on their way from one state to another. In his rush north, he had yet to consider just what he was going to do when he got there. There would be a lot of explaining to do. He had set Kevin loose, not quite knowing what might happen. The thought of bringing together two unknown entities was daunting. He glanced down at the small battered black case on the floor of the passenger side. There were ways of dealing with problems. He just hoped it didn't come to that, one way or the other.

The news of Fred Taylor's being alive had sunk in that morning. Paynter hadn't seen him in over 24 years, but that was how they had planned it. Now, that old sense of over-paranoia was in his chest. Were they simply being flushed from the cover they had so carefully built over the years? Paynter stopped moving after seven years. He made the decision that if they really wanted to find him and kill him, he would at least be relaxing in a comfortable home with a drink in one hand and a good book in the other. But, by the time he had stopped running, he was already an old man. They had scared his youth from him and it was only the approach of old age that had stopped the running. He stretched deeply and glanced at the eyes in the rear-view mirror. The smile lines around them were only slightly deeper than the worry lines across his forehead. Where had the time gone? Was he really sixty-three? Only on the outside, he thought.

He tried to imagine what Fred Taylor looked like now. The diminutive man had lost his hair young, which had aged him even twenty plus years ago. It wasn't hard to picture him a little grayer, a little stooped, and a little gaunter. The years of running must have worn him down to nothing, thought Paynter. They had been good coworkers, but Taylor had always been a private man. His wife, a rather attractive, if not painfully shy, petite brunette woman, had died rather suddenly before the age of 35. Breast cancer. Though never one to socialize frequently, Paynter noticed his friend sink into a downward spiral of reclusiveness. He delved into his research like it was going to keep him alive. If he had known the consequences, he might have walked away. But, instead, he catalyzed the research with his obsession and desire for perfection. Paynter and the others knew damn well that they would have never succeeded without Taylor's diligence. Of course, then it got most of them killed.

A car came up on his left, distracting him from his reverie. The mile marker showed that he had another 5 miles until the

Virginia border. The clock said 5:45 PM. At this pace, he would reach his destination at approximately 1:00 AM, without traffic. He watched as the lines of the road went in and out of focus. Daylight was fading and he was on his 10th straight hour of driving, minus two stops for gas. Perhaps, he thought, if he tied the steering wheel straight, he could just take a little nap. He rolled the window down and waited till he was shivering before rolling it back up. He cranked the clearest radio station he could find. The weather forecast was looking grim. The last thing he needed was to get stuck in a Nor'easter. He pressed down on the pedal till he was doing a steady 80 mph and hit the cruise control.

Chapter 8

They ate, drank and told stories well into the night. James and Kevin had a lot more in common than they would have initially believed. Both had sold sneakers as a part-time job in high school. Both had played the clarinet. Both had sung in the school choir. Nicole was amazed that the two, having lived so close, had not somehow bumped into one another. Kevin called it fate, but James responded that it was just "dumb ass luck." When the bottles of wine were empty, they decided to retire for the evening. James had already decided to call out sick the next day. They wouldn't miss him for a day. Not really.

James was not aware of the time of night when Nicole was suddenly on top of him, shaking him abruptly awake, her hand pressed over his mouth. At first, he thought she was being playful. Part of this was due to that fact that the alcohol he had consumed less than three hours earlier had not worn off and he was in the middle of a bizarre dream upon awaking. In fact, for a moment, he was certain that she was just another part of his dream.

"What the hell?" James hissed through her fingers.

Nicole shook her head, her eyes large in the darkness. She leaned close to his ear.

"Shhhh…listen," she hissed.

Through the fogginess of sleep, what remained of the alcohol, and the sudden rush of adrenaline, James could barely hear a thing above the racing beat of his own heart. For a moment, there was only the pleasant immediacy of having

Nicole pressed so close to him. But he could feel and smell her fear. She was shaking, and even in the blurry paleness of the night, he could see that she was a shade paler. He sat up a little, pushing against her weight, which was now acting to keep him in the bed. He frowned at her and shifted her gently to the side as he swung his legs over the side of the bed.

Straining now to hear anything, he thought he heard the squeak of shoes across the kitchen floor. Nicole must have heard something as well, because she tensed against him, pulling him closer.

"It's Kevin," James said, his voice barely audible.

"I checked…he's still in the next room…sound asleep. I got up to pee and…I thought I heard something."

"Why didn't you get me?"

"I was frozen. I didn't want to move. Shhh."

They listened again and by straining, James heard the slightest notion of movement from the kitchen. He made to move up in the bed, but Nicole pressed herself tighter to him.

"There was someone rattling at the back door. I thought it was my imagination, but…" she said before James put a finger to his lips.

In the recesses of his mind, between hearing what Nicole had said, in the silence of the house, James was certain that he had heard his name called. He shivered. Then he heard it again. It was clearer this time, and it was coming from the bottom of the stairs. There was someone in his house in the middle of the night on a cold December day, and they were calling him out

56

by name. If there was ever a time to wake up from the dream, he wished it were now. All the little hairs on James body stood at attention. He shuddered again.

"Oh my God," whispered Nicole.

James stood, not knowing what else to do. He stepped toward the open bedroom door and walked out into the hall to the top of the stairs. Nicole clutched the back of his shirt and crept behind him. He stared down at the figure at the base of the stairs. It was a man, according to the dim light from the kitchen. A small man with little hair left on his head. His glasses reflected thickly back up at him. The man held a gun loosely at waist level in his left hand, the barrel aimed at the steps in front of him.

"Hello, James," said the man.

James felt Nicole move behind him. He watched as the man's eyes caught her movement. He seemed unconcerned with her.

"Is the gun necessary?" James asked.

"Troubles arise."

"So, you know my name, where I live, but obviously nothing about me," James said.

"I know enough. Besides, you're forty years my junior. Kids tend to be a little quicker."

"But, a gun? Were you expecting some resistance?"

"Why wouldn't I?"

"Well, you are…" James stopped and turned at the tug on his arm. A bleary-eyed Kevin was leaning against the wall. He was shaking his head and whispering. James leaned in closer and watched his lips. *It's not Paynter.*

"I've already called the police," James said, turning back suddenly.

The man had watched James with great interest. He now had a bemused look on his face.

"You shouldn't lie, James. It isn't becoming. There's three cell phones in the kitchen and there is no line to the second floor...I checked," the man said, giving his gun an absent wave.

"What the hell do you want?" James said, his fists clenched, a feeling of weakness forming in his stomach.

"First, I want the girl to come out where I can see her," the man said, and his tone had changed from one of indifference to one of muted menace.

James glanced over his shoulder, knowing that Nicole would have heard him. She crept out of the hall shadow and moved in behind James, peering over his shoulder. She suddenly became conscious of the fact that she was only wearing a t-shirt, panties, and some wooly socks. She tugged at the t-shirt, trying to make it cover more than it was ever meant to.

"Where I can see you, Miss," the man said, using the gun as a pointer, "That's it."

"Happy?" James said, passing from elation that the man didn't know Kevin was there to fear that he was still holding a gun.

"Quite," said the man, "Now I just need you to get me your birth certificate and we'll be on our way."

"Uh...birth certificate? I don't know what you're talking about," James said.

"Don't be a fool, it's not worth it," the man said.

"No, I'm...I'm telling you. I've never seen my birth certificate before. My mother told me it was lost years ago," he said. Nicole wrapped her hands around his arm and squeezed tight enough for it to hurt. In the dull light from the hall window, James could see a look of concern build in the man's face.

"I don't carry a gun for my health, James. We can do this one of two ways, and I'm sure you'd rather it be the easy way," said the man, the gun now held more firmly, but still pointing down.

"I'm telling you, I don't know what you're talking about," James said, and at this statement, the man no longer held back any emotion.

"How the hell...I told them not to lose that envelope. I explicitly told them. Of all the things...of all the stupid things to do."

"What difference does it make? It's just a piece of paper!" James said.

"You're lying...you've got to be. God dammit," he said, raising the gun now and pointing it at James, "you better be lying, or--" He stopped in mid-sentence, his eyes suddenly shifting to the open hallway to his left.

James heard a *click* sound from somewhere below and then all hell broke loose.

Chapter 9

With a slight change in his route, Dr. Robert Paynter entered New Jersey at around 2 AM, from northeastern Pennsylvania on Route 80. He had made the conscious decision to avoid the direct path of Route 95 with the idea that if he were being followed, he might delay the inevitable by taking an indirect path. He cruised along the interstate in the northwest part of the Garden State. It was here that there still remained some of the land that reflected the nickname. The road was quiet and the sky thick with clouds. The almost-full moon, which was now at its peak, illuminated them from behind. Paynter kicked back the last of his fifth cup of coffee, knowing damn well the caffeine was of little use now. He'd been awake for twenty-two of the last twenty-four hours. He was done. He could only hope that a warm welcome and accompanying bed awaited him.

He looked at the directions again. He had never forgotten the address, though he had never been there in his life. Even after almost twenty-four years, he had not forgotten the one piece of information that had linked him directly to his past. 601 Hamilton Drive, Hackettstown, New Jersey. Home of the Masterson's. And home to a baby boy name James. *Not such a baby anymore.* And, though Paynter had never seen the boys in his lifetime, he could imagine their build. After all, he'd seen the mold.

They would be about six feet tall, dark ragged hair, stark eyes, strong chin, and a bit of a slouch in the shoulders, as if they were afraid to stand up straight. Though, on further thought, Paynter wasn't quite sure that a trait such as that would have been passed on.

The Allamuchy/Hackettstown exit was soon upon him, and he drove onto the ramp with a renewed sense of urgency. He was finally within sight and it energized him. He was going to meet James and Kevin.

The drive from the exit was about five miles. He pulled off of the county road onto a side street, clicked on his overhead lamp and glanced quickly at the map. He might have known the address by heart, but he'd never bothered to memorize its exact location in the town. That had seemed a bit too much trouble for a task he had felt he would never have. Just a few more blocks, according to the map.

The streets were empty, as most small town streets are at 3 AM. He slowed as he approached the house. To his surprise, there were two cars in the driveway, outside of the garage, and a third late model muscle car across the street that had started up noisily on his turning onto the end of the street. He was still half a block away when it lurched around the corner of the block ahead. Paynter shut off the engine and coasted to a stop in front of the house. There was a light on at the back of the house.

Reaching down to the passenger side floor, he fumbled with the assembly of the gun. He was relying on the prep work he had done the previous day. He couldn't afford a mistake if he needed to use it.

He walked out into the driveway, silently cursing the nearly full moon that he had just been admiring earlier. Any night owl looking out of their window would be able to clearly identify him. None of that mattered now, though.

He spotted footprints in the remaining snow along the side of the house. They trailed around to the back of the house. There were no other tracks in that part of the yard. He followed them to the back porch and pushed the kitchen door, which was already open. Seeing fresh mud tracks weaving their way through the room, Paynter moved across the kitchen floor. He paused at the entry to the hallway. He could hear the conversation clearer now. Someone upstairs was conversing with someone in the hallway. Paynter moved to the doorway of the kitchen.

Paynter raised the Pneu-Dart Model 179 Projector with an unsteady hand. He had never once fired it at a living object. His arm felt stiff, and his finger slippery. He shook off the fear and stepped out further into the hall. At the bottom of the stairs was a short, balding man with glasses with a large chrome-plated gun held in his hand. He was aiming up at the top of the stairs, and only flinched slightly when he finally saw Paynter.

"You...," the man said, without a hint of surprise in his voice. Paynter had taken aim. When the gun moved, Paynter pulled the trigger.

Chapter 10

James watched as the man at the bottom of the stairs turned, eyes narrowing. There was another audible click and a tearing sound that cut the air. The man lurched and grasped at his throat, slumping against the wall.

Nicole screamed and tried to pull James back from the top of the stairs. Kevin came around the corner and the three watched the man at the bottom of the stairs slide slowly down the wall, his hands still clutched to his throat. They could see something sticking out between the man's fingers just beneath his chin. Inaudible words escaped curled lips. His eyes bulged in a mixture of horror and fear. He wrenched what looked like a dart from out of his neck, and stared at it, his lips now mouthing soundlessly like his voice had been muted. His eyes slowly rolled into the back of his head and he collapsed the rest of the way to the floor. Nicole let out another cry.

James put his foot onto the next step down, which elicited a shudder from Nicole, her whole body shaking in disbelief. Even Kevin looked dismayed at the thought of descending the stairs. James turned slightly, gave her hand a squeeze then froze at the sound of another man's voice.

"James?" said the new voice.

James threw his hands up.

"Jesus Christ! Why does everyone know my fucking name around here?"

"Paynter?" Kevin called out.

A taller man with a full head of grey hair materialized over the slumped, drooling, unconscious man at the bottom of the stairs. He too held a gun in his hand.

"What the hell is going on?" James shouted.

"Did he hurt you?" said the man.

His voice was anxious, but not aggressive.

"No. Who the hell is he, and who the hell are you?"

James pointed nervously at the new man. The man shoved his own gun into his coat pocket, then reached down and picked up the intruder's weapon. He leaned the small man's head back, as if he were examining his handiwork.

"I...am Dr. Robert Paynter. I'm the one who sent Kevin to find you. He...is the man who has stirred the hornet's nest, so to speak, and...he could be the death of us all. He was supposed to be dead. We were all supposed to be dead. And, it's somewhat amazing to actually see anyone still alive, especially him...after twenty-four years. That...is Dr. Fred Taylor...such as he is," Paynter said, waving a hand at the motionless man.

Paynter suddenly turned, walked back into the downstairs hallway and out of view. James took another couple of steps downward to see that he had gone to the front door. Paynter peeked out of the window then reached for the door and pulled it open. There was a sound of a revving car engine and accelerating wheels on the road outside. He closed the door and returned to the base of the stairs. He stared up at the three, with

66

what James might have mistaken for awe if the situation hadn't been so strange.

"Is he dead?" Nicole said, pointing to the heap of a man at the base of the stairs.

The man called Taylor had slumped nearly horizontal, his mouth lolling open, a thin strand of spit that hung from his bottom lip was just about to reach the carpet.

"Oh, no," said the man, pulling the bulky, fake-looking gun from his pants, as if that itself were an explanation.

"Tranquilizer," he continued. "He should be out for a good hour or so with the dose I gave him. Nowhere near enough to kill…but, he'll have a heck of a headache when he wakes up. Now, get packing. We haven't much time."

"Right," James said, "so…what?"

"We need to get the hell out of here," said the man. "That car outside wasn't just a curious neighbor."

"And I would want to go somewhere with you because…?"

"Because, after I've had some time to tell you what I know, you'll want to come with me."

"James, he did bring us together," Kevin said. "That's gotta say something for the guy."

"Start talking," James said, folding his arms across his chest.

"We don't have time for this. Once they find out that…"

"They? Who's they?" James said. Nicole stirred behind him, and came down the few steps to his level.

"You do have the envelope, don't you?" said the man.

"Again with the envelope? What's so special about this friggin' envelope! It's a ratty old envelope that held my birth certificate," James said.

"You lied to him?" Nicole asked.

"Taylor asked for it? That's troublesome. Listen, I'm here to help. I promise. I just need to know that you still have it," Paynter said. James looked into the man's eyes. If he was lying, he was well practiced.

"I keep it in my mother's old lock box. I've seen it a hundred times…what's so important about my birth certificate."

"It's the envelope that matters, not the birth certificate," Paynter said.

"What is all this?" James asked. "Why are people coming into my home and threatening me?"

"I'm sorry, but you…have information…that is possibly harmful…," Paynter stammered.

"You're lying," James said.

"No, it's true. We are in a lot of danger here. If we're not moving, we're asking to be caught. That's why we have to go. Now. There are people who want that envelope…people who would kill to get it," Paynter said.

"Like him? Taylor?" James asked.

"Well, I never thought so…I don't really know why he's here…that's a completely unexpected development. It doesn't

make sense that he was threatening you…and that bothers me,"
he said.

"Then who *else* is out to get me?" James said.

"I'm not one hundred percent positive, but I have a few
guesses. We'll probably find out soon enough," Paynter said.

James saw the lie, or at least the hint of it, but he chose to
not call it out.

"And I have this information," James said.

"Yes…you…all…both have it. It's only strength is in the
cumulative," Paynter said.

"And people are just coming after it now?" Kevin asked.

"Power matrixes shift. The information is more important,
or rather, detrimental now to those in power than before,"
Paynter said.

"Those in power? Did you say we all have it? I'm so
confused," James said and he dropped down onto the steps."

"So, why don't you take your information and leave?"
Kevin said.

"Because, Kevin, that information is probably more
important to you…and James…than either of you could ever
imagine," Paynter said.

"Why should I come with you? Why can't I just call the
police?" James said.

"James," Kevin said, as if asking for a break.

"They are the police," Paynter said.

James folded his arms across his chest.

"You still haven't convinced me. Why should I come with you? How do I know this Taylor guy wasn't the one I was supposed to trust?" James asked.

Paynter paused before answering right away. He held up the dart that had been fired from his gun.

"Because the bad guys don't carry tranquilizers. Because there is more truth waiting for you out there than you will ever find waiting around here."

"Truth," James said.

"I can…lead you to the truth," Paynter said.

"That sounds like a bad line out of a cheesy movie," James said.

"I have a better one," Paynter said, and a sly look took over his face, the corner of his mouth rising.

"Oh?" James said.

"Yeah," Paynter said, folding his arms to match James' stance. "Kevin isn't your only brother."

Chapter 11

James sat in the back of the Chrysler 300M. No matter how far Nicole moved the seat up, James legs were cramped. It fit his mood, so James didn't say a word. He alternated his stare between the back of the driver's seat, and the back of the man's head in that seat. He had not said a word since they got on the road. It had been apparent to Dr. Paynter that they needed to leave the premises as soon as possible, as someone would eventually show up for the man with the gun. He told them all to pack an overnight bag. Paynter gave Nicole no choice. She had to go with them, or risk being used against James. Before they left his house, the doctor dialed three digits into Dr. Taylor's cell phone and threw it on top of the still unconscious man. It looked so new and unused; he might have purchased it the previous day. Paynter smiled wryly as they left. James didn't smile back.

Paynter's only request as they enter the car was that Nicole drive. She was the least intoxicated of the three and he was struggling to stay conscious. He gave her the simple directives of "drive due west" and "don't speed." Within moments of being in the passenger seat, he was asleep. James fumed silently in the back seat. Occasionally, he would make eye contact with Kevin, who could only shrug. Eventually, Kevin stopped looking at him. Nicole played the radio softly and tapped along on the steering wheel. She tried to adjust the rear view mirror so she could catch his eye, but he shrank lower in his seat.

71

"Oh, why don't you cry about it," she whispered.

"Maybe I will," James snapped back.

"Children…please!" Kevin said, noticing that Paynter had stirred.

James turned his back to Kevin and curled up in the corner the best he could, closing his eyes. He couldn't make out a hushed conversation between Nicole and Kevin before sleep took him.

James was jarred awake by a sharp cry of laughter. He tried to stretch, then, realizing where he was, gave up. He sat up straight as best he could, and saw that Nicole was covering her mouth with her hand. Paynter was wide awake and smiling broadly. James glanced out the window to see the morning light illuminating snow covered fields in both directions.

"Glad we're all having a good time," James muttered.

"Oh, I'm sorry, sweetie. Really...it's just that...Bob was telling a funny story...and...," Nicole said, trailing off and shrugging her shoulders.

"Oh, was *Bob* telling a funny story? I fall asleep for a bit, and when I wake up, we're on a first name basis? Nice. Well, Bob, by all means...don't let me interrupt."

"Somebody woke up on the wrong side of the car," Kevin said.

"Whatever," James said.

He caught Nicole's frown in the rear view mirror. Maybe he was being an ass, but he wasn't apologizing. Not yet anyway.

As they hurtled on through central Pennsylvania, the conversation blossomed again. Nicole didn't seem to mind Paynter one bit, and now, as James sat in the back, almost hiding in the collar of his coat, she was cheerfully relaying the difficulties of her Psychology finals just days before. James stewed as she rattled on about the field's most recent discoveries like someone had pulled her string. Paynter smiled and nodded knowingly, adding comments, and generally seeming to enjoy the conversation. Kevin chimed in on occasion, and Paynter and he talked readily about the current hockey season.

After another hour of riding in the confines of the back seat, James started shifting uncomfortably.

"I'm going to stop, ok? We're getting low on gas," Nicole said.

"I think that's a good idea. I think we could all use a breather," Paynter said.

They pulled off of the highway. There was a gas station right across the road from the exit ramp. The old snow was deeper up here. It looked to be about ten inches. Nicole maneuvered past a large mound of snow, across the lot and up to the first available pump. They all got out at the same time.

"Might as well ride in the trunk," James said, in a low voice, not really trying to hide his displeasure.

Nicole scowled at him. Kevin just rolled his eyes.

"I'll switch with you," Paynter said, but James barely acknowledged that he had spoken.

"No, I'll be ok. I gotta piss something fierce, though," he said.

Paynter stood next to the pump, stretching his arms above his head and yawning. James gave a quick nervous glance back at Nicole, then back at him. It didn't go unnoticed.

"Do you want her to go with you?" Paynter said. "I'm not going anywhere without you, James, so go do what you have to and let's get back on the road."

James blushed and turned away.

Try as he might, James could find no sign of insincerity in the man's voice or demeanor. But, the time was coming for him to own up to what this was really about. Then, thought James, then we'd see what he was made of.

James walked into the gas station store, rubbing his hands against the cold, dry air. There was a young guy behind the counter with a bag of sunflower seeds. He looked bored, and his crooked nametag read "Jo-n", as if the "h" had fallen off at some point and he'd just never bothered to make a new one.

"Bathroom?" James asked.

"Yep," said Jo-n, and he pointed to a hallway in the back of the store.

By the time James came back out, Kevin and Paynter were standing at the counter. Paynter had pulled out a rather large clip of bills. James gave the clip a sideways look.

"Knew it was gonna be a long trip," Paynter said in response.

"Guess so," James said.

"Do you want anything? Something to snack on?" Paynter said.

"No," James said, quickly, then added, "Thanks."

"You haven't had anything to eat today…you must be running on empty," Paynter said.

James looked at him, trying to imagine the man as someone's grandfather.

"Yeah, thanks, that's ok, I'll be fine. I'll just ask Nic if she wants any--"

"She's already come and gone," Paynter said, a smile lighting his face. "I can't imagine she eats that crap all the time, with a figure like that, but she must've had a craving…or something."

Over Paynter's shoulder, James saw Jo-n smiling and nodding, as if it was the funniest thing he'd seen in a long time.

"Two bags of stuff!" he said, half a sunflower shell flying, unnoticed by him, from his lips. He grinned broadly at James with another black shell still covering one tooth.

"Right," James said. "I'll be in the car."

He walked out to find that Nicole had already taken over the rear seat. He stuck his head just inside the door. She was sitting with an open bottle of root beer in one hand and the half-eaten remains of a Twinkie in the other. Despite his cheerless disposition, she smiled at him. There was a smudge of white cream on her cheek.

"Is there room for me back there?" he asked, the anger melting away for a moment.

"No. Kevin's sitting back here. Maybe he'll even hold my hand," she said.

"That's not funny," he said and slid into the seat beside her, pulling an empty wrapper out from under him.

"You can't just hide away back here, James," she said through a mouthful of Twinkie.

"Well, why not? I don't feel like talking," he said.

"Because it's going to be a long trip and..."

"To where? Where the hell are we going?" he said.

"I don't know," she said, "but I trust him. I think he's really a nice man. There's something very sincere about him. You were asleep. We talked about a lot of things. He really opened up to us. He wanted to tell Kevin something, talk to him about what it is we're doing, but said it would be unfair to talk without you being awake for it."

"How can you trust him?" James said. "This man, pushing sixty, walks into my house and shoots another man with a poison dart?"

"That guy had a gun on you, and you want to persecute your savior? What is wrong with you, James? What is it that's bothering you?"

At that moment, both doors opened. Paynter got in on the driver's side and sat down, turning to look at the both of them.

"Gas prices are outrageous," he said.

Both James and Nicole nodded wordlessly. Kevin sat down in the passenger seat without a word and stretched his legs. James didn't take his eyes off Paynter.

"Right," Paynter said, "First-off, I pushed past sixty a few years back. I'm sixty-six. Second, that dart had Risperdal in it, not poison…though some might argue otherwise. And third, you've got a pretty powerful voice when you're angry."

James turned away and glowered out the front window.

"I have every reason to be angry," James said.

"You deserve answers," Paynter said.

"Then why don't we hear some," James said, no longer trying to hide how he felt.

"Fine," Paynter said, and turned in his seat.

"Are our parents still alive?" Kevin said, suddenly.

Paynter frowned sympathetically at him and shook his head to the negative.

"No. In fact, their deaths are why we're here," Paynter said.

James focused on every aspect of Paynter's face. This was where he'd expose his lies, James thought. Paynter continued.

"Your real parents were military folk. They had no extended family, so when they were both killed a week after—
"

"How?" James interrupted.

"Car accident," Paynter said too quickly for James.

"Oh," Nicole said softly, biting her bottom lip.

"Anyway, the government stepped in and made some…bad decisions. What they had planned was immoral and unethical and those of us involved decided to put a stop to it. Myself, Dr. Taylor, and a woman by the name of Agnes

Richardson formulated a plan to…hide you. It was crazy, but apparently they hadn't seen it coming. By the time we were gone, the trail was cold. They chased me around the country for a while, but after a half dozen years or so, I stopped running…and they seemed content at giving up the chase. Then I received a phone call from an old friend. Agnes Richardson, who'd been living under a fake name, was murdered the other day…and the rumor was that it was a professional job. Why someone would go to the trouble of killing a woman in her early seventies beats me. Poor Agnes…," Paynter's voice faded and he seemed to lose focus.

"Why now, though?" James said. As hard as he had looked, James could pin no insincerity on the man…and that bothered him.

"I'm afraid we might have Dr. Taylor to blame for that. I'm not sure he ever stopped running. Tired of it, I think he might have mailed some documents to a couple of the big newspapers. If the papers tried to vet the information, it might have knocked the cobwebs off of some old files…and some forgotten fears," Paynter said.

"So, now what?" Kevin asked.

"Now we go to find your brother," Paynter said.

"Three of us, huh?" James said.

"Yes…three," Paynter said and James wondered why the man had suddenly hesitated.

"Cool," Kevin said.

"Yeah…well, we'd better figure out where we are headed," Paynter said.

"What?" James said.

"You're the one with the directions, James," Paynter said.

"Ummm…ok. I don't understand."

"The envelope," Paynter said and he started the car.

"It's an empty old envelope," James said.

"Sometimes you gotta think outside the box, James…or in this case, outside the envelope." Paynter said

James unzipped his coat and pulled the envelope out from the inside pocket. He held it in his hand. Opening it, he pulled out the fake birth certificate and dropped it into his lap. He held the envelope up to the window as if to look through it. Nicole leaned over his shoulder, straining to get a better look.

"See anything?" Paynter said.

"No," James said, straining to make something out of the nothing he was seeing.

"Good, that's how it was designed," Paynter said.

"And you designed it," James said.

"Well, yeah, I guess I did," Paynter said, as if that was the first he had ever thought of it that way.

"So, what am I missing?"

"Pull the envelope apart at the seal…as gently as you can," Paynter said.

"You mean where the paper's glued together?"

"Yes," Paynter said and he reached down to his left and pulled out a compact US map.

James pulled at the center point of the envelope and gently tore the glued edges apart. First one, then the other. Then he saw it. In faint lettering visible beneath the glue, there were several letters, seemingly written in pencil. HUBBARDOH. James read the letters out.

"I don't get it," he said.

"It's a location," Paynter said.

"O-H," Nicole said, "Ohio?"

"Not exactly cryptic," Paynter said, with a little laugh, and he scanned the map in his hand. James continued to look at the envelope, his head cocked to one side.

"And this is?" James said.

"Where your other brother lives," Paynter said, "It sounds right. I'm not quite sure...it has been twenty-four years." James shook his head.

"Great plan you have here," James said.

"It's worked so far. You're alive aren't you?"

"This was meant to keep me alive?" James asked.

"Give the guy a break, James," Kevin said.

"So, where in Ohio is this?" said Nicole.

"That I don't know. What I do know is that this map is useless. We'll need a more detailed Ohio map."

"Think the store has one?" James said.

"I gave a quick look before, knowing that we'd need a map eventually, but I didn't see any. We might just have to wait until the border."

"Great plan," James said, tossing the torn envelope on the floor.

"The idea was to keep people away from you," Paynter said.

"Including yourself," James said.

"Yes," Paynter said, quite seriously.

"Why?" James said.

"So they couldn't use me against you," he said, and started up the car.

Chapter 12

Samuel Isaacson stood at the end of his driveway, wearing nothing but his pajamas and thin summer robe. Despite the month, and despite the weather, he just couldn't be bothered to get his winter robe down from the attic. Besides, he only ever wore it to get the paper in the morning. It usually took him all of a minute to complete the task. The driveway just wasn't that long. Today, however, he had stopped at the end of the driveway long enough to feel the chill. Something had caught his eye.

The light on in the neighbor's kitchen should not have bothered him as much as it did now. The neighborhood had been a quiet place to live for the past forty some odd years. You couldn't change your cologne without someone knowing about it, but at the same time, they were all good people. They had all stopped by to give their condolences when his wife had passed three years earlier. Some of them even left food. One of the young couples had even added him to their Christmas card list, and he'd never had the heart to tell them their mistake. They were good people, and you just couldn't take that for granted. The Masterson's were good people too and living next to them had never been cause for excitement. That is, it hadn't been, until the other night.

The previous morning, there had been a knock on Samuel's door as soon as it was light. The officers were polite, if not a little brusque. Yes, he had heard the sirens, but only briefly. No, he hadn't looked out the window, despite the flashing lights. He takes medicine to sleep at night and anything less than eight hours and he's a zombie. Yes, he knew the boy lived alone. His mother was a wonderful woman and his father had always been there when Samuel needed something fixed around the house. He missed their presence, but he was sure they were with God. No, he didn't know the boy well. He was a polite, respectful boy who had offered to shovel his driveway every time it snowed, but they hadn't actually spoken much. Samuel felt bad for him, having lost both parents at such a young age. No, he didn't know where the boy might be. As far as Samuel knew, the boy had a job. He had an uncle who lived somewhere in the Midwest. He had been down for the funeral a few weeks before, but that was all he really knew of that. No, he really didn't know where James might be, or why he would have left his car, or why he might have dialed 911 in the middle of the morning and then disappeared. Yes, if he saw James, he would be sure to contact the police.

"Is the boy in trouble?" Samuel had asked.

"No, we'd just like to ask him some questions," was the response they gave him.

Of course, Samuel thought.

So, now, as he stood looking at the light coming from James' kitchen, that had not been on first thing this morning, it occurred to him what the officer had said. Samuel should call the police. Not because he had said he would, but because of the chill that had run through him upon seeing the light on. It hadn't been from the cold after all. It was something else.

He gripped the paper and found himself moving through the snow, across the space between his driveway and James' back porch. He paused when a figure moved quickly past the window. He cursed his forgetfulness, remembering his glasses were on his kitchen table. But, who the hell needs glasses to fetch the paper? He moved forward again, squinting in a vain attempt to gain some focus. His eyes remained on the window. He was almost to the back of the house when the kitchen light went off. The leather of his slippers seemed to be frozen to the snow, as he found it difficult to move. The thumping of his heart was deafening in his own ear and for a moment he imagined that the person in the house had heard this and run.

Samuel stepped up onto the back porch. With the light no longer on, the kitchen was obscured in the darkness. He looked at the back door. The handle looked damaged, though maybe he was just imagining it to be worse than it really was. Over-reactive fool, Samuel thought. But, when he reached for the handle, it gave a little too much and the door pushed open with little effort. He called out weakly and then cleared his throat to try again.

"James?" he said, though still not very loudly. He stood just inside the door and listened. He thought he could hear someone talking and called again. The talking stopped. Samuel walked further into the dark kitchen. He glanced around nervously. There were a few dirty dishes in the sink, but as far as he could tell, there was nothing out of the ordinary. No sign of struggle, no pool of blood. He glanced at the dinette and stopped once again. The teacup was placed at the edge of the table. The spoon was still in it, steam rising steadily from the lip. He heard the voice again, coming from the living room. It sounded a lot like James', which emboldened him.

"James?" he called louder and strode to the living room.

When he rounded the corner, he saw a man with his back to him, sitting hunched on an ottoman in the middle of the room. It was James; at least, it looked like James. It was hard for Samuel to tell, without his glasses. But, this man had the same hunch in his shoulders that made James appear to be about an inch shorter than he probably was. But, he was dressed like Samuel had never seen him dress before. And, there was something about his hair. Something not quite right. He realized the man must be on the phone, and he spoke again, with somewhat less conviction.

"I'm sorry to bother you, James--" but the man, James, cut him off by standing up and suddenly speaking very loud. It confused Samuel.

"I said, there's an intruder in my house!"

The man spun around on his heels with his arms spread out to both sides so suddenly that Samuel staggered and dropped his newspaper. This was not James. At least, this was no James he knew. His eyes didn't need to be in focus, nor did they need the full light of day to know this was not James. But, it could have been his grandfather. Then, the spell was broken by what he knew to be a gun in the man's left hand.

"James...you're not..."

"Thank you," the man whispered, and he quickly raised the barrel of the gun. Samuel barely had time to register the pain of the first two rounds when the third brought darkness.

Chapter 13

When he awoke, Dr. Fred Taylor reached for his neck, half expecting to find a large hole oozing what remained of his blood onto his neck. Much to his temporary relief, though still painful, his hand came back sans blood. Then he remembered why he was prone, what he had just been doing. He sat up quickly, a flash of white light tearing at his eyes and head. He wavered a moment, trying to blink away the pain. He couldn't see for the stars, but he heard a voice behind him.

"The good doctor rises," the man said.

The sarcasm was evident to Dr. Taylor, but when he responded, he was in no way fit to question its reasoning. He kept his eyes closed, focusing on his words.

"Who are you?" Taylor asked.

"I am your goddamn guardian angel, Doc."

Dr. Taylor tried to think through the pain in his head. It was letting up, or perhaps he was just growing used to it. He opened his eyes again, just a crack. He was no longer in the Masterson house; that much was certain. He still could not see the man who was speaking to him. He decided that, for now, it didn't matter anyway.

"Where am I?" he asked.

"At the rattiest little motel I could find in the area. They don't even ask you if you want them super-sized, they just come that way," said the man, who followed the remark with a hoarse laugh.

"Why am I here, and not still on the floor in that house," said Dr. Taylor.

"Because I wasn't hired to kill you. But, you got in my way, and now you're going to help me finish the job," the man said.

"You weren't following me?" Taylor asked.

"No, but I guess I should have. I was right there...and you went and fucked it all up."

"It's not over," Taylor said.

"You better believe it's not over. That's why I saved your ass," the man said. Taylor could see smoke and smell the cigarette.

Dr. Taylor touched his hand to his neck again, still expecting a Monty-Pythonesque stream of blood to start shooting from it. It still hurt. His whole neck and back hurt.

"You should've just left me on the floor," Taylor said.

"The police were already on the way," the man said.

"They called the police?"

"In a sense. You must've scared 'em pretty good to get 'em to leave in such a hurry. But, the boy was smart enough to drop your cell phone on your lap and boogie on out the door before anyone showed up. Luckily, I was right around the corner, waiting for said departure."

"The boy? My cell phone? Jesus Christ...it probably wasn't him...it was Paynter," Taylor said.

"Paynter? Dr. Robert Paynter?" the man asked, a new enthusiasm in his voice.

90

"The same…who do you think shot me?" Taylor asked.

Dr. Taylor looked to his left. The large mirror next to the TV reflected the figure of a man reclining on the other bed in the room. He was light haired and medium height by the looks of it. The man was wearing blue jeans, but everything else looked black. Black boots, black shirt, black jacket, and a black newsboy cap. He was smoking the last of a cigarette, and by the look of the ashtray besides him, it might have been the end of a pack. There was something disconcerting about his face, but Taylor couldn't make it out.

"Who do you work for?" Taylor asked. The man almost spit.

"So many questions, Doc, so little time. Now that you're alert, or at least conscious, you can tell me where we're headed," the man in black said.

"We? You think I'm that stupid?" Taylor asked.

"Do you really want me to answer that question truthfully, or would you like me to smile and lie to you?"

"Listen asshole…" but Dr. Taylor did not finish.

The man closed the distance between them in a heartbeat, cigarette still at the corner of his mouth, and grabbed the collar of Taylor's trench coat, shaking him, his face contorted on one side.

"Excuse me? I think you were about to say something stupid. Am I right? I suggest you think about your situation here, Doc, and understand that you are in no position to be calling anyone, especially me, an asshole. Dragged your sorry ass out of that place when I could've gotten busted myself. And for what? To have some over-educated pussy call me names? I don't think so."

He released the collar from his grip brusquely, pulling the cigarette from the side of his mouth that seemed to function. Dr. Taylor winced as a fresh cloud of pain and smoke marred his vision. He raised a hand up to his face. He wasn't sure if it was just his head, or whether his hand was actually shaking.

"Wh...what time is it?" Taylor asked quietly.

"It's almost one...in the afternoon," the man said.

"Dammit," Taylor whispered.

"You know where they're headed," the man said.

"Yes...roughly, and at this rate, they'll be there way before us."

"Roughly? Which way, roughly?"

"West," Taylor said. The man laughed.

"You're gonna be a hard nut to bust, aren't you, doc? I have other sources, y'know. Don't *really* need you."

"Take interstate 80 to Ohio."

"Well, that poses a problem, now doesn't it? Are you sure that's the way their headed?"

"I'd bet my life on it. Without a doubt. Why do you say it's a problem?" Taylor asked.

"Big ol' storm headed in from that way. Can't really avoid it now. They're calling for snow out the wazoo."

"Then maybe we have some luck on our side," Taylor said.

"Or we're up a shit's creek," the man said.

"What do you plan on doing once we find them?" Taylor asked. The smile, if you could call the crooked line on the man's face that, told Taylor everything he needed to know.

"You leave that up to me, Doc. Like I said, I represent a concerned party. I'll deal with their concerns. You deal with yours. Now, we'd better get our boogie-shoes on, hadn't we?"

"Right," Taylor said, staggering to a standing position. He reached for the dresser to prevent a fall.

"Don't worry, Doc, you'll be able to recover in the car."

The man pulled his cap off, ran a hand through fading auburn hair, then placed the cap back on his head. He pulled up the collar of the black pea coat and opened the door of the motel room. The light, though not truly bright for a cloudy winter afternoon, made Dr. Taylor cringe. Then he saw the car. The man in black had a black car. An old black sports car.

"I'm going to recover in that?" said the doctor.

"C'mon, Doc, you must've seen a few of these when you were a young man."

Admittedly, the doctor had, but they had all belonged to people he didn't really socialize with or, more specifically, didn't want to socialize with him. It was a jock's car, which was fitting, because the man in black seemed like a jock. A jock who still thought that cars like that got him women and respect.

"Sixty-nine Barracuda, Doc. A goddamn pussy-wagon. Original Formula S package with the 383 in it. It's a goddamn dream, you'll see."

"I can't wait," Taylor said.

"You'll see, doc…you'll see. By the end of this little trip of ours, you're gonna *love* this fucking car."

Chapter 14

It started as a slow crawl that developed into a stand still. The two lanes of interstate traffic became a solid wall of vehicles, snow, and billowing plumes of exhaust. For the first time, James thought that Paynter looked worried.

"Can we find somewhere to stop?" James said.

"I don't think we can risk it," Paynter said.

"Do you really think they're that close," Kevin said.

"In cases like this, I think it helps to think that they're in the car behind you," Paynter said. Kevin glanced back nervously.

"They. They. You keep referring to 'they'," James said, "Do you have an idea as to who 'they' are?"

"They could be several parties. That's what worries me. It's an unknown quantity at this point. Fred Taylor was a complete surprise. I did not expect to find him at your house. I don't know what he was hoping to do. Certainly nothing like the man I used to know," he said.

"Not exactly the rabble-rouser type?" James asked.

"No…he's scared…or just plain tired. Tired of hiding. Those are the only two reasons I can think of. Otherwise, he would have never exposed himself in this way."

"Expose himself?"

"James, we've been in hiding for over twenty years. People thought he was dead…hell, I thought he was dead, which was probably convenient. Most dead guys get left alone. But, by coming out like this, he's really opening the bag."

"And your coming out won't?" Nicole added.

"It's all in the timing. Hounds usually chase the first fox out of the hole," Paynter said.

"Trouble is, they usually catch the slowest," James said.

Paynter was sitting, the driver's seat leaned back a bit more than before. His hands lay idle against the wheel. Traffic hadn't moved in over half an hour. They had all zipped their jackets back up as the car's engine tried to create enough heat against the bitter cold outside. Nicole had set herself against the side of Paynter's seat, facing James.

"I still don't understand the connection with James and Kevin," she said. "Why are they trying to get at him? I mean, do you think that Fred guy would have killed him?"

"No," Paynter said, waving a hand. "At least I don't think he would have. I think the gun was just for his security."

"*His* security," laughed Nicole.

"Cuz I'm such a dangerous kind of guy," James said.

"He didn't know what to expect," Paynter said.

"You could've gone all kung-fu on him," Kevin said.

"Yeah," James said, "with all that kung-fu I don't know."

"I could've hit him with a frying pan," Nicole said.

"In a fight, I'll take your frying pan over his kung-fu any day," Kevin said, rubbing his forehead.

They all turned as a police car went past them in the emergency lane. It was announcing something over its loudspeaker, but they all missed what it had said. Another soon passed, more slowly. The highway was being shut down due to the storm. Cars were being directed off at the next exit.

"Great," Paynter said.

"Well," James said, "at least they won't be able to follow us."

"Don't bet on it," Paynter said.

"Where there's a will, there's a way," Nicole said.

"If anyone is following us, they'll have to get off here too," Kevin said.

"Yes. That's what we have to think," Paynter said.

"Traffic's moving," James said, and the cars ahead of them starting showing signs of life.

It took another half hour, but they managed to move the final half mile of the highway to the next exit. The sign was covered with snow, making it unreadable. Off of the exit ramp, the traffic seemed to all be turning to the right. Paynter headed left.

"Reverse psychology?" James said.

"Common sense," Paynter said, smiling. "Any lodgings in that direction will be full by now."

"We're stopping?" Nicole said.

"The side roads will be just as bad as the highway," James said.

"The distance we can make tonight would be negligible," Paynter said.

"Don't you need a credit card to get into most hotels nowadays?" Nicole said.

"Don't you worry about that," Paynter said, the wry smile on his face again. "I've got enough identities and credit cards to go across the country and back, and they'd still be looking for a Mr. H. Potter from Small Flinching, Wisconsin."

"Nice," Kevin said.

"Aren't you just the James Bond type," Nicole said.

"You learn a lot when you run for your life," Paynter said.

Twenty minutes of slow crawling through blinding snow and poorly plowed roads made James realize why the traffic had gone the other way. There was nothing in this direction. Houses were few and far between. They had almost reached the Ohio border when they exited the highway, but the further they drove, James was fairly certain they were becoming lost. He could read the concern on Paynter's face. They came to a crossroad. A sign at the side of the road was obscured by caked-on snow.

"Kevin," Paynter said, a finger raised at the sign, "would you do the honors?"

Kevin nodded, pulling his collar up. They watched as he stepped out into the whiteness. He was immediately enveloped in the snow, as if the white powder had detected his presence. He bundled a hand in his sleeve and knocked on the corner of the blue sign. There was a Shell station three miles to the left. A hotel two miles to the right. Kevin climbed back into the car, trying to brush the snow from himself without getting everyone else wet.

"Looks like we're in luck," Kevin said.

"Call it what you will," Paynter said.

Chapter 15

James stared out of the car window at the snow falling against the cooling windshield. His eyes focused at the clumps of flakes as they tumbled against the glass. He tried to focus on the flakes themselves. Perhaps that would clear his mind. Enable him to gather all of what had happened so far into a malleable form that he could shape into something that made sense. If he could only concentrate. He let his eyes cross and lost his focus, leaning his head against the rest.

"Are you all right?" Nicole said.

Her hand drifted to his forehead and she gently brushed aside a stray hair.

James watched as Paynter walked back across the crowded parking lot toward the car. He turned and looked at Nicole, blinking.

"Yeah," he said, trying to force every bit of confusion from his face, "I'm fine."

"Liar," she said.

Paynter opened the door and climbed in.

"They have a room at the back," he said. "There's no parking back there, though, so we'll have to walk around."

James looked at him, an eyebrow cocked.

"Guy said we got lucky. The weather has him full up for the night. Last room available. Lucky us."

James looked at the shabby white building. "Yeah, lucky us."

"No questions?" Kevin said.

"I think he'd been napping. He didn't seem all there. Didn't even ask how many we were," Paynter said. He waved a silver key on a nondescript ring.

"Wow…not even your standard magnetic strip plastic card? Can't wait to see what this looks like," James said.

"It's late and there's a warm dry place to lie down. Let's go," Paynter said, and he moved to get back out of the car.

James reached out quickly and grabbed his arm, steadying himself against the back of the driver's seat. It was an awkward position from which to exert force.

"James," whispered Nicole.

"Jesus, James," Kevin said.

"If this is something stupid," James said, "If this is…some sort of ploy…"

Paynter looked into James' eyes, and the corner of his mouth raised in that funny way that James wasn't sure he liked. He wasn't resisting James' grasp, but James could feel that it probably would have been no trouble for the man to break it. He felt Paynter relax.

Paynter offered him the room key. James glanced at it. It might have been a show of good faith, but James couldn't shake the possibility that it might still be bait in the trap. Paynter had drawn heavily on James' trust, and now he felt like the account was drying up. This was such a bad situation, or at least had the possibility to be bad. A stranger and a car that belonged to someone who didn't exist in the middle of

Nowhere, Pennsylvania, with a key to a room that had no measure of trace. James released Paynter's arm.

"Sorry…lead the way," James said.

They all got out of the car, greeted by a bitter wind and thick snow that was made pale pink by the pall cast by the solitary streetlight nearby. It was a surreal snowscape. Every car in the lot was covered or close to being covered. A lonely looking phone booth stood at the edge of the parking lot, accompanied by what looked like a mail box. Like an old couple waiting for a bus that would never come.

James handed Paynter the key and followed the man as he led the way to a doorway around the back of the building. Nicole carried an overnight bag she had packed. The door was unmarked and certainly did not resemble a normal hotel room. There was one small window, with plastic blinds. There was no mark on the door at all. Not even a peep hole. Paynter brushed the snow from the door handle and inserted the key. He pushed the door open and groped for a light switch. It relieved James slightly to see the man so uncomfortable. Paynter cursed under his breath. The room was dark and there were no lights behind the building to aid them in their entrance.

"Smells like my Dad's bathroom in there…yum," Kevin said.

"Here," Nicole said, and brushed past Paynter.

She stepped through to a table that neither Paynter nor James or Kevin had seen, and pulled the switch to a table lamp. Paynter stood in the doorway a moment, giving Nicole a look.

"You boys need to eat your veggies. Vitamin K gives you good night vision," she said, and shrugged.

"Alrighty then," Kevin said.

"I'll say," Paynter said, and he shut the door after Kevin.

It was an old storage room and smelled every bit as Kevin had described. Everything about the room screamed off the books. There were two single beds and the sheets looked like they might crack if anything touched it. There were dead bugs along the bottom of the wall, throughout the room. There was a TV in the corner of the room on the floor that James' would have bet was black and white, if it had worked. Two chairs that looked to be refugees from the 80s kept dust off the far wall. A doorway at the rear of the room suggested the existence of a bathroom that James had no desire of exploring.

"Glad I didn't bother to bring pajamas…wouldn't want to get them dirty," Kevin said.

"Funny," Paynter said, frowning slightly, "but this will do. Not exactly the Ritz, but it'll do."

"I've never stayed at a Ritz, but if it's the opposite of this, then maybe I have a clearer picture," Nicole said.

"At least it's warm…ish," James said, blowing on his hands.

Paynter threw his coat over the back of a chair and glanced into the bathroom. Again, he batted around for a light switch, only this time there really was no light.

"That might be a good thing," James said as he watched.

Nicole touched the blanket on the bed furtively. It didn't bite, though she didn't look too sure. Paynter settled himself into one of the chairs. It groaned under his relatively light weight. Nicole eyed James with what he thought might have been guilt.

"You take the bed," James said.

"Ooo, thanks for the treat," she said, lifting the moth-eaten pillow from the bed.

"Would you prefer one of the comfy chairs Dr. Paynter is modeling?"

They both looked to Paynter, who had settled as best he could into the chair.

"I can sleep just about anywhere," he said, "doesn't bother me. I've slept in worse."

James looked around. "That's a frightening thought," he said.

"I don't think I can sleep sitting up," Kevin said.

"Take the other bed," James said. He turned to Nicole. "You too."

"Thanks," Kevin said.

James walked over to the door and checked the lock. There was no deadbolt. He looked around and quickly spotted what he was looking for; he picked up the flimsy metal trash can and placed it directly in the path of the door. He turned to find his three companions gazing at him in various stages of wonder.

"I...ummm...just thought that maybe we'd hear if someone was trying to sneak in," he said.

"Personally…I'd rather not know ahead of time if someone was going to shoot me. Seems like a lot of senseless screaming on my part," Kevin said. Nicole and Paynter were smiling at James.

"Shouldn't you people be asleep?" James asked.

Chapter 16

James sat in the chair, willing the discomfort in his lower back to go away. He had locked himself into one position after quickly discovering that there would be no truly comfortable position. The chair reminded him of one from his childhood. His grandmother, on his father's side, had a chair just like it out in the carless garage in Vermont. They had only been there once, when he was eight. But, he could remember the layout of that garage as if he had been there the day before. It was what he found himself relating everything in his life that was 'old' with. That garage was age and everything that could be older than him. He had wandered through the garage, touching everything, absorbing the lack of newness. There were two old bikes, the tires flat, the chains rusty, and the seats cracking from dry rot. He had become aware of the difference between an old toy and a new toy and had realized that nothing he had was truly old even if he thought it was. He drew a finger across the seat of the closest bike and rubbed the dust between his thumb and forefinger. This was old. No matter how messy his room had been, his toys had never had this kind of dust on it. It was like a mark of age. He spent the entire three days in and out of that garage, much to his mother's dismay. When they finally left, he had cried himself to sleep on the way back to Jersey. Something inside had told him he would never return. And he hadn't. His grandmother died the following year, and the house was sold in an estate auction. Years later he asked his mother about the house, and how come she had sold it. She had avoided the question, and never truly answered. He often thought that he might go back someday and find it, perhaps even buy it if it were still standing. But, what he really wanted was that garage and the things it held. And more so, he wanted to return to that feeling of wonder, though he knew he had probably left that behind with his childhood.

James didn't realize he had been sleeping until he jerked awake. He blinked into the darkness of the room. His eyes were slow to adjust to the darkness. What little light came from a small gap in the curtains. James must've seemed unsteady because Paynter spoke softly to him.

"You ok?" he asked.

James looked from him to Nicole on the bed closest to the window. He could just make out that she had made a pillow out of her coat. She had determined the blanket to be of fairly good, relatively clean quality, and it was pulled up to her ear. By the steady rise and fall of her body, he could tell she hadn't had trouble sleeping. Kevin was curled into the fetal position on the nearest bed. James looked in Paynter's direction, not quite able to make out the man's eyes.

"What time is it?" James asked. Paynter flicked his sleeve off his wrist.

"Three-ish," he said.

"I didn't realize I had nodded off," James said.

"You always talk in your sleep?" Paynter asked. James shot him a quick look.

"Don't know…never been awake to listen. Did I say anything good?"

"Nothing too clear," Paynter said, but he could tell the man was lying.

"Did you sleep? You've got to be running on empty," James said, stifling a yawn.

"A little. I did have that power nap this…I mean yesterday morning. I'll sleep tomorrow too…in the car. When you're driving," Paynter said.

"You trust me?" James asked.

"I trust you…I trust you want to know what's going on. And that you know by now that if I was out to hurt you…well, I've had plenty of opportunity," Paynter said.

James nodded.

"So…we know where we are headed, right?"

"Yep, and by the looks of this map I found--" Paynter said.

"You found a map?" James asked.

"In the lobby. Not exactly a Rand McNally, but it'll do us for now," Paynter said.

"Ok, so now we have a town. But, what good does that do us without a name?" James asked.

"Who said we didn't have a name?" Paynter said, and the corner of his mouth lifted. James cocked an eyebrow at him.

"Oh?" James said.

"I could probably rattle off all of them, though I never saved a shred of evidence. Taylor was the one who told me. He was the one responsible for transporting most of you," Paynter said.

"All three of us," James said. Paynter nodded slowly. "Yeah."

"Scattered to the wind," James said.

"I guess it wasn't the greatest idea, but we had to separate you. There was just no other option at the time," he said.

"I still don't understand. What were their plans? What is it they were going to do with us...that someone now thinks they have to get rid of us?"

"It's complicated, James. And, it's late. Try to get some rest."

"Sure...rest...cuz this stuff is easy to just let go of," James said.

"You're talking to someone who's spent the last twenty-four years thinking about it. You'll get no sympathy here," Paynter said

"I guess not. So, you gave each family an envelope."

"Yeah, we set up all the adopting families. About a year later, I sent out the bogus birth certificates. It was Taylor's idea, but he never knew...or at least I didn't think he knew that I had followed through on it. I think he just guessed. Never really knew where to contact him about it, and that wasn't exactly part of the plan anyway."

Something surged within James at those words. He had been adopted, though like most infants, he was not made aware of it until he was at an age that his parents felt he would be ready to understand and absorb the information. He was nine. It was one of those days that seemed to stand out in a lifetime of vague childhood memories. He could remember what he was wearing (a red and blue polo shirt and a ragged pair of Lee jeans his mother would throw away no less than a month later), the weather (it was a warm, sunny, spring day), and the meal his mother had cooked that he had watched become cold on his plate (pork chops, white rice, and boiled peas). It was a day that he had set his life by. There were events that had happened before his knowledge of his adoption and those that came after. He could date things by their relation to that day of his life. And there was a sense of consciousness that related to that day and the words that his mother said to him. There seemed to be consequences after that. An absurd sense of importance that related to everything he did. He became serious about school and sports and everything else he did. He had moved forward with a sense of purpose. Until recently, that is. Until his father died. That had been the end, hadn't it? It was like a light had turned on. His father had died, and the sense of importance that had driven James until then had faded. His mother's death seemed to take whatever was left. That was what Nicole had seen. She hadn't been around for the initial blow, but she had known, sensed, that something major had happened to James with the death of his mother. He'd been unable to move on from her death because he had never really come to grips with his father's death. He blinked at the tears that had welled in his eyes. It was a damn fine time to have a moment of revelation, James thought. He closed his eyes and drifted briefly.

As if on cue, Nicole made a small groan from the bed that disturbed James. He sat forward and looked at her figure stirring slightly on the bed. She had rolled over, facing away from them. James looked back at Paynter who smiled.

"Too many Twinkies," he said, and James could see the crooked smile in the dark.

With that James settled back in the chair.

"So, what's his name?" James asked.

"Doug," Paynter said, "Doug Peterson--"

The words had barely left Paynter's mouth when the quiet of the room was pierced with a guttural shriek. James' heart leapt to his throat and he stood up. His legs tingled from the night's stillness. Nicole was pointing at the window, pushing herself back to the edge of the bed. Paynter was on his feet as well.

"Hey…hey, hey…What is it?" James said, running to her and pulling her to him. She shook uncontrollably.

"Oh my god…there was someone…someone at the window, I swear, peeking in through the crack in the blinds," she said through heavy breaths, still pointing.

Kevin lurched from his bed, looking inebriated.

"What the fu--" he said.

"Shhhh!" came from three mouths.

James looked at the blinds on the window then to Paynter. He looked skeptical, but moved to the door, a finger raised,

112

listening. He removed the trash can, braced the door with a foot, and cracked it a hair, trying to look out. Though dim, the light from the front of the building made the evening seem darker than it was. The snow wasn't falling quite as heavily, but a small amount fell onto the floor of the room. Paynter ventured to open it further. Nicole stood now, still shaking under James' arms. She pulled her coat off the bed and put it on.

"I swear… I swear I saw something through the blind. Maybe….maybe it was just a shadow."

"No," Paynter said, who quickly closed the door again. James looked struck.

"What?" James asked.

"There are fresh tracks leading up to the window, and away. Someone was there," Paynter said.

"Jesus Christ. You're kidding. Out here? Do you really think?"

"I told you, James. These people are professionals. Why the hell else would anyone come sneaking around here?"

"Someone found us? Here? How? How could they know?" Kevin said. James looked to Paynter with the same question.

"No time to discuss semantics," Paynter said, pulling the car keys from his pocket and handing them to James. "Take these. You three go out the door to the left and around the far side of the building. Get to the car. The tracks seem to lead back around the near side. I'll go that way. Give me two minutes. If I don't show, go without me. No…don't look at me like that…I'm serious. If anyone else approaches you, go without me."

"But…," Nicole said.

"I'll be fine. They aren't after me, and…you don't really need me anymore," Paynter said, and James thought there was a brief flash of sadness to go with the lie.

"Remember, James. Doug Peterson. Try to be indirect. He doesn't know you two from Adam. Remember how you felt when you first met Kevin. Doug's a Midwestern boy. Might be a little more of a shock."

"I'll meet you in the parking lot," James said.

"With luck. Remember, if anything happens to me…anything…go, find your way. Doug will have what you need…another envelope."

They quickly gathered what little belongings they had brought into the room. Though they couldn't quite see the snow yet, they could feel it and the cold of the night, as it struck their bodies. James watched as Paynter disappeared around the right hand side of the building, retracing the way they had come in. He grabbed Nicole's arm firmly and headed in the opposite direction. Kevin trudged along close behind. There really was no other light than that of the streetlamp in the front parking lot, and the light it gave off was only bright due to the snow. It illuminated the edge of the building in stark contrast to the rear. James froze at the shadow's edge and peered one eye around as quickly as he could.

It was the man with the gun. The man who had been in his house. The man who Paynter had shot with a tranquilizer dart. Dr. Taylor was standing, waiting for them. He had known to wait there…somehow, which meant that Paynter would run into someone else. James dared another quick look, then realized that the man had been distracted. He was about fifty feet away. James grabbed for Nicole's hand and placed the car key into her cold fingers as quietly as possible. He could see her eyes like beacons of danger in the light from the lamp.

"When I distract him," James whispered, looking between Nicole and Kevin "you two go for the car."

Upon saying this, her eyes welled up, and she whispered a slow, quiet 'no'.

"I'll be ok. I'm not going to do anything stupid. I didn't play fifteen years of soccer for nothing."

He patted her hand in a gesture that he found both useless and comforting only to himself. She was there. She was real. Everything else was not. He turned and bolted around the corner as if he had been sprinting. The move surprised Nicole and she yelped, but fell back against the building with Kevin.

Taylor was slow to react, as if he hadn't expected their plan to work. James eyed up a large row of bushes that he could easily put between himself and the man. Taylor shouted something James didn't hear and started running through the nearly knee-deep drift of snow towards him. James quickly glanced back at Nicole, then bolted for the cover of the shrubbery. He could hear the man shout after him in pursuit. Had he expected James to just give up?

James crossed the street to a row of small houses that might have looked picturesque at another time. Now they looked like a wall he was trapped against. The road had been plowed recently, and James splashed across through half-melted slush. It would probably refreeze by morning. He felt his legs moving steadily beneath him on the surface of the road, but he hadn't expected the curb. The pain from his ankle made him abandon his balance, and he tumbled into a snow covered trash can at the curb. The metal lid skidded out into the street clanging loudly as James hit the ground hard, clutching his leg. Taylor rounded the bushes and spotted James across the street. James tried to duck behind the can, feeling foolish as he did so. He knew it was no use. Taylor carefully crossed the road toward him.

James looked about for something, anything to use in his defense. A light had come on in the nearby house, presumably the owners of the can he had just crashed into. Call 911. Call 911. Wait, do they even have 911 out here? Then Paynter's voice spoke in his head, "They are the police." Crap.

"Don't try and get away, James," Taylor shouted.

"You're persistent," James said, standing and wincing at the pain in his ankle, "I'll give you that."

"Paynter isn't here to rescue you now," Taylor said.

"Oh, I wouldn't rule that out," James said, and he heard the car before Taylor did, "I have a few more friends than you."

"Oh, I--" Taylor said.

Then, he not only heard the car, but saw the Chrysler 300M slide haphazardly out of the hotel parking lot, tires spinning, and into the road, headed right toward him.

"...shit!"

James watched as Taylor stared at the car in disbelief, grappling with the choices of capturing James or being run over. The car made a bead for him and the man lifted the gun toward it. The engine was gunning, and the tires were furiously fighting with the snow to hurtle down upon the man. He leapt out of the way as the car skidded between James and the man. Both doors opened, and Nicole and Kevin were both screaming something unintelligible. James didn't need the hint. He threw himself into the back seat and slammed the door behind him. He heard her foot pound the gas pedal. The tail fished in the slush, but the tires found some traction, throwing James back in his seat. He massaged his leg as he tried to sit up. He realized Nicole was crying furiously, wiping her hair from her damp face. She was possessed, turning every few blocks, and gunning the engine along snowy side streets.

"He killed him," Kevin finally said, his voice low.

"He shot him...in the parking lot..." Nicole blubbed.

"Paynter?" James said, and Nicole nodded, her hair flailing.

117

"A man in a black coat and hat," she sobbed between words, "The gun…it didn't make…a sound. He just raised it and…and shot him…square in the chest and…and then walked away."

Chapter 17

Taylor watched as the car sped away, fishtailing up the road and violently around a corner. He wiped his cold, damp brow and quietly cursed himself. He rolled onto his side and pushed on the ground to get up. A shove to the back threw him back down into the snow. He tumbled into the slush on the road and pointed the gun in the direction of his would-be assailant. The man in black kicked him again and barked a harsh laugh.

"Use it, ya fool! I don't know why you even carry the goddamn thing," he said, the light from the hotel parking lot, casting a shadow under the brim of his cap.

He brushed some snow from his own gun. The silencer barrel gleamed in the light from the street lamp. A window opened on the second floor in the house nearest to them. The owner loudly recommended that they finish their business and move elsewhere or he would have to notify the authorities, only in much more colorful terms. The man in black turned to the crew-cut coifed man leaning out the window. That man had just realized that both of the men in the street were carrying guns. The silenced weapon was brought to level with the second story window.

"Now, that wasn't very nice, was it?" said the man in black.

The man in the window cursed and ducked out of view just before two rounds pierced the sill.

"Holy shit," Taylor said and he moved quickly to his feet and started toward the parking lot.

"Where are you going?" said the man in black, as he strode to catch him up.

"Where's Paynter?" Taylor said.

"He's dead."

"What?"

Taylor spun on his heels, stopping the man in black in his tracks. They were nose to nose, though Taylor gave up at least four inches.

"What's the matter, Doc? Still have some of those old feelings for your pal?" the man spat.

"He didn't...need to die," said Taylor.

"Need. Need? Why does there always have to be a need? He was on the list. There's your need."

His smile disappeared. He moved so quickly, that it took a moment for Taylor to realize that he was no longer holding his own gun. The man in black had disarmed him and wrenched him by the collar.

"If I believe there is a need for someone to die, then I will make it so. Paynter was in the way. Those kids become that much less to deal with, without him. They have nothing without him."

"You sound so sure," said Taylor, the tip of his lip bleeding down his chin.

"I am, that's why they sent me," and the smile returned as he loosened his grip on the doctor's collar.

120

"And what of Paynter?" Taylor said.

"What of him?"

"You're just going to leave him there?" Taylor asked.

"Um…let me think about that one…yeah, let's go," the man in black said without really thinking.

They walked like men on a casual stroll back to the parking lot. The man in black handed Taylor back his gun.

"Try not to shoot your dick off," the man said.

He stopped suddenly and threw a hand against Taylor's chest to stop him. It knocked the wind out of Taylor for a moment and he rubbed the spot, looking at the man in black with renewed hatred. Just as quickly, the man started moving again, this time with a quicker pace.

"Better get our boogie-shoes on, Doc. The po-leece are on their way."

Taylor hurried after him into the parking lot and toward the Barracuda that was slowly accumulating a new layer of snow powder. He walked over to the passenger side of the car. He waited for the man in black to enter the car, but he didn't. He was staring over Taylor's shoulder. Taylor spun around, but saw nothing. Nothing at all.

"What…?" blurted Taylor, just as he realized what it was. "I thought you said you shot him? Where the hell is he?"

The man in black walked to the front of the car, peering around the parking lot. He could see several sets of tracks. There was no body. And there was barely a sign that the man had been there at all. No pool of blood. No red-streaked snow.

121

The sirens were growing louder. The man in black smacked the hood of his car, then ran back to the driver's door and jumped in.

"God dammit, how could I be so dumb. God dammit! Must've had a vest on or something. God dammit. You stupid mother…God…*dammit*!"

They pulled out of the parking lot just in time to avoid immediate pursuit. The man in black pounded the steering wheel, cursing so furiously that it made Taylor fear for his own life. He imagined asking the man if he was still as sure as he was before. He also imagined the beating he would receive for it. It could wait. His time would come.

Chapter 18

"Where are you headed?" James asked.

"No clue," Nicole said.

"Maybe you should pull over," James said.

"No," Kevin and Nicole said at the same time.

"Okay. Maybe we should at least try and find out where the hell we are."

"Where's that map?" Nicole asked.

There was a feeble search for it, but the three seemed comfortable with just getting away from where they were. Nicole continued to drive, though with less emphasis on speed. She gripped the wheel so hard that James thought her hands might go numb. She broke out every so often in a fresh set of tears. Kevin stared out into space, occasionally uttering the same phrase, "Unfuckingbelieveable." James didn't know what to say to either of them. He felt stupid. He felt like he'd been shown a set of choices that should have seemed obvious and yet he had chosen poorly anyway. He wasn't used to that. He had never needed to make the tough decisions. Not these kinds of decisions at least. James had been suddenly ripped out of the comfortable world of easy decisions to one where every decision could turn the course of his life…or what was left of it.

"Turn right!" shouted James, startling Nicole into a turn that nearly ran them into the ditch on the far side of the road.

She struggled with the car, allowing it to come to a complete stop in the middle of the road. The windshield wipers squeaked against the glass, brushing uselessly at the heavy wet flakes still falling. Kevin looked over at Nicole. Then they both looked back at James.

"Next time," Kevin said, looking back at Nicole, "don't listen to him. Jesus, James! Could you be a little more…oh, I dunno…timely, with your directions?"

"We've got to keep going," she said.

"I know, but let me drive," James said.

She nodded and opened the door to get out. James climbed out of the car after her, grasped her hands and was surprised by how cold they were. She was shaking and he couldn't be certain it was from the cold night air. Tear streaks had dried on her cheeks, but her eyes looked ready to provide fresh ones. The snow was catching in her hair. Everything he had felt in the last few hours seemed to be reflecting back at him in her face. Something had changed. She would never look the same to him, and something that had existed for her inside of him had died. He turned to pull the driver's seat back for her, afraid that she might see that feeling in his face.

She climbed into the back seat. He looked to her for some sort of response, but she simply curled herself into her jacket and turned her back to them. He looked to Kevin, but he was staring blankly out the front window. Kevin looked like he was ready to cry himself. James told himself that their reaction was natural and completely understandable given the circumstances. But, despite what he tried to think, he felt that they were really turning their backs on *him* and leaving *him* alone when he needed them the most. Then he felt guilty for thinking that. The stress was starting to affect them all. He put the car in drive, but only inched forward a foot before stopping again.

He looked around at the sign that had made him turn. The familiar blue and red shield of the interstate system. The same one that had brought them here in the first place. He assumed this because the snow obscured exactly which interstate highway that it was. Being Pennsylvania, the choices were limited. James considered the situation. There was a state of emergency declared, which made driving a problem. At least on a major highway. He stared back over at the sign. It wasn't clear from where he sat. He gingerly reversed the car several feet to the corner. Interstate to the left. State highway 44 to the right. He reversed some more, hearing the tires struggling to grip the increasingly snowy road. It hadn't seen a snow plow in at least an hour if not more.

"Heads or tails?" James asked.

Kevin just shook his head.

"Unbelievable," he said.

James hunkered down behind the wheel and focused on what he could see of the road. With sunrise still several hours off, it would be a long, dark, and quiet remainder of the night.

Chapter 19

Agent John Norris awoke to the sound of a disturbingly loud telephone placed too close to the head of the bed. An accompanying light flashed along with the ring, in case he was so deaf that he could not hear the ear-splitting bell. Only the cheapest motel in the area could provide this added bonus of discomfort. His rapid attempt to silence the racket was nearly fatal for the phone. His crumpled pants cushioned the three-foot fall that the phone made to the floor. He pressed the receiver to his head and spoke, or at least tried to.

"John?" said a somewhat familiar, though tinny, voice on the other end.

Norris pulled the receiver away and coughed out the night's congestion. This took several hacks that a chain-smoking emphysema sufferer would have been proud of. He tried again.

"Hello?" he said.

"John? You ok?" came the familiar voice.

"Damn cold. Started coming on last Tuesday. Can't seem to shake it," Norris said

This was followed by another round of phlegm-dislodging coughs. He placed the receiver down, went into the bathroom, and proceeded to spit the contents of his lungs into the toilet. He returned to find that the familiar voice had begun talking to the end table.

"Den? Start over."

"Why'd you turn your cell off?" Dennis asked.

"Because I didn't want to talk to anyone," Norris said honestly.

"Well, I had a hell of a time tracking you down, but I have my ways," Dennis said.

"Careful, Den. That's misappropriation of…errr…something I'm sure," Norris said.

"I thought you'd approve," Dennis said.

"What's going on, Den?"

"We have something in your area."

"You gotta be kidding," Norris said.

"No. Something came in over the wire this morning. 'Round five. When I found out where you were, well…with the storm and all, it'll be a bit before they can get someone in from Pittsburgh or Cleveland."

"Out here?" Norris asked.

"Listen, it's not far up the road from where you are. A place called Springfield."

"And the locals can't handle it?" Norris said.

"Well…according to the police, witnesses saw a man get shot."

"Wow. A shooting. Go figure," Norris cracked.

"Point blank in the chest," said Dennis.

Norris put his glasses on and took two deep swallows from the glass of water at the side of the bed. He knew that the water was clean because it tasted just like chlorine.

"Impressive," Norris said, picking up the remote and turning the TV on.

128

"Then he got up and walked away," Dennis added.

"Nice. Why are they wasting my time with this sort of shit, Den. Just because I got stuck in the middle of fucking nowhere in a snow storm, they gotta go and throw something like this in my lap? I'm supposed to be reporting to the Cleveland office today, remember? You know, Cleveland? Where the real crime happens?"

"John, c'mon, don't shoot the messenger," Dennis said.

"Nice pun. I'm sorry, Den. I'm just not in the mood to go looking for a body. Can't they just follow the blood trail?" Norris said.

He flicked between Headline News and The Weather Channel. Neither seemed to offer any good news.

"There wasn't one," Dennis said.

There was a moment while Norris waited for the explanation. There wasn't one.

"And?" Norris said.

"And, there's a slim chance it's our man," Dennis said.

"How's that?" Norris said. He turned off the TV.

"Someone spotted a '69 Barracuda. Could be a coincidence, but--" Dennis said.

"How far am I?" Norris coughed again, the phlegm refusing to cooperate with this sudden burst of conversation.

"Couple miles. Listen, there's a couple witnesses."

"How many?"

"Three."

"How many saw the shot?" Norris asked.

129

"One…from about a hundred and fifty yards…through a thin curtain," Dennis said.

"That'll be useful," Norris said.

"Saw the shot. Saw the victim fall."

"Didn't see him get up and mosey on away?" Norris mocked.

"Nope."

"Of course not. Too busy trying to dial 911 on his rotary phone. Any descriptions?"

"Vague. It was at three this morning. Poorly lit parking lot. The other two who saw *something* gave conflicting reports as to how many people were there."

"Great."

"The only solid stuff we have is the description of the vehicles."

"Who's the contact?"

"A lieutenant by the name of Fields. Chief's out of town on vacation or something like that. Sounded like the kind of guy who joined the police force in his home town for the uniform and not the potential gunplay."

Norris laughed harshly, which then turned into a cough and another fit.

"Great. A small town Buford and a walking dead man. Where's Mulder and Scully when you need 'em."

"And John, keep your head up on this one."

"Oh?"

"They don't know I'm calling you on this."

"Seemed a little small for bureau work," said Norris.

"Yeah, so don't stir the pot too much. A flash of the badge and then in and out. Don't go pissing 'em off. You haven't even checked in yet for Christ's sake."

"Alright, Den. I'll check it out. I'll call you in a couple of hours. Let you know what's going on," Norris said.

"Okay. Keep your nose clean, alright?"

Norris reeled with a volley of chest-splitting coughs.

"And, Jesus, do something about that, will you?"

"Yeah, hey, no problem."

Norris hung up the phone and placed it back onto the end table. He sat on the edge of the bed, boxers and a t-shirt on from the day before. His pants, shirt, tie and jacket lay in a pile on the floor. He breathed deep and felt the air catch in his lungs. He coughed again, the phlegm deep within his chest. Some cold, he thought.

He stood and walked to the curtains. They were that triple-layered burlap design that managed to block out all possible light no matter what time of day. He pulled back the circa 70s fabric. The light from outside was more snow than sun, but he was pleased to see that the abundance of falling flakes had abated. He was less pleased to look down into the parking lot and see that his car was now beneath three feet of snow along with several others parked right next to him.

"Son of a bitch," he said and closed the curtain as a fresh wave of coughing hit him.

Chapter 20

"Nic."

It took a moment for the response, but eventually she responded in a quiet, hidden voice.

"Yeah."

"I need you to be with me, here," James said. "I need both of you to be with me on this."

Kevin stirred and looked at him and he could hear her turn around in the back seat. She had been still for at least an hour. James had let her do it. Had given her that chance to come back by herself. She hadn't, though, and it was starting to bother him. The road was still dark, though the snow had let up. And on more than one occasion, he had considered finding the interstate and just turning back. Forget the whole thing. Just drive back to Jersey and live in his parents' house for the rest of his life, as short as it might be. At least he'd be comfortable. But, then he knew it wasn't that easy. Knew he wouldn't just be left alone. And besides, that house would always await his return. It and nothing else awaited him back there. At least while he was out here, wherever here was, he was not alone. At least not yet.

"Are you ok? Are you lost?" Nicole said in a voice that was not completely her own.

"You could say that," James said, "I think we passed into Ohio a ways back and…and I just need to hear a voice…something. The radio's just not doing it for me anymore."

"I'm sorry," she said.

"Sorry, bro, that shit was...well, it was fucked up back there," Kevin said.

"Don't I know it. But, don't apologize...I won't hold it against you. I just really need you to both be with me in spirit as well, instead of just in body." She grasped his shoulder and he could hear the hesitation in her voice.

"Pull over," she said. "Kevin, can I sit up front?"

Kevin nodded.

James pulled over, finding as clear a spot as he could on what little shoulder there was. He put the car in park and helped her as best he could with the seat. She climbed in and wrapped him around the head with both arms. He returned the hug and they just sat like that for a while, awkward as it was with Kevin in the back. He inhaled deeply of her and felt himself relax for the first time that night. There was something he was chasing here. There was something to be found at the end of it, and it might not just be the promised other brother, or the remote hope of family. Nicole let go first and as she sat back, James could see fresh tears streaking her cheeks.

"It was my fault," she said, choking back a sob.

"Oh Nic, you couldn't have done anything--" James started.

"I must've...pushed the dial button...on my cell phone...sometime in the night," she gasped.

"But..." she wouldn't let him speak though.

"It was to my home number and the answering machine is unplugged. I have the ringer on so low, you have to be on top of the phone to hear it. It just kept ringing. It was nearly dead by the time I got in the car. It had been ringing for over two hours." She couldn't hold anything back and began sobbing furiously. James sat looking at her, the pieces trying to work their way together through the clouds of sleeplessness.

"The signal," Kevin said and Nicole nodded her head without looking up. "They could have triangulated the position within a couple miles depending on where the nearest towers were."

James looked back at Kevin, an eyebrow cocked.

"I watch a lot of Discovery Channel," Kevin said.

"Right. But, how would they know to be looking for you, Nic? There's got to be another explanation," James said and leaned out to Nicole and gently stroked the side of her head.

The sobs were coming less frequently now. She pulled his hand to her face and rubbed her cheek against it. Her face was warm and damp. The lights that suddenly appeared behind the car startled James.

"Get down," he hissed and they obeyed.

He looked back at the road and realized that, despite his attempt to pull over, he still took up most of the lane. He rolled down his window enough to stick his arm out and wave the car by. They didn't seem to notice, or care. The car pulled up right behind the 300M.

"No way," James said, "No fucking way. Sit back up…slowly" and as if to answer, the car was suddenly flooded with red and blue flashing lights. James felt sick as his body moved hurriedly from fear to relief and back in a matter of moments. Paynter's voice was still clear in his head, 'They are the police.'

Nicole made to straighten her face and hair in vain. Her eyes were red and puffy from all of the crying she had done that night, and her hair was everywhere. She sat forward and pulled on her seatbelt. Kevin looked especially nervous. His hands rummaged in his pockets for something that wasn't there. He turned away from the driver's side door as James rolled the window down the rest of the way. He watched in the side view as the officer got out of his car and made the slow walk up. He tried to move the shifter into drive as smoothly as he could. The car gave it away with a loud "Thunk!" The officer stopped short of the door, his hand suddenly at his holster.

"Put the car into park, sir." James hesitated for only a moment then did as he had been told. He made a split decision that he wasn't feeling that brave.

"Sorry officer," he said, placing both hands up on the wheel.

The officer, a local from what James could make of his uniform, relaxed his position only slightly.

"Bit far from Florida tonight?"

"Florida?" James said, his mind trying to make some sense out of the word.

"Yes…yes it is, officer," Kevin said from the back seat.

He shone a large black flashlight into the back seat. Kevin waved as cheerily as he could.

"Are you aware of the current state of emergency, sir?"

"State of Emergency?" James said, wishing he could do more than spit out a question to answer a question.

The officer moved closer to the window, bent down and got a good look at Nicole.

"Are you all right, miss?" said the officer. His free hand was still on the top of his unbuttoned holster. James tried not to look uneasy. It wasn't working. In the suddenness, none of the consequences of what was happening had occurred to him until now. The officer would routinely ask for a license and registration. James would provide it to him, upon which the officer would realize that the car was not registered to either of its occupants. Then he would run the plate, and discover that the car belonged to a man in Florida named Reed. Oh yeah, and the three in the car just happened to fit the vague description of three from a crime scene about a half hour away. They would be arrested. The officer would probably call for backup, and this whole escapade would end with James in jail.

"Do you want to see my registration, officer?" James blurted out.

"I asked the young lady a question, sir, and I'd like her to answer it."

"She's not feeling too well," James said. The officer looked at him.

"Have you been drinking, sir?"

James' laugh was a little quick and a little too high pitched. The officer took a step back from the car. His name-badge said Williams.

"You were going to ask me for my license and registration, so I just thought I'd save you the trouble of asking."

The officer's free hand nervously fingered the snap that kept the 9mm holstered.

"Step out of the car, sir," Office Williams said.

"I'm sorry, Officer Williams," James said, his voice faltering with the knowledge of what he was about to attempt, "I just can't do that."

"Sir?"

"James...what are you doing?" Kevin whispered.

James could tell that his answer had somewhat stunned him. As James looked at the man, he realized that he wasn't really a man at all. At least, not in James' definition. He might have been a year or two older than James, though the smattering of facial hair gave him the look of a few more years. He had most definitely never fired that gun at anything but a target, or perhaps some poor four-legged creature, and the sudden prospect of being forced to pull it out now, and possibly using it against another man, seemed daunting. James was betting on it.

It was a clumsy move. Amateur at best. James turned toward Nicole quickly and leaned over the center console, saying something about the registration being in the glove compartment. The officer wasn't expecting the sudden movement or the refusal to leave the car. With his body blocking the view of his hands, James reached with his left and slammed the gearshift down with his right.

"Sir?" Office Williams said again, his voice cracking a bit. James could hear the sidearm slide out of the holster.

His foot was on the pedal down to the floor. It was done. It wasn't pretty. But, it was done. Nicole screamed. Kevin gripped the back of the seats like they might fall off if he let go.

The all-season radials fumbled about in the snow before finding anything resembling traction. The tail of the car fished about on the road in front of the stunned officer.

The car righted itself and was twenty feet away before Officer Williams had raised his gun half-heartedly to bear on the car. He considered firing a shot into the rear of the car, but then he remembered the girl. He stood there in the snow, choosing not to give chase. He would not report it. He did not want to waste the paperwork. As he sat in his car, convincing himself to forget all about it, his in-dash monitor lit up. It was a brand new APB out from the Springfield police department, about a half hour away. They were looking for a couple of vehicles involved in a possible homicide; one of which was a green Chrysler 300M with two young men and a woman in their early twenties.

"Sonofabitch."

Chapter 21

"That fucker," mumbled the man in black. It had been less than two hours since the incident in the hotel parking lot. Taylor had watched as his captor had rolled through every level of anger possible. He had gone so far as to slam both fists against the wheel, nearly sending them off the road. It was too much for the doctor to handle anymore.

"Alright! Get over it," Taylor said, lashing out, "You're such a fucking expert. You didn't think he'd see something like this coming? Fuck him. He's out of the way. He'd be a fool to follow now. Focus on those boys. They're all that matters. They're all that ever mattered."

The man in black stared back across the car at Taylor, but Taylor did not flinch. He merely tried to meet the man's gaze without faltering. The slow wicked smile crept across the man's face.

"Growing some balls, doc," he said, the smile only fading slightly. "I like that. You're gonna need 'em."

Taylor looked away from him. He felt ill. His inability to stop James from continuing on, and the escape of Paynter had turned a bad day into a worse night. He had not wanted this man in black to kill Paynter. He had told himself that repeatedly. And he had felt a sense of relief when he realized his old friend had escaped. He had not felt so relieved by James' deliverance. He did not want to kill James, but the thought had grown that there might be no choice in the matter.

"I need to stop," Taylor said.

"Tough shit, doc," said the man in black, his humored look wiped clear of his face.

"Might be tough to get off the seats," Taylor said.

He watched as the man in black turned toward him, turned away, turned back, and pulled roughly onto the side of the road, cursing under his breath. A cloud of snow and steam billowed into the glow of the headlights as they came to a stop. They were surrounded by rolling fields of what might have been corn during the summer. Taylor opened the door, the drastic difference in temperature snapping at his exposed neck. He looked back at the man in black, who was lighting a fresh cigarette.

"Don't be gone too long, Doc," a sneer peeling his lips back across his teeth, "I don't wanna be losing you out here in this lovely weather."

"Wouldn't that be a shame," Taylor said.

"Yeah, especially if you lived to tell about it," the man said.

Taylor stepped out of the car, trying to ignore what the man had just said. He had known it from the time he woke up in that room days before. Taylor was not going to survive this trip and the man in black knew it as much as he. There was a certain sound in his voice that sometimes disappeared, but always returned to remind the doctor of its purpose. Sure, he needed him to get to James, but Taylor wondered if even that was true.

No, thought Taylor, he knew where he was going, or at least he had an idea…and someone was definitely feeding him information. How else would he have known to look at that particular hotel in the middle of nowhere Pennsylvania? Taylor served a purpose though. Perhaps he was simply a convenient secondary target that might draw fire away.

Taylor expelled a large breath into the cold air and watched it whip around his head before dissipating. What little hair that was left atop his head was blown around like grass in a storm. He would start shivering soon. He had started walking aimlessly out into the field where they had stopped. Amongst the lonely remnants of corn stalks, he was emboldened. He could run for it. But, he wasn't exactly dressed for a romp through the snow in the middle of winter. He still had his wingtips on. He might make another two hundred feet into the field before the man came after him. And where would he be then? Dead in the middle of a corn field. As opposed to being dead somewhere else, he thought. Dead in the trunk of a '69 Barracuda found at the bottom of Lake Erie? Nah, he'd never give up his baby.

The cold was starting to make him shiver uncontrollably. The notion of relieving oneself in such weather was really beyond Taylor. Even if he had been able to maneuver his fly open with his now frozen fingers, he could not imagine performing in these extreme conditions. He stopped walking. He fingered the revolver still in his coat pocket. It was useless in his hands and he knew it. Near the stock was the small folded piece of paper with six sets of letters. A jumbled mass of numerals that only he understood. He didn't need it. He could still remember the cross-country hike. *Had it really been twenty-four years ago?*

"Doc," said the man in black.

His voice was low and deadly even at fifty feet. Taylor made a quick glance to make sure that the man had not crept up on him. He had not. The man in black sat against the side of the car, still smoking the cigarette. Taylor made to pull up his zipper. His hands aged in the cold air, feeling like they might break if he bent the knuckles. He turned to face the man.

"Cut the show, doc. We got miles to go yet," said the man in black.

"I needed a breather," Taylor said.

The man was silhouetted against the car, his cap pulled low over his face. The cigarette burn brightly with one long drag, then it was tossed on the ground. The man got back into the car. Taylor squinted his eyes against the wind. Before him, the sleek blackness of the car merged with the darkness of the night, contrasted by the white of the earth. Its eyes the taillights, gleaming red, its breath the exhaust. I'll grow to love this car, thought Taylor. Only if I'm behind the wheel...and he's under it.

Chapter 22

When the mileage markers for Cleveland read 20 miles, James knew he needed to stop. He was probably a half hour late in making the decision. The snow had stopped but despite his plea for a bit of company, Kevin and Nicole had both drifted off into uneasy sleep. The rest area was a welcome sight. It offered the comforts of a bathroom and food, even if it was a public stall and a Burger King. His eyes were ready to fall out of his head. He had intermittently opened the window to keep himself awake. He'd heard Nicole cry in her sleep and it killed him to be unable to comfort her. Kevin stirred for the first time in an hour.

"You awake?" James said, barely above a whisper. He had pulled into the first cleaned-out parking spot he could find.

"Yeah," Kevin said, without turning away from the window.

"Did you sleep?" James asked.

"On and off. You staying awake?" he said.

"Barely," James said.

"You're doing a pretty good job."

"Amazing what you can do when you need to."

"I need my bladder to be about a half-gallon larger. Think it'll happen?" Kevin said, grabbing his crotch with a pained expression.

James shook his head 'No.'

"You'd better go before you wet your seat," James said.

"You comin'?" Kevin asked. They both glanced back at Nicole. "She'll be ok…you wouldn't even know she was in here--"

"Unless you were looking for a girl in a green 300M," James said.

"Gotcha…I'll try and hurry," Kevin said.

"By the looks of it, hurrying won't be your problem," James said.

Kevin got out of the car and made for the nearest restroom. James watched him walking away. The rest area was a simple collection of buildings. He had made an effort to park farthest from the main building that housed the food. When Kevin had opened the door, James got a faint whiff of fried food and his stomach had shouted at him. It had been a long time since his last proper meal. The one Nicole had cooked the morning before. That seemed like a lifetime ago. Paynter had been alive then.

"Where are we?" Nicole asked, her voice strained as she stretched her legs the width of the car. James glanced back at her and saw that what little sleep she had gotten had not really been what she needed. By the looks of it, she needed a week of sleep. Her face was pallid, the rosy color of her lips muted. Her eyes were glassy and her lids puffy. Her naturally tousled hair was looking flat and tired.

"I'm so sorry, Nic," James said.

She looked at him, but refused to meet his eyes in the rearview mirror. He could see her shoulders shrug.

"Let's not talk about it anymore, ok? I think there's some more important stuff to deal with right now. Why'd we stop?"

"I...ok...I stopped because I think we are really lost this time. I need to find a map or something," James said.

"How far are we from...what was it? Hubbard?"

"Yeah. Well, I think we might be about twenty miles past it. Paynter...he said it wasn't far over the Ohio border...and we passed that a little while ago," James said.

"We'll have to find a phone book, or maybe they have an information desk here?" Nicole said.

"And then what?" James asked.

"What do you mean?" she said.

"I mean exactly that. Then what? What the hell are we going to do?"

"Well, we're going to drive to this Hubbard and you're both going to go meet your brother," Nicole said.

Kevin approached the car and got in, releasing a long satisfied sigh.

"Much better," he said.

"You make it sound so easy," James said.

"What'd I miss?" Kevin asked.

"After all this? James...gimme a break," she said, laughing humorlessly.

"Ummm...hello?" Kevin said.

"James is worried about meeting Doug," Nicole said, folding her arms and reclining once more in the back seat.

"What if he freaks?" James asked.

"Of course he's going to freak…a little. You freaked," she said.

"Well, he does have a point, Nic. I mean, what if he has a girlfriend who wants to brain us with a large kitchen appliance when she sees us? I mean, this could be dangerous," Kevin said, massaging the still noticeable lump on his temple.

Nicole tried to look angry at him for a moment, but quickly broke into a smile. They laughed like it was water and they were thirsty. It eventually tapered off into giggles.

"You've been driving too long if that's all you're worried about," she said.

"You're right about that," James said, "I have been driving way too long. And I need to piss. And I'm hungry. Anyone want Burger King?"

"James, we can't risk…" Nicole began.

"We can't risk all of us passing out from exhaustion and lack of food either. I've been feeling light-headed for the last ten minutes. If one of us goes in, it shouldn't be a problem," James said.

"He does have a point. I could go an egg sandwich. You know what…just get me whatever you're getting. I'd eat just about anything now. Ooo…and a large coffee…black with sugar," Kevin said.

"Now it's getting complicated. Hon?" James said.

Nicole looked wary but gave him her order anyway.

"I'll be right back," he said as he closed the door.

To the East, James could see the faint promise of dawn struggling to be seen through the winter glom. The snow had stopped falling, but the wind was blowing the powder hard enough to make it blizzard-like. James pulled at the collar of his jacket, the chill cold running quickly through him. He wished he had listened to his mother's constant advice and worn a hat. The warmth of the rest area was a welcome relief even after only a short walk outside. He found the bathroom and relieved himself, then stood in front of the near-vacant Burger King counter, deciding what to order. A TV overhead was broadcasting regional news to no one in particular. The place was empty. He picked up a few sandwiches from under the heat hood, got Kevin's coffee, and went to the register. He handed his cash to a young black woman named Chanice. Somehow, she looked more tired than he felt. He tried to smile at her when she handed him his change, but she didn't make eye contact.

He turned to leave, but paused when he heard the news broadcast.

"…disturbing news that begins with a report out of New Jersey…"

James turned and slowly looked up at the monitor. His heart dropped into his feet. He watched as a young woman spoke into the camera, his house clearly visible in the background. The multicup coffee holder in his hand swayed and he had to steady himself against a nearby garbage can.

"…events that took place at this home in rural New Jersey. According to police, they received a call from the home's owner, twenty-four-year-old James Masterson, early yesterday morning. Based on the 911 tapes, police were able to determine that Mr. Masterson believed that someone had entered his home. That someone turned out to be 77-year-old Samuel Isaacson, Mr. Masterson's neighbor. What happened next you can hear for yourself…"

A map of New Jersey appeared with Hackettstown marked in proximity to New York City. Then the recording began and James steadied himself again, fearing that he would just fall over in the middle of the rest stop and draw the sort of attention he certainly didn't want now. He heard someone whispering about an intruder, then there was a pause and he didn't have to be told that Samuel's voice was calling to him in the background. The old man had been James' neighbor all his life. They'd had picnics at his house when he was a boy. Then the caller suddenly spoke loudly. "…there's an intruder in my house!" Samuel spoke again, this time much clearer due to his apparent proximity to the phone. He seemed to recognize James, but his voice was confused. James jumped when the first gun shot rang out, making white noise of the recording. The 911 dispatcher screamed. It was followed by two more in evenly spaced succession. James' head swam. Samuel was dead. It hadn't been him, but someone pretending to be him. And they killed his neighbor. For no apparent reason, they had killed his neighbor. He glanced back up at the screen and

150

flinched. His photograph, about six years old by the looks of it, appeared blown up on the screen. James looked around, eyeing up the two people nearest to him. Neither was paying any attention to the TV. He almost bolted for the door, but thought better of it. He staggered his way back to the car, so much so that Kevin and Nicole came out of the car to help him. He had no sooner handed the food and drinks to Nicole when he turned, fell into the snow and vomited.

"James!" Nicole cried. Kevin stood in the snow next to him, a hand under his arm.

"What the hell happened?" he asked.

"I'm on the news," James spat. He wiped his lips with the sleeved of his jacket. He spat again, trying to get rid of the bile taste in his mouth.

"What? How?" Nicole said. She had placed the food in the car and now was crouched down beside him. He looked up at both of them.

"They killed my neighbor…someone…they killed Mr. Isaacson. And…they think it was me," James said, looking between the two of them.

"But, how?" Kevin asked.

"There was a 911 call from my house…it almost…he thought it was me. Then he shot him. Whoever made the call shot him…three times! He was an old man. They killed him…because of me. And now, they think I did it," James said, turning now to sit in the snow.

Kevin tugged on his arm to try and lift him from the ground, but James resisted.

"James, honey, we need to get moving then," Nicole said.

"Why are they doing this?" James asked.

He stared at Nicole and his eyes began to well with tears.

"Why are they ruining other people's lives…because of me? I didn't…I didn't do anything. Why can't they just leave us alone?"

He turned his head and wiped the tears away.

"I wish I had an answer," she said and wrapped herself around him.

Kevin crouched down and put his arms around both of them.

"James, I don't want to be a prick…I'm sorry for your loss and all, and as much as I'm into the whole hug fest, could we move it to the car? My balls are gonna crawl up into my stomach in a minute."

"C'mon," Nicole said. They stood, half lifting James from the ground.

James trudged back to the car and slumped into the back seat. In his mind, he could see and hear Samuel Isaacson's last moments, repeating over and over. He screamed at the top of his lungs.

Chapter 23

Norris pulled the wool hat tight over his head. The snow might have stopped, but a bitter arctic wind had chased it down from Canada, or so the weatherman would have you believe. It was supposed to creep back up above freezing later, but that would be accompanied by rain.

Large sections of the parking lot of the hotel in Springfield, Pennsylvania, had been cordoned off with yellow tape. Judging by the size of the town, Norris figured they had raided the local hardware store for the extra rolls. He pulled out his badge as he approached the line. A lone officer who, to Norris, looked barely old enough to break the law, let alone defend it, pulled his collar about his ears, glanced at Norris' badge and nodded. He pointed to the hotel, where there were three men standing, looking at the ground as if all three were in deep thought. Norris thanked the deputy and lifted the yellow tape above his head.

He had crossed three quarters of the lot before a fit of coughing took him over. The pain wracked his body, shooting from his chest down through to his ass. He blinked tears from his eyes and he wavered in his tracks for a moment. He didn't see the office approach, but was glad for the hand of support that had gripped his elbow.

"Can I help you?" the man said in a deep baritone voice.

Norris hacked one last time, then bent away from the man and spit into the snow. He looked down at the bulge of bloody green mucous, then kicked some snow over it. He wiped his mouth with the exposed back of his free hand. *Shit*.

"FBI. Agent John Norris, for what it's worth" said Norris, flashing his badge again. He forced another cough back.

"Deputy Robinson. If you don't mind me saying, Agent Norris, you don't look too good," said the officer holding his arm. Norris turned to look at the man.

A square-jawed, clean-shaven, black man, Deputy Robinson wore a look of genuine concern on his face.

"Deputy," said Norris, "I don't feel so good, but the sooner I can get my work done here, the sooner I can worry about that little problem. Make sense?"

"Right," said Robinson, releasing Norris' arm slowly as if waiting for him to need it again. Norris straightened himself, and pulled his hat on tighter.

"The one you want to talk to is Lieutenant Fields. He's right over there."

As he said this, Lieutenant Fields turned and strode toward them.

Lieutenant Fields was a tall young man of about thirty, Norris guessed. He looked too good to be a local cop, and Norris thought he might have puffed his chest up before he turned, which meant he was either dumber than a box of rocks or there was something else fundamentally wrong with him.

"Lieutenant…Agent Norris, FBI," Robinson said.

"Agent," Fields said, extending a hand. Norris looked at it, then at Fields who seemed to have lost some steam.

154

"Don't want to leave you hangin', Lieutenant, but you don't want what I've got," Norris said.

Fields smiled wanly and pulled his hand back into his coat pocket.

"What can I do for you, Agent?"

"A little bird told me you had some trouble. Thought I'd stop by and see if I couldn't help," Norris said.

"Well, I think we've got things under control," Fields said.

"You have a fairly large area cordoned off, Lieutenant."

"We've got footprints everywhere."

"Snowfall didn't obscure them?" Norris asked.

"A little, but there was only a dusting after the incident," Fields said.

"What have you made out so far?" Norris asked.

Fields shot a look to Robinson that was hard for Norris to not notice. He hesitated.

"Lieutenant…we're all on the same side here. I already know you've got a missing body. Otherwise, I wouldn't be here. Spill."

Fields considered this, then spoke.

"Well, the night manager's a little skittish. He…wasn't exactly on duty per se. Had a little nightcap and dozed off when this all went down. He's afraid he's going to become some sort of accessory for doing what he did," he said.

"Which was what? Drinking on the job?" Norris asked.

"He boarded some people last night off the books. Took cash for a little room around back that's really an old storage closet. Said there was only one guy who came in to check in, but he was pretty sure there were a few more people in the car," Fields said.

"Small town to try and keep secrets in," said Norris.

He slipped a hand into his coat pocket and pulled out a wrapped cough drop. He fumbled with it, his ungloved hands stiff in the bitter cold morning air. Just as he managed to raise it to his mouth, it slipped in his fingers, grazed his outstretched lips, and fell into the snow at his feet. He stared after it for a moment like a kid who has just dropped his ice cream on the pavement and considers the possibility of rescuing it. He looked up at Lieutenant Fields who looked down at the ground with a small look of sympathy. Norris pulled out another cough drop and handed it to Robinson pathetically. The Deputy didn't bat an eye. He peeled the wrapper off and dropped the candy into Norris' outstretched hand.

"Much appreciated, Deputy," Norris said.

"People still try…to keep secrets that is," said Robinson.

"But, it wasn't locals," Norris said.

"No. Night manager said the guy was tan. Definitely not from around here. Two of the witnesses corroborated on the plates. The sedan had Florida plates. The classic was from Texas."

"A Barracuda?"

"How'd you know that?" Fields asked.

"Call it an educated hunch," Norris said.

"One of the witnesses is a local mechanic. Said he'd know one from a mile away in the fog," Robinson said.

"Is that so?"

Norris tried to pull his coat tighter to himself. The cough drop had done the trick for now, and he breathed in deep on the cold air.

"Said he thought it might be a '68 or a '69," Robinson said.

"Huh," said Norris.

He could remember the '69 well. It was intimidating next to cars twice its size. It had balls even if the driver didn't. But, that wasn't what was intriguing Norris.

"It was black?" Norris asked, knowing it was.

"Yep," Robinson said.

"Tinted windows?" Norris asked.

"Yes," said Fields, cocking his head. "Familiar to you?"

"Nope," said Norris, not having to try hard in covering the lie with a cough. The cough turned into an actual fit, and he turned away from the deputy, nearly spitting out the cough drop. He recovered. "It's a familiar layout for that car. Probably a couple hundred like them left in mint condition."

"But, at least we can narrow it down to Texas," Robinson said.

"Probably a waste of time," said Norris, wiping the water from his burning eyes. "Did anyone get a number on the plates?"

"No. They were either too far away, or too busy dodging bullets," Robinson said.

"Someone fired at a witness?"

"One of the witnesses decided to try and scare him away by telling him the cops were on their way. He didn't take kindly. He didn't miss by much," Fields said, pointing to a row of houses nearby.

"He didn't miss," Norris muttered.

"What's that?" Fields asked.

"Nothing. So, what's the timeline?"

"What we can figure from the tracks and the witnesses is that there were two confrontations. The first occurred at approximately 2:30 AM. Our missing dead man confronted the shooter at the front of the building," said Fields.

He pointed to an area close to the front right wing of the building. There were two yellow plastic pyramids, typically used to mark shell casings on the ground near one another.

"One witness actually saw the shots and watched the man fall into the snow. Didn't hear a single report though…suggesting they were silenced. He went to call the police. No less than five minutes later, they were all gone."

"No one saw the dead man walk," Norris said.

"No," Fields said.

"And no blood," Norris said.

"Nope," Robinson said.

"He was wearing a vest," Norris said.

"Pardon?" Fields asked.

"He was wearing a bullet proof vest. It's the only answer, Lieutenant," Norris said.

"But, that would mean he was expecting to be shot," Fields said, his face screwing in confusion.

"Strange world we live in, Lieutenant. Tell me about the second incident," Norris said.

Robinson cleared his throat.

"The only witness to get a real good look at any of them. Heard his garbage cans being knocked around and got up to look out. He saw two men in the road. One older man with a gun and one younger man without. He went to call the cops and when he was on the phone he saw a car come out of the parking lot and nearly hit the man with the gun. The young man jumped in the car and fled the scene. Our shooter, dressed in a black jacket and cap joined our man with the gun. The witness then made the nearly fatal mistake of shouting at the armed men in the street."

Robinson said. Norris nodded thoughtfully.

"Agent, I'm still not sure why you're here. Though we don't exactly deal with this kind of thing on a regular basis, we are still trained for such occurrences. Last murder was over ten years ago...and that was nothing like this," Fields said.

"And how old were you, Lieutenant?" Norris asked, smiling.

Fields blushed visibly and pursed his lips.

"Sixteen, maybe," he said.

"Well, have no fear, Lieutenant, your streak's still alive. You've merely had an attempted murder. That man is still alive…somewhere."

"He's gotta be hurt though," Robinson said.

"Ever taken a bullet, Deputy?" Norris asked.

The deputy chuckled a bit, then stopped, seeing the look on Norris' face.

"No, sir," Robinson said.

"Well, a vest only cuts down on the blood loss. You're still gonna take a pretty mighty wallop. And, judging by the range, ten…fifteen feet max, I'd imagine our dead man walking is wishing he *were* dead. Where's the nearest hospital?"

"About five miles," Fields

"Might want to send some of your men in that direction. Check for tracks leading that way. Probably off the road. He won't have walked on the road. And, he won't have checked in. If he has, he's a fool. And, a man who wears a vest…well, this one's not your typical fool," Norris said.

"I don't have too many men to spare, Agent Norris. With the chief out, there's only a handful of us," Fields said.

"I doubt you're going to have a return call, Lieutenant. By the sounds of it, you'll have a lot to tell the state police. Attempted murder, attempted assault, weapons offences, etcetera."

"Don't forget the attempted vehicular assault, Agent Norris," Robinson said.

"The sedan?" Norris asked.

"Sure…we don't know the circumstances, but we can't just assume…" Robinson said.

"Did any of these kids have a gun?"

"I…none of the witnesses said anything like that. No, I don't think they did," Robinson gave Fields a look as if seeking forgiveness.

"And our walking dead man?" Norris asked.

"We're fairly certain he didn't," said Fields.

Norris looked at Fields, who looked away.

"Fairly certain, Deputy?"

"There were no reliable accounts," Robinson said.

"Gotta love it. People can tell you what clothes Oprah wore for the last three days, down to her shoes, but ask them something important, and…anyway, my point here, Deputy, is that we might do more harm than good by putting heat on the kids. Let's let that one slide a while."

The Deputy and Lieutenant did their best to avoid eye contact for a moment. Fields shifted his eyes to the ground and kicked some snow with his boot. Norris saw for the first time just how young this man was. Thirty might have been a stretch. Norris couldn't help but sigh. He looked from Fields to Robinson and back.

"Deputy, you did what you were supposed to. Next time give it some thought. The book is a great tool…a guide for us all, but remember that it was written by someone who sits at a desk all day. You'll remember that next time. I'd like to take a quick look around and then get out of here. My balls are about the size of peas," Norris said.

"Rob, hang here at the line. Now that this is down the wire, we might have some gawkers swinging by. Hold 'em at bay," Fields said.

Robinson turned back toward the yellow tape, a hangdog expression in his shoulders.

Fields and Norris walked toward the yellow markers. Beneath each was a copper shell casing. The Deputy stepped to the left of the markers and raised his arm, as if he were holding an invisible gun.

"We already took all our measurements, Agent, so I'm not messing anything up."

"That'd be your problem, Lieutenant, not mine. Go on."

"Two bullets. Standard 9 mm. Nothing fancy. Same stuff you can buy over the counter at Wal-Mart," Fields said.

"Makes sense," Norris said.

"We'll dust the casings," Fields said.

"You probably won't find anything," Norris said.

The Lieutenant ignored that comment and walked over to where the victim had fallen. The snow evidence was still clear.

"He fell almost flat. Then, by the looks of it, he just got up and walked away.

"Which way did he head?"

"We only followed them out to the road, but then he must've hopped around in some tire tracks or something cuz they sorta just disappear," Fields said.

"Start looking in back yards...you'll find 'em," Norris said.

"We'll do that."

"And no blood was found, right?" Norris asked.

"Not a goddamn trace," Fields said.

Norris walked a pace around the corner and stopped, looking down at the tracks in the snow.

"Agent?" Fields said, giving Norris a tap on the shoulder. "Do you want to see the room?"

"Mmmm? Oh, yeah. Don't know what good it'll do, but...sure. Lieutenant?"

"Yes?"

"You put an APB out on both vehicles, right?"

The deputy nodded, though almost apologetically.

"I don't know what good it will have done though. At least not until now. With the weather, and the state of emergency, there isn't too much manpower to spare. They could have slipped by anyone in the night. Especially the sedan. But, now that it's daylight..." Fields said, trailing.

"And you haven't heard anything?" Norris asked.

"No," said Fields.

Norris scratched the three-day-old scruff on his cheek. It wouldn't be long before something came up. The question was who would be caught first, and how would that go down. He figured they hadn't stopped the Barracuda yet. They would have definitely heard something by now. But, that meant that the sedan could have made it out of the state by then.

"Lieutenant, you keep doing your job here. The evidence you collect here will probably be needed down the road. It might not point to the pot of gold, but it's part of the rainbow, y'know?"

The Lieutenant shrugged.

"Consider it a training exercise. Now, where's this cozy little room? I guess I'll have a peak at it."

Norris tried to laugh, but coughed, then gagged on the chunk of phlegm that had come up to his mouth. He turned away, coughed again and spit into a pile of pristine snow. He didn't bother to examine it this time. When he turned back to Fields, the man's eyes were watering and he looked somewhat paler. Norris wiped his mouth with the back of his hand again.

"Sorry 'bout that, Lieutenant…please…lead on."

Chapter 24

James' had not closed his eyes with the intention of sleeping, but his body must have argued otherwise. He dreamed of his mother, standing in the kitchen pouring a cup of tea with one hand, holding a gun in the other. It was pointed at him, and she was saying, in a voice that was not hers, that she should have done this when James was born. She pulled the trigger, but he couldn't move or scream, and he lurched into a new sequence. He was a small child; perhaps only three or four. His father was there, standing with his Uncle Ted, the two men towering over him. His uncle reached down as if to pick him up, but he picked up someone James had not seen. It was a boy, and his uncle turned quickly away with the boy, and James was running after him, trying to see the boy's face, but his legs were getting bogged down in the suddenly waist deep grass. He was crying hard enough to sob, but when he turned, the yard, *his yard*, was gone, replaced by an endless sea of grass. They were gone. It was all gone. A voice called to him. It was Nicole. He could hear her, but he couldn't see her through fog that had seeped in. She called out again, this time more clearly. She was afraid. His voice broke, 'I don't know where you are!'

"James."

"What?" he said, jerking awake in the car seat, half annoyed, half frightened.

"James, wake up."

He shivered, squinting to focus on the glimmer of light that was coming through the window. The car was stopped, that much he knew. He blinked several times before looking at Nicole. She smiled weakly at him from between the front seats. He sat up straight.

"What's wrong?" he said.

"Nothing," she said, looking frightened at his response, "you were having a bad dream."

"Why have we stopped," James said, looking around the street as if expecting to see flashing blue and red lights.

"We're here," she said.

"Here. Where's here?"

"Chicago, can't you tell? Windy city? That *is* where you pointed to on the map, wasn't it? I told her she was probably wrong, but nooo," Kevin interrupted.

For a moment James was ready to believe him. He sat back in the chair and breathed out heavily, glancing out the windows suspiciously.

"We're here?"

"There seems to be an echo in here," Kevin said.

"Nice little Ohio town by the looks of it," Nicole said.

James looked around the street. Other than being blanketed in nearly two feet of snow, the block could have passed for his own, back in Jersey, though maybe a little flatter. The yards and houses were still that pristine, clean, untouched white snow.

"What were you dreaming about," Nicole said.

"I don't...remember," James lied, the false feeling of loss for Nicole still uncomfortably fresh in his mind.

He ran a hand through his mop of hair and had a strong desire for a mirror. He looked into the window for a reflection of any kind. Even in the dim glare of morning light, his eyes looked tired and he felt like he could curl up and sleep the rest of the day. He was so tired it hurt. He saw Nicole watching him and he reached for her hand. They leaned toward one another and their foreheads met.

"What next?" she said.

"Now we find Doug," James said.

"Doug?" Kevin asked.

"Doug Peterson. That's the name that Paynter gave me," James said.

"And he lives here?"

"That's what the envelope said," James said.

"Of course, that was twenty-four years ago," Kevin said.

"Well, if he's not here, we can at least get a bead on him," James said.

"Hopefully, he hasn't moved to Idaho or something like that," Nicole said.

"This whole thing is a joke," James said.

"Jokes are supposed to be funny," Kevin said.

"Right," James said, glancing up and down the street they were on, "did you pass a gas station or anything on the way here."

"There was a 7-11 back on the main road," Nicole said.

"Let's go back that way. Maybe we can find a phone book," James said.

"Let's hope they still have the endangered North American pay phone," Kevin said.

The lot to the 7-11 had already been plowed hours ago, and the mid-morning traffic was fairly heavy considering the weather. Hanging just outside the front door was the blue and white sign indicating a pay phone. Nicole carefully backed into the spot, something they might have questioned on a different day. Not today. They were going to wait for James in the car with the engine running.

"You going to be ok?" Nicole asked as he slid out from the back seat.

"Sure, so long as they all haven't been watching news out of New Jersey," James said.

"Here," Kevin said, and handed him a baseball cap. It was an uncomfortable blue color with the words 'Ted's Towing' emblazoned in gaudy red lettering.

"Uhh…thanks. That's totally random," he said, curling the brim, placing the cap on his head, and pulling it low over his eyes.

"No, man. Push it up. Otherwise, you look shady. We're going for average guy here. Faithful, hard-working employee of Ted's towing. Not creepy outsider who pulls his cap over his eyes," Kevin said, the hint of a smile on his face.

"This would've been a lot easier if you hadn't shaved," James said.

"You're right, but I'm not going to grow a full beard in the next ten minutes…go," Kevin said.

James jogged nonchalantly across the parking lot and went inside. The pay phone was just inside the door of the store. James glanced at the three people in line and the tired looking clerk behind the counter. He wondered if it was the beginning of his shift or the end, and if it would ever matter to either of them. No one even looked at James when he walked in. Just another tired looking kid who didn't have to worry about the typical nine-to-five. Out partying the night before probably. Just another kid going nowhere. He wanted to shout at them, wake them up to the potential danger. But, it was he who was facing danger. It was he who had been tossed over the protective fence. He was on the outside, on the wrong side, looking in jealously at the ones who were still safe. The ones who could go about their daily lives without being chased and shot at. He pretended to become interested in the phone book.

It was in pristine condition. Hot off the presses, or perhaps Ohioans just didn't have the urge that Jerseyans had of destroying phone books. Not that anyone but drug dealers used pay phones anymore. James flipped through to the P's. He blinked at the first page he found. 'Pederson,' followed by the 'Peterson' page. Paynter had told him the name, not spelled it out to him. There was almost a half-page dedicated to each, but luckily it was restricted to a small area; just the town and one or two nearby townships. James stared at the page, a growing fear creeping into his already tense shoulders.

He needed two pages from the book. The first page tore out neatly with little effort. James glanced over his shoulder, knowing that it was a sign of guilt, but not being able to resist the urge. He was still invisible as far as anyone was concerned. The second page ripped as he tried to pull it out slowly. He began to sweat as his fingers struggled with the paper. Finally, feeling like he was becoming more and more obvious, he tugged the page from the book with a jerk of his hand, creating a loud ripping sound. He turned to leave. The two people still waiting in line and the guy at the counter were looking at him.

"What?" he said in a louder voice than he had intended, and walked out.

In the car, Nicole quickly scanned the pilfered sheets of white pages.

"We can't sit here. Drive," James said.

"Popular name. There's gotta be over fifty choices here," Kevin said.

"At least it isn't a hundred," James said.

"Do you think we can risk using a cell phone?" Nicole asked.

"I don't think so, but it's not like we have a ton of change for a pay phone to call a hundred numbers," James said.

"Better start dialing," Kevin said.

James reached into his coat pocket. There was nothing. A sinking sensation ran through him. He rummaged through his other pockets. Nothing.

"Where's my cell?" he asked.

"When did you have it last?" Nicole asked.

"I had it last night…I think," James said.

"Before or after all hell broke loose?" Kevin asked.

"I don't remember…I think I had it in the hotel room, but…"

"Maybe it fell out in the snow," Kevin said.

"Maybe…I think I took it out of my pocket though. Jesus…I hope I didn't leave it on the table in that room," James said.

"Here, borrow mine…I hate making phone calls," Kevin said and smiled as he handed the phone back to James.

Chapter 25

James stared out the window, the cell phone held up in front of his face. A slip of paper was half-crushed in his other hand, a dozen of the likeliest numbers scrawled haphazardly on it. He listened to Nicole calling the numbers on her list so nonchalantly it made him embarrassed for her. He hated having to do this. He loathed calling strangers, let alone strangers who he needed to lie to. He had managed to call two numbers on his list. The phone just kept ringing on the first one. With each ring, he prayed that no one would pick up. He hung up, and then tried the second number reluctantly. This time, the owner answered before the first ring was complete, startling James. The man explained to him that his name was Darryl Peterson, and that he was tired of receiving calls for other people and that James needed to do something about his database. James began stuttering through a ridiculous made up excuse when Kevin turned in his seat and motioned for him to just hang up. Now, as he hesitated to dial the third number, he was acutely aware of how much be had begun to sweat.

They had found an empty spot in a nearby public parking lot. There, they tried to analyze the pages of phonebook James had pilfered. They had eliminated several that were outside of town, but it still left more than a couple dozen. They split it up as evenly as possible between the two phones. Now he watched as the occasional car passed by on the road. A cold-looking lady walked her cold-looking dog about a block away. She was stopping at every tree to give the dog a chance to go. The dog would make to lift his leg, then change his mind. The dog was right. Sometimes it was just too cold to even piss. James looked back down at the paper. I can't do this. He suddenly realized Nicole and Kevin were both watching him.

"Just dial the numbers…the rest is easy," Nicole said.

"Yeah…after they answer, you just move your mouth and make some words come out," Kevin said.

"Thanks," James said.

"Listen, I could--," Kevin started.

"No. No thank you. I can do this. I'm just…I don't know. Mental block or something," James said.

He tried to smile, but judging by the looks on their faces, it wasn't convincing.

"Right, just dial," James said, and did so.

Of the next four numbers, one was a business, and three politely told him there was no Doug Pederson/Peterson at that residence. He tried the fifth number and it was four rings before James heard anything. His first assumption was that the answering machine had picked up, but there was a faint cough, and the voice of an older woman spoke.

"Good morning," she said.

"Oh," James said, already expecting to hang up, "I'm sorry. Is Doug there?"

"Doug?" said the woman, "Might I ask who's calling?"

James' stomach fluttered. Another brother. Who am I again? He pushed back at the feeling in his stomach and exhaled away from the phone.

"My name is…Jim. I'm an old friend," James said.

"An old friend," the woman echoed, a sound of humor in her voice.

"Yes," James said, blurting out something generic before he could take the words back, "I'm in town for a couple of days, and I thought I'd give him a call."

"At 10 AM on a Thursday morning?" she asked.

"Oh, well, I know it's…early? But…" James stammered.

"Oh, sweetie, you should remember that's midday for Douglas. He's been up and out for over six hours," she said.

James' face flushed and the phone itself felt extremely hot. He tried in vain to clear his dry throat and tugged at his collar. He avoided looking at Nicole and Kevin, who had both turned in their seats to watch. Frowning at them, James turned to look back out the window. He needed a sign, any sign. The cross street nearest to them was Michigan Boulevard.

"So, then he still works at that place on…Michigan?"

He could almost hear her thinking it through. James was ready to hang up when she spoke.

"You've been out of town a while," she said.

Something had changed in her voice. He had passed the test.

"Yes, Ma'am, I have."

"Well, it's a block over from Michigan, over on Wisconsin. Would you believe they built a Dunkin Donuts across the street?"

"You're kidding," James said.

"Like they need two places selling bagels and coffee on that block!"

"It's a commercial world, Mrs. Pederson."

"Say hello to my boy for me when you see him," she said.

"I will," James said.

He hung up and leaned back against the car seat, a forced smile coming across his face. Nicole and Kevin looked at him expectantly. He shivered, suddenly feeling the dampness from his sweat meeting the cool air of the parked car. He could see his breath rising in rhythmic bursts.

"Well?" Kevin said.

"He's a block away. Bagel shop by the sounds of it. His mother calls him Douglas," James said.

Chapter 26

"My name is James Masterson. My name is James. Doug, right? My name is James Masterson. I don't know how to tell you this. Dammit. James, my names is James. Jesus Christ. I know you don't know me from Adam, but guess what? Look at me. I look like you. We must be brothers. This is fucking ridiculous!"

He pounded his hands against the back of the seat. They were parked no more than a block away from where Doug Pederson's mother had told them her son worked. They had been there for over twenty minutes. The sight of a police car had made Nicole nervous.

"James," she said, crouching down in her seat, "we haven't exactly got all the time in the world."

"I know, I know! I just…" he mouthed wordlessly.

"You could always do it the way I did it," Kevin said. James didn't even respond.

"We came all this way, and *now* you're going to have cold feet?" Nicole said.

"I could use a little support here," James said.

"What do you want me to do, introduce you to him? He's not going to need an introduction, James. You're identical twin…uh…triplets."

"Thanks," he said after a moment, and opened the door, "C'mon, Kevin, back me up on this one."

Nicole grabbed his arm.

"What are you going to do?" she asked.

"No clue. Maybe I'll just order a couple of bagels and walk back out," James said. She frowned.

"You can't just do *that*," she said, and he turned back to the car.

"Why not?" James said, his hands falling slackly to his sides.

"Do you really want to broadcast this to a bunch of strangers in a small town bagel shop? Might as well put an ad out in the paper," she said.

"Now you're full of bright ideas?" James asked.

"I thought you had a plan!"

"My plan was to sleep in this morning and go to work on Monday. Ever since that plan got shot down…no pun intended…I haven't had a plan!"

"I'll go in. You two look for a back entrance. I'll send him out," she said.

"Good Lord! You can't do that! He'll think we're there to jump him," James said.

"Yeah," Kevin said, "How the hell are you going to convince him?"

"I don't know…I'll use my girlish charms," she said.

She winked at them, and James was too tired to keep arguing.

"C'mon," Kevin said. "It's probably our best shot."

The walk to the bagel shop seemed too short for James. He walked methodically, aware of everything and nothing at the same time. He pulled the collar of his coat up. His legs felt stiff as he walked. Too many hours spent in the car. They walked along the street; nearly no other people were visible. A car passed and they crossed the street behind it.

The bagel shop was now one building away. It was hard to miss; a huge fake bagel hung above the doorway with the word 'Bagels' in large cartoonish letters. James and Kevin slowed their pace, spotting an alley on the nearest side of the shop. James felt a burning inside, somewhere above his gut and below his neck. If he didn't already know how nervous he was, he might have thought he was having some sort of seizure.

They were now standing on the sidewalk, paces from the front window of the small store. James wanted to just look in. Just to sneak a peek. He looked at Nicole and for the first time she looked hesitant.

"We could figure something else out," James said.

"No," she said. "I got it. Go round the side. There must be a rear delivery door or something."

James walked to the edge of the front window and peered in. There were shelves blocking most of the all-glass window, but between the bins of fresh rolls, and stacks of wrapped bread, he could see the front counter. The smell of fresh baked bagels was overpowering and his stomach suddenly reminded him that he hadn't eaten much more than a Slim Jim in the last twelve hours. The window was fogged with the heat from inside. He wanted nothing more than to walk in and get a tea and a fresh bagel. His mouth watered.

At first, James saw no one, but his stomach dropped with the sight of a man that he almost immediately determined could not be related. He squinted through the hazy glass. This man was probably in his early forties, maybe even late forties. His face was round and squat with what looked like several days beard growth. The apron that used to be white looked like a tight fit on a body that had seen too many of his own product. He walked behind the counter carrying a large tray of what looked to be onion bagels. The tightness in James' chest was followed by a growl from his stomach.

Footsteps to his right forced James to turn away. A bell announced the customer as he pulled open the door to the shop. This was followed by muffled hellos and a back-and-forth conversation that made everyone in the shop laugh.

His chest was pounding hard now. He was close enough to the window to make out some of the banter going on between the man behind the counter and the customer. Then he heard it. The fat man called out to someone in the back to bring out a fresh something-or-other. The name he had used was Doug. James pressed close to the glass, eyeing the counter between a loaf of rye and a loaf of wheat. Someone came out of the back, but ducked beneath the counter before James could see him.

James' stomach leaped again. He caught a glimpse of a young man. His back was to the front of the store. There was another carbon copy of James…and Kevin. He stood slightly taller than James, as well as he could guess at this distance. He had the same not-black, not-brown, crazy hair that James had always lamented. There was something different about him and James realized that this new incarnation of himself bested his weight by at least fifty pounds. Doug Peterson was a taller, broader version of himself. Then James saw him misstep. At first, he thought that it was just something to do with working behind the counter. But, the more he watched, he could see that he had a distinct limp in his step. He stepped away and rounded the corner, where Nicole and Kevin were waiting.

"It's him. He's a beast. Makes Kevin look downright scrawny."

"Dude, that ain't sayin' much," Kevin said.

"He's got me by fifty pounds easy," James said.

"Jesus! Too many bagels?" Nicole said.

"Maybe, but it looks like he might have been in shape once. He's got a limp too."

"Oh," said Nicole.

"You still got this?" James said.

She hesitated, but nodded.

"Yeah, you two go. I got this. Really," she said.

"Just tell him some old friends are here to see him," James said.

"Right, and they don't want to come to the front door like civilized human beings," Kevin said.

James and Kevin walked around to the back side of the building. They stood outside two large steel doors that looked like they had been given a layer of grey paint every year since they had been installed. The alley was quiet, only disturbed by the distant sound of machinery running and a faint stench from the nearby dumpster permeating the chill air. They didn't need to speak. Kevin looked at James and shrugged nervously. James blew on his hands and stomped his feet to keep them warm. He wished he had brought a winter hat. After two minutes, James began to worry. After five, Kevin started to look worried. There wasn't even a hint of sound from behind the doors. So, when a voice called out just behind them to the left, both young men jumped, twisting around.

"Jesus Christ!" James said.

Kevin clutched at his chest.

"Who..." Doug Pederson stammered, a hand leaning against the brick wall, a door opened behind him to their left.

"Who the...who are you? I thought she said there was a delivery?"

Even in the morning cold, a bead of sweat was trickling down Doug Pederson's cheek. His face was red at the cheeks. He was still wearing his bagel apron and a paper hat that covered most of his hair. Upon a second good glance, James could see that his counterpart was a good two to three inches taller. He took a step toward Doug, who now looked ready to hit something.

"Doug, right? James. My name is James," James said, extending his hand.

"And this...this is Kevin."

Plumes of breath filled the air between them. James' hand was left suspended between them. Doug looked at the hand warily.

"Don't leave me hangin' here," James said, his face breaking into a nervous worried grin.

Doug smiled at James sheepishly, then looked back at the hand, still worried.

"Have you ever seen *Time Cop*? Jean-Claude Van Damme? No? Never mind," Doug said, and he finally wrapped a warm meaty mitt around James' cold hand.

"Doug, everything ok out there?" The short fat man stuck his head out the door, not really looking closely at the trio out the back.

"Yeah, Leo. Everything's fine. Just some…old friends."

"Thought she said delivery," Leo said, hoisting a bag onto his shoulder.

"Yeah…she did…not what she meant though. Don't worry about it," Doug said.

"Alright. Take fifteen if you need it. Shop's slow."

"Thanks."

He turned back to James, taking the two in, looking them up and down. He took an awkward step toward James, favoring his left leg, and patting James' shoulder as if to test its tangibility.

"How do you know my name? Where did you come from? How come we've never met before? Who was the girl?"

It was rapid-fire with a lot of pointing, and James couldn't help but be awestruck by the simple experience of watching this version of himself act. He almost smiled.

"And, what's that look for?" Doug said.

"It's amazing," James said.

"It is kinda amazing, isn't it," Kevin said.

"It's freakish," Doug said, the hint of a smile.

James frowned. To him, it had all the makings of a life-moment. One of those times he would look back on and remember to his dying day. This was supposed to be one of those moments. But, somehow, he now felt short-changed as he stood feeling as perplexed and confused as Doug looked. He wanted him to recognize it as something important. But, maybe that was asking too much.

"Come with us, Doug," James said.

"Where are you going?" Doug asked.

"That…I'm not really quite sure," James said.

"Why would I come with you? I don't even know who you are," Doug said.

"Who do you think I am, Doug?" Kevin said.

"You look like someone who might be…who should be…my brother," he said, his face translating the thought process from understanding to confusion and back.

"And I *am* your brother," James said.

"And, I…am your father…dude, I'm joking. Jesus…this guy's touchy," Kevin said.

"How is this possible?" Doug asked.

184

"That's a bit of a convoluted story. But, so far, everything that's happened has led us here…to you," James said.

"But, James," Doug said, a pained expression on his face, "My parents never had another child."

"But, Doug, isn't it obvious? You were adopted, just like Kevin and I…" James said.

The words seemed to gain weight as they left James' mouth, and they seemed to hit Doug square in the chest. He coughed out a plume of breath, but surprised James by breaking out into laughter.

"Adopted! Ha! That's a good one," he said, removing his bagel hat and slapping it across his knee. "That's a riot."

James and Kevin stared fixedly back at him.

"You mean to tell me your parents are still alive?" James said, "That woman I spoke with is your…our…"

"Now hold the phone," Doug said, "I didn't say that."

"Oh, so we just happen to look just like you, almost to the last mole, give or take fifty pounds and an inch or two, but it's just a freak of nature. I don't think so, Doug. I was told my parents died right after I was born. And, now here you are, and you're telling me that your birth parents are still alive?"

It was all just too much for James. Had he really come all this way to discover, not only that he had *another* brother, but that his birth parents were still alive? He had a sudden appreciation for the fear Kevin had expressed just the day before. It wasn't a good feeling.

"I'm sorry," Doug said, quietly.

185

"It's ok…it's just been a trying couple of days," James said, feeling guilty for getting loud.

"James," Nicole said, coming around the corner from the alley. "We need to get going before someone sees the three of you."

"Sees us?" Doug said.

"Yeah, I'll explain in the car," Nicole said.

"Listen, I gotta get back to work."

"No," James said, startling all of them, and grabbing Doug's wrist, "you don't understand."

"Whoa," Doug said, breaking his grip without a show of effort, "Listen, I don't know what you three are about, but…"

"Doug, please. It's you who has to listen to us," Nicole said. "We've traveled a long way to find you before anyone else does. For all we know, they're waiting around the corner for us."

"Who's they? Us? Me? I don't understand," Doug said, still looking as if he were two steps to high-tailing it back into the bagel shop and locking the door behind him.

"Like I said…it's a bit of a long story," James said, weakly.

"There was a man who brought us together…a doctor. He pointed me in the right direction to find James…then he told us to find you. Told us that we were part of some…government experiment. That doctor was killed because he helped us. He told us that there would be people after us. And, if we didn't find you first, well…," Kevin said.

186

"What? Why? What does…finding me…have to do with anything? I live at home with my mom and dad and work at a bagel shop. What do I have to do with people getting killed?"

He took a half step back from them.

"Man, if you only knew the half of it," Kevin said.

"It's really been a rough couple of days," Nicole said, looking from James and Kevin to Doug.

"I'm sorry, I don't want anything to do with this," Doug said, raising his hands apologetically. "I can't get caught up in something like this. I can't. I'm…sorry."

"It's not that simple, Doug," James said.

"They're coming after you too," Nicole said.

"Who?" Doug said.

"A doctor and some other dude with guns," chimed in Kevin.

"They've been following us since we left New Jersey," Nicole said.

"New Jersey…that explains a lot. Why don't you just call the police?"

"They are the police," Kevin said.

Doug wrinkled his nose.

"Sounds like a bad movie line," he said.

"Yeah," James said, with a sigh, "that's what I thought."

"It only sounds funny when you aren't on the run," Kevin said.

"I wish I could help, really," Doug said.

"Doug," James said, "We're not here for your help. As stupid as it might sound, we're here to…save you. I can't tell it to you any other way, and I know it must sound crazy coming from someone you met five minutes ago, but I need you to hear what we're saying. There's an answer to this somewhere, somewhere here," and James gestured between the three of them.

"Don't you want to know what this is all about? Don't you think your parents might have some answers? If you tell me no, I'm going to go over to your house and knock on the door myself," Kevin said

"You wouldn't…" Doug said.

"Oh, he would," James said, "I understand your sense of confusion…trust me. But, you haven't lived through the past forty-eight hours that we have. I've left everything I had behind. Such as it is. I can't go back to that life now. It doesn't exist. Besides the fact that I've no family to return to, Doug. This is it. I'm looking at it…right here. This is what's left of my family…for what it's worth."

There was a long awkward moment, where the two young men looked one another in the eye. It was Doug who looked away first. He looked over his shoulder, as if back into the bagel shop.

"He's going to kill me you know," Doug said.

"I know some other people who might kill you too, only not in the figurative sense," Kevin said.

"Our car is around the corner," James said.

Doug took off his apron and his hat and turned away from them without speaking. He went into the back door. James looked at Nicole and they exchanged a look that questioned whether he had high-tailed it out the front door. But, he returned a moment later in a khaki Carhart jacket, an orange wool cap, and a simple wooden cane.

"You forgot your shotgun," Kevin murmured and Nicole elbowed him so hard that he coughed.

"I'll take you to my house. I think my parents…might have some explaining to do," he said.

James said nothing, but they all turned down the alley toward the car.

Chapter 27

The house at Seventeen Lawrence Square Drive was
almost as James had imagined when he spoke to Mrs.
Pederson. It was a small cape-style house with a tiny front
yard. The houses along the entire street were all no more than
ten feet apart on either side and cookie-cutter in size, shape,
and quaintness. It was white-bread Middle America.
Something fluttered in James as they approached the front
door. Kevin looked completely uncomfortable and hung back,
looking around nervously. Nicole seemed to sense James'
mood, and squeezed his arm gently. She looked at him as if
grasping at the same hope that Doug's parents were his too.
James had decided on the way over that he didn't want them to
be. That would certainly be harder to take than if they had
simply lied to Doug. It was a selfish thought, but James didn't
think he could handle any other answer at this point. He looked
at Doug, wondering if his physical size equaled the strength it
might take to comprehend the possibility of his parents not
being *his* parents. James didn't want to see him crushed and he
certainly didn't want to feel responsible.

Doug unlocked the door and the four of them stepped into
a small foyer.

"Mom? Dad?" he called.

"Douglas?" a woman's voice called out from somewhere
at the rear of the house. James stomach flopped in place, and he
wasn't quite sure if it was nerves or the fact that they hadn't
eaten in so long. The warm smell of baking bread was almost

overwhelming, and the country-blue décor made the home overly welcoming. He fought the urge to turn and run out.

"Douglas? What are you doing home so early?"

The voice came from behind James, and as he turned, he locked eyes with a retirement aged woman with salt-and-pepper hair, an oversized denim shirt, and glasses that made her eyes look strangely large on such a small woman. "Is there something...oh my."

"Mother, I've brought some...friends," Doug said.

The woman didn't seem to know her son was there. She stared, mouth agape, at James and Kevin. James stared back at her, not knowing quite what to do or say. Her hand went to her mouth and the other found the back of the pale blue couch she stood next to. Her face paled and James could see her chin tremble.

"Oh my," she repeated, then moved around to the front of the couch to sit down, her legs looking less and less stable.

"Mother?" Doug said, and he walked over to her, placing a hand on her shoulder.

It wasn't until this point that she stopped looking at James. Her eyes were looking watery, and she covered her mouth as it was visibly starting to shake.

"Oh my," she managed again, this time nearly inaudible. There was no other sound in the house.

"Mother, it's all right. This is James...and Kevin, right? They've come a long way. And, that's James' friend...ummm," Doug said, offering Nicole an apologetic look and a sheepish smile that James recognized too well.

"Nicole. My name is Nicole," Nicole said, offering her hand. Doug's mother looked at Nicole's hand as if it might bite, then took it, gripping it briefly, and let it go. She pointed to a box of tissues that Doug retrieved immediately. She removed a fistful to blot her eyes and nose. She stared up at James again, her eyes welling with fresh tears. She opened her mouth, but said nothing.

"Mrs. Pederson, I...I'm just looking for some answers. I'm not looking for anything more than that," James said.

But, he had seen it in her first shocked look. This was not his mother. Nor was she Doug's, and inside she was now dealing with the old lie that had unraveled right before her eyes. Doug was still very much confused and when he looked to James for some explanation, James looked away to Mrs. Pederson.

There was no physical resemblance between either of them. She could have as easily called Nicole her daughter as James, Kevin, and Doug her sons. She stared so fixedly at James, but he wouldn't look away. He couldn't read her, but he was positive there was now a note of hatred welling somewhere behind the watering eyes.

"He told me...warned me not to do it. That I should just tell you the truth. I was such a fool...such a fool. He told me that something like this might happen...just not...good lord, if

I had known. Triplets?" she said, and pressed a wad of tissues to her face to stem the new flow of tears.

Doug pressed a soothing arm over her shoulder. His attempt to smile faltered.

"What are you saying, Mom? Who told you?" Doug said.

"Someone told you we might come?" James said.

"Douglas, I'm…so sorry," she said, grabbing him and pulling him into an awkward hug. She sobbed into his shoulder, "I've been such a bad parent."

"Mom…momma, c'mon," Doug said, patting her should.

He again tried a half smile, looking around at Nicole and James for some sort of consolation. They didn't return his smile.

"What's that supposed to mean, Mom?" Doug asked.

It was then that steps and a voice came from an unseen doorway. It was a deep baritone voice.

"Douglas? Is that you, son? What the hell are you doing home so early? Leo send you home early? You ok, son?"

It was a flurry of questions that came out all before the man could be seen. He entered the room, almost having to duck inside the doorway. James felt that he had suddenly eaten the mushroom that makes you small without knowing it. The man, with slick silver hair and an angular face and glasses to match those of his wife, towered over James by a solid foot at least. He was lean and lanky because of his height, with a pleasant demeanor that shadowed upon seeing James and Kevin and his crying wife.

"Sweet mother of God," he said, suddenly looking stiff. He rubbed a finger across his lips and settled himself slowly into an oversized easy chair that seemed to be custom made for someone large, but still smaller than himself.

"Oh, Jair," whispered his wife.

"Alice," he said, his resolute voice carrying to every corner of the room, "we knew this day might come."

She only seemed to sob harder into her son's shoulder.

"Dad?" Doug said.

He had sat next to his mother and gently rubbed her back like someone who doesn't know what else to do. His father and he stared one another down for what seemed to be a long moment, as if one was trying to pass the word silently to the other. His father looked away first and Doug frowned. James felt a wave of embarrassment burn up through his chest. He pulled at his collar, his jacket suddenly feeling extremely constricting.

"Douglas," he said, after some time, "Son…your mother and I…there's something…we should have told you this a long time ago. It would have saved us a lot of grief and anxiety. But, ignorance is all the more bright when looked upon with fading eyes."

"I don't understand," Doug said.

"Nor will you," said Gerard Pederson, and he turned to James, "your name?"

"James, sir," and James stood to shake the man's hand. The man offered him a firm handshake and an awkward smile. He turned to Kevin.

"Uhhh…Kevin. Yeah," he said and offered a quick handshake.

"You must realize that we cannot be your parents," he said, as James sat down.

"I think I understood that before we walked in the door, sir," James said, turning to look at Doug.

"I still don't get it," Doug said. "Then…"

"Douglas," said Gerard, "your mother and I were…fools. This should have never been a surprise."

"Such is life," James breathed more to himself than the group.

"James," said Gerard. "What did your adoptive parents tell you of your blood parents?"

"That they were killed in a car accident on the way home from the hospital after having me. I somehow survived," James said.

Gerard puffed through his nose sardonically.

"Such a tale. We were told to tell Doug the same thing. That it would be easier that way, especially if his brother should arrive to find him."

"Dad?" Doug said.

"Son," said Gerard, and he leaned forward in his seat, pressing his fist to his mouth before speaking again. "As much a son to me that I could have ever wished for."

At that, Gerard Pederson stood up, walked over to his son and knelt by his side, enveloping his wife and child in his tangle of arms. James, Kevin, and Nicole stepped slowly out of the room as one.

"Are you ok?" Nicole said in hushed tones, reaching the hallway past the foyer.

"Am I ok? I feel like I just took a Sharpie to the ceiling of the Sistine Chapel," James said.

"Like we just told The Beav that Ward and June weren't his parents," Kevin said.

"Look at this place! Look at them. We've come in...and *ruined* it all in one fell swoop. They're devastated. How am I supposed to the feel? This was selfish. We should have never come," James said

"James, don't. You couldn't have known. Paynter never told us this, any of this," Nicole said.

"And, now I've met him, now what? It was too easy. Something inside me knew it was too good to be true. After all of that crap, I knew it couldn't be this neatly wrapped package."

"But, a part of you wanted it to be true," she said.

She placed a warm hand behind his neck and rubbed gently, but he pulled away.

"That doesn't make it ok," he said.

He pulled open the front door and welcomed the crispness of the cold morning air.

Chapter 28

Dr. Paynter sat in a supply closet on the third floor of the cardiovascular ward. As far as he could tell, he was now in the Our Lady of Mercy Medical Center in Lewiston, Pennsylvania. He hadn't moved for over six hours as best as he could tell. The numbness from the cold and the miles of walking had worn out midway through the night and he could only remember one other time being in so much pain. He was sixteen, left wing for the varsity soccer team in Norfolk, Virginia. It had been an unusually cold and rainy November day for a game. He had been a late replacement for one of the regulars and he had played his butt off. With the final minutes of the game ticking down, his team was down a goal when they earned a corner kick. The fullback had lobbed up a high slow one and he positioned himself to make the leap. He hadn't seen the defender and the goalie heading toward him. The three young men collided in mid-air, the ball glancing off of Paynter's head and the goalie's fists, one of which caught Paynter on the temple. He didn't see the end of the game. They lost and he spent the following days in bed recovering from a concussion, four broken ribs, and a high ankle sprain. If that was the worst, he thought, he'd had it pretty easy. This wasn't even close.

He'd spotted the blue 'H' hospital signs along the road and used them as a guide. He had ducked in and out of places where tracks would be hard to follow, or behind shrubs and bushes where it was possible. It had felt like a journey that wouldn't end. At times, he had to use the cell phone in his pocket to see in the dark. He had done that sparingly, so as to save the battery life. He didn't have a chance to tell James what he'd done. His cell phone had just been sitting out in the open on the table. Paynter had slipped it into his pocket when the commotion began. It was instinct and he wasn't quite sure why he had grabbed it and James hadn't.

Now, he looked at James' phone and hoped the young man was safe and that he hadn't needed it. Given the circumstances, he saw the true dumb-luck brilliance of it. Paynter didn't know James' number, but he knew the number of the phone in the glove compartment of his car. At least he should have.

It was only a brilliant plan if he could remember his own number. Several times during his walk, he stood cursing at his luck. He just had to remember ten digits, but between the cold and the pain he was in, nothing he did changed the fact that he couldn't remember the last four numbers of the phone he'd had for the last seven years. Throwing the phone into the snow seemed like a good idea several times that night, but he decided to keep walking until he could do something for the pain. The hospital would be where they would look for him first, but it was also the only place he could help himself. He'd checked out the wounds. Broken ribs were his best guess, a couple of surface lacerations, and deep tissue bruising to go with it, but he figured it still beat the alternative.

The hospital was barely stirring when Paynter first saw it from a distance. Set out at the edge of the small town, it had looked like a beacon in the dark when he came across it. At the same time, he knew it could also be a hub of activity. Someone might be there, waiting for him already. He had relied on his knowledge of general hospital protocol. There were certain areas more heavily monitored than others. And, hospitals out in The Sticks sometimes had more lax rules regarding visitors. He couldn't simply walk in the front door, but with a straight face, he might make it in through a service entrance and find what he needed.

Paynter watched for about a half hour from the rear parking lot. There was little activity back there and he thought that he had timed it perfectly to go in before the shift change. He saw a particular service entrance door close ever so slowly. He timed it. It took all of forty-five seconds to close after being opened wide. Moving as quickly as he had all day across the parking lot, his chest fighting the cracked ribs, his cold fingers caught the edge of the door before it shut. From there, he was able to avoid major hallways, doorways that required a pass, and what few security cameras he spotted. The first utility closet he came to was locked. The second was ajar. Another security violation laid bare. Should do this for a living, he thought.

The closet contained the typical cleaning and sanitation supplies, but had been expanded to store unused or possibly broken beds and gurneys. It gave Paynter some space to conceal himself. Even if someone came in to get something, they'd have to be looking for him. He hoped that he didn't smell as bad as he thought he might and that maybe someone would mistake it for mop mildew if they noticed.

When he settled onto the floor in a corner furthest from the door, he thought it might have been the most comfortable block of tile he'd ever rested on. He would try and sleep first, then make his way to find something to dull the pain, and maybe some athletic tape for the ribs. He just hoped his self-diagnosis had been accurate enough to not get him killed. During his walk, he had half-expected to just drop dead from some major internal injury he had not felt. Now, as the desire to sleep overwhelmed his sense of pain, he remembered that he still needed to call James…if only he could remember that number. Sleep would do the trick. Maybe the numbers would come to him in a dream.

Chapter 29

It was nearly thirty minutes before any of the Pederson family was ready to talk again. Nicole leaned outside and beckoned James back inside. His cheeks and nose were red and he sniffed loudly as the warmth hit him upon reentering the house. He rubbed his hands together. Mrs. Pederson motioned them into the kitchen, her eyes still a bit red. Coffee was offered and poured and they sat without speaking so long that Kevin turned toward the wall as if to assess the quaint village scenes on the wallpaper. James shifted uneasily in his chair before speaking.

"I need Doug to come with me…us," James said, dabbing the corner of his mouth with a napkin. "I need him to help us figure out just what exactly is going on."

The three Pederson's all seemed to stop what they were doing to look at James. James stared resolutely back at Doug.

"You're all the family I've got, and I'll be damned if I came all this way to still be left hanging. Something…screwy…has happened here, and many lives have been tossed into the fire."

"I can't just leave, James," Doug said after a moment.

"I understand that, and I'm not talking about something permanent, but, what I need for you to understand is that I can't just leave you now. You're my brother, Doug. That much should be very clear. My brother," James said.

He laughed a little and said the word again.

"Brother. I spent all my life wondering what it would be like to have one and in a matter of twenty-four hours I have two. Yes, Virginia, there is a Santa Claus."

"Douglas needs to keep his job if he's to finish school," said Mrs. Pederson, walking over now and placing her hands on her son's shoulders.

"I don't want to get in the way of your life, Doug, but please try and see this from my...our...point of view," James said.

Doug tapped his mug on the kitchen table. The kitchen, like much of the rest of the house was country décor to a fault. The curtains in the windows were as white as the snow outside. The border around the top of the ceiling had a boy and girl figure holding hands amongst cows, sheep, and barns. It was all so pristine; the kind of immaculate that made tidy look filthy.

"I can't get into something like this," Doug said.

"I hate to tell you, but it might be too late to decide whether you *want* to be involved or not," Kevin said.

"My parents still don't know where I am. Gone two days and no word, they've probably called out the air national guard," Nicole said.

"Sweetie," said Mrs. Pederson, "You can use our phone if you need to call."

James shot her a look, before shaking his head.

"I'm sorry...we just can't take that kind of chance. I don't want them to be able to trace us back to you," James said.

She made a dismissive wave of her hand.

"These people are serious, Mrs. Pederson. They've already killed a man who was traveling with us."

He had done it on purpose of course. James had considered the odds and decided that dropping that bomb on Doug's parents was possibly the only way to get Doug to change his mind. He allowed the words to sink in. James had never seen someone's jaw drop, until he watched Mrs. Pederson's slowly yawn open and stay that way in a frozen look of utmost awe. Nicole shifted uncomfortably at his side.

"K...killed?" she stammered.

"The man who led us to Doug was killed last night by men who were out to stop us from finding you. They killed him without regard, and I'm afraid that the same fate may await all of us," James said.

Mrs. Pederson gave a little cry. Mr. Pederson sat stoic, glancing between the three boys. Doug looked nonplussed.

"And, you think they'll eventually seek Douglas out?" Gerard said.

James laughed harshly.

"I have no idea. I don't know what they want, or why they would be willing to kill, but yes...they are definitely after us...all of us. There's something they want kept secret, and they're willing to kill us to keep it that way. None of it makes sense to me, and the one man who could have made some sense out of it...well, he's dead."

"Then maybe your problem's gone away," Gerard said.

"I wish I could believe that," James said.

They all sat, dwelling on their own thoughts. The ring of the phone startled James out of his chair, and everyone else jumped.

"Who knows you're at home?" James said.

"Everyone, James," Gerard said, striding out of the room, "we're retired."

James sat back down, Nicole patting his arm. He felt a bit of the fool and at the same time an anger welled up inside. He had never lived like this. Never had he been so on edge. Would he ever get a decent night's sleep again? As if in response, Nicole yawned into her hand. Gerard stepped back in the doorway.

"That was Leo at the shop. He was wondering where the hell you'd got to."

"I'll drive you back," James said, "it's the least I can do."

Doug looked across the table at him. They were really quite alike in the most bizarre ways. They even had the same funny little ridge of cartilage at the top of their left ear.

"I have to go back," Doug said.

"I understand. I just…hope that you understand I'm not being entirely selfish here. I'm concerned for you…for your family. At least if we're together…well, I don't know…maybe I am being selfish," James said.

"No, James," Mrs. Pederson said. "It's we who've been selfish. None of this is your fault, son."

James smiled. He hoped she couldn't see the hollowness he felt inside.

They stood and said their goodbyes. Mrs. Pederson hugged Nicole and Kevin without hesitation, as if they were family. Kevin blushed and said nothing, moving quickly toward the door. She held James at arm's length and looked him up and down.

"You could do with a few more pounds on you," she said. The anger in her eyes was gone.

"My mother used to say the same thing," James said.

"Used to?" she said.

"She passed…recently," James said, and though he didn't want to, he felt the emotion well in his chest. She saw this and pulled him back into a hug. He hugged her back without saying anything.

"You're always welcome here, sweetie. When the trouble passes, and it will, you'll have to come and stay for a while. And Kevin too."

He thanked her and gave her one last hug. She shuddered back a sob as they broke away. Gerard gave him a firm handshake, but said nothing. His eyes said it all. Take care.

The rest were waiting outside for him. He looked at Doug as they walked toward the car.

"They're good people. I hope you can…forgive them," James said.

"Forgive them…yeah. She's my mom…he's my dad…no matter what…y'know? I'm sure it hasn't quite sunk in yet, but

I don't know how much I'll have to forgive. They did what they thought was best. Maybe they were right," Doug said.

"Two days later and I still keep waiting to wake up, but so far…" James shrugged.

James made his way to the driver's side door, but Doug caught his arm with his cane.

"Mind if I drive?" Doug said.

"Uh, sure…I guess. It's not that far back, though. I think I remember."

"I know…" Doug said and he smiled sheepishly, "I just…don't get to drive too often." He waved the cane as if that might explain things.

"You don't have a car?" Nicole said.

"Had one…a while back now, though. Wrecked it."

"And that's the reason for the cane?" Kevin said.

"Yeah…pretty much ruined my life," Doug said.

"If you don't mind my asking…" Nicole said, her question fading in the cold air.

"Oh, well, I used to be a pretty good footballer. I…uh…don't like to toot my own horn, but I was *really* pretty good, I guess. Had the scouts looking at me. Division 1-A. Free ride pretty much anywhere I wanted to go. Then there was the accident and they had to replace my hip and put pins in my leg to keep it from falling off. That pretty much shot my football career. I rehabbed, but nobody was looking at me anymore. I couldn't pass a metal detector, let alone a physical."

They stood looking at him for a moment. Doug just shrugged and tapped his cane in the snow.

"You know...you could've just said you really like driving. You didn't have to come up with a bullshit story like that," Kevin said, having a hard time not smiling.

He laughed and jumped in the back seat.

"How the hell can I say no to a story like that?" James said, a smirk on his face. He tossed Doug the keys, which Doug caught deftly.

"I was hoping you'd say that," Doug said.

He climbed in, somewhat awkwardly, to the driver's seat. He placed his cane on the floor of the back seat.

"I walk to work, normally. Saves money. Helps me pay for college. Anyway, driving is sorta like a treat now. When you don't do it every day, you don't take it for granted."

They were all piled into the car now, Nicole sitting in the back with Kevin, rummaging through her stash of junk food and handing out sandwiches from the full lunch bag Doug's mom had packed them. Doug settled in behind the wheel, adjusting the mirrors and the seat, frowning at the automatic transmission shifter.

"Yours?" he asked.

James shook his head slowly.

"Dead guy's," he said.

"Oh...then I guess it would be pretty inappropriate to comment on his choice of wheels," Doug said.

"Yeah, it would," Nicole said.

Doug started the car with a relish James had rarely seen. He even goosed the engine a little as they waved to the house. Despite the cold, Doug's parents came out and waved from the porch.

They drove off slowly in relative silence. When James heard the chiming sound, he nearly jumped.

"Stop the car...stop the car! Pull over!"

"I only got a couple blocks...I'm not driving that bad, am I?" Doug said.

"James?" Nicole said.

"Shhhhh," James hissed.

There it was again. A distinct sound that could only mean one thing.

"Cell phone," James said.

James opened up the glove compartment. A small flip phone sat on top of a stack of papers. A light was flashing at the top, and as Doug reached over to pick it up, it chimed again. He flipped it open and turned it to James.

"James?" Nicole said.

"What's the number?" Kevin said.

"It's mine," James said.

"The cops?" Doug asked.

"Paynter," Kevin said.

"That's impossible," Nicole said.

"Just like having a twin brother," James said slowly.

"Answer it!" Doug said.

"What if it's not him?" James said.

"Then you hang up…it's called the magic of the end key," Kevin said.

He pressed a button and said nothing.

"James, listen and listen good. I don't have time to explain and the longer we're on, the longer they'll have to pinpoint both of us. I'm in a hospital, about five miles from the hotel we were in. Our Lady of Mercy Medical Center in Lewiston, Pennsylvania. They'll figure it out sooner or later. I need you to come get me," Paynter said.

"You're alive." James said.

Nicole inhaled quickly through her teeth.

"I am," Paynter said.

"You're registered?" James said.

"Nuh-uh. I snuck in through a service entrance. No one knows I'm here…and I'd like to keep it that way," Paynter said.

"You stole my phone," James said.

"I *took* your phone….there's a difference. And, as it turns out, it was the smartest thing I did. Listen, you'd better high tail it here. I think I've already heard cops in the building."

"We're on our way," James said.

"Did you find Doug?"

"We did," James said.

"Did you get his envelope?"

"Envelope? What envelope?!"

"Shit…I have to go. Someone's coming. Send a text when you get here. Just get here…"

211

"Dammit!" James said, but the line was already dead.

He turned in his seat. Nicole was quietly hugging Kevin, her head buried in his shoulder. For his part, Kevin looked like he wanted nothing more than to be a million miles away. He rolled his eyes at James who reached back and patted Nicole's shoulder.

"He's alive," she mumbled from Kevin's jacket.

"And kicking," James said. James turned to look at Doug. "We could use you, y'know."

"James…I…" He turned away and looked up the road.

"You think I didn't have a life back in Jersey? It wasn't much, and it certainly wasn't this exciting, but I did have a life. All this, though…this changed everything. It made me realize what a gap there was in that life. I had no real family to speak of anymore. Now I have more than I know what to do with! And…there must be another."

"What?" Kevin, Doug, and Nicole spoke at the same time.

"Didn't you hear me?" James said. "Paynter asked if we had gotten Doug's envelope."

"What envelope?" Doug said.

"Your parents must have it," James said.

"It's an envelope they were sent. My envelope led to you. Yours…I can only assume, leads to someone else…brother number four?"

"Four?" Kevin said.

"That can't be," Doug said.

"It's fucked up," James said, "But, there you have it."

"What do you say, Doug?" Kevin asked.

Doug stared into his lap for a moment, then looked out the front window at nothing in particular.

"I don't want you to think I'm more than I am. I was a football hero, but it sort of ended there," he said, quietly. "I'd been drinking the night of the accident. It was sort of a…celebration party a bunch of my buddies threw. They knew I was headed off to State that fall. I had a handful of beers and figured I was ok to drive. My blood alcohol level wasn't over the limit, but I was tired and…well, I fell asleep. At the scene, everyone knew who I was. The cops, the EMTs, even the doctors at the hospital. They'd all heard about me and most had watched the state championship game on TV. They didn't charge me. I was a local hero, and they weren't about to have their golden boy tarnished by a stupid mistake. After all, I had only hurt myself, right? I told all of them that I would make it up to them…go to college…become a big star. Well, that didn't happen, now did it? I see them all from time to time, and there's nothing worse than seeing the disappointment in their eyes. Oh, they don't really show it…at least not when I'm talking face to face. It's when they think I'm not looking. They can't hide that what-might've-been look."

"We all make mistakes, Doug," James said.

"We're not taking applications, bro. You're in. You just have to say so," Kevin said.

"This could be your shot at redemption," Nicole added.

Doug chuckled humorlessly.

213

"That's a load of bull. But, it might be my only shot at wiping that look off their faces."

"It might be replaced by one you don't like, though," Kevin said.

"How so?" Doug asked.

"Well, for now, you're poor Doug Pederson, the kid who could've gone far and didn't. Tomorrow, you might be Doug Pederson, the kid whose parents lied about where he was from, oh and who has at least two, maybe three, identical siblings, oh and who's being chased by people trying to kill him, oh and the brothers are cray-zee!"

"You are?" Doug said, looking at Kevin.

"I meant James. Can't you see it in his eyes?" Kevin said.

James laughed, but stopped quickly when he saw that Doug hadn't even cracked a smile.

"He's kidding...at least about the crazy part."

"I want to come with you," Doug said.

"But–" James said.

"No buts. I'm serious. I do want to come with you...I don't think I knew how much until just now," Doug said.

"That's great, Doug. That's really good. You're sure?" Nicole said.

"I am. I really am. This...this is good. It'll be good," Doug said.

Nicole reached up and squeezed Doug's shoulder.

"We're in this together, y'know?"

Doug shrugged, smiling.

214

"It's gotta beat flipping bagels," he said. "Speaking of which, just let me call Leo and let him know…"

The phone call was short. Leo seemed to be a man of few words and, though none of the others caught on, wasn't taking the news too kindly. Doug hung up.

"He's pissed. He'll get over it, but he's pissed."

"He'll forgive you," Nicole said.

"We need to go back to your parents' house," Kevin said.

"What will you tell them?" James asked.

"The truth…they have to respect that…after all this," Doug said.

They returned to the house, but Doug insisted that he be the only one to go back in. The visit was brief and there was a shadow on his face when he returned. Doug handed the envelope to James who hastily tucked it into his coat pocket.

"You ok?" Nicole asked when he had gotten comfortable again behind the wheel.

"Yeah…I think I've seen about as much of my mom crying as I can take in a day though," Doug said.

They said nothing as he readjusted his seat and ran his hands across the steering wheel. A grin took him somewhere far away from the present and James felt bad interrupting his brief reverie.

"We need to get going, Doug," he said.

"Sorry…just trying to remember," Doug said.

"Gas is on the right…brake is on the left," Kevin said.

"There's always a comedian," Doug said.

"Trying to remember what?" James asked.

"My first go behind the wheel. Might've been ten years ago now. Dad would let me pull the car out of the garage before a long trip. It was all fine and dandy till I ran over my own bike one day. Hee-hee! I think that was the first and last time I cussed in front of him," Doug said.

He slipped the car into gear and eased back out onto the road. Five blocks down, James began scanning every side street they passed. He was reminded of the feeling he used to have while walking home from school. Terrified of dogs, he would take a certain path through town just to avoid dogs *he knew* were locked behind a fence. But, it was those times when one would appear in the open, come out from behind a house or out of a side street. That heart-skipping, stomach-bottoming moment that made him feel ill. That feeling he would later read about in Psychology 101. The fight or flight instinct. It was his body's attempt at getting him to do something. Anything. As a child, he had learned quickly that flight was often a catalyst to being chased. So, more often than not, he would simply freeze as soon as a dog came into sight, then continue on as if he hadn't seen it, the fear pouring off of him thick enough to bottle. Sometimes it worked, sometimes it didn't. Some dogs just don't like to be ignored.

Now, with every street they passed, James felt his stomach lurch in waves. Nicole noticed and reached a hand out to touch him. He flinched.

"Sorry," he said. "Little nervous."

216

"James, it's…oh, shit!" Nicole said, pointing through the front windshield.

James turned around. Five blocks ahead, approaching them from the opposite direction was a black 60s muscle car. Just like the one Nicole had described. James cursed.

"What?" Doug said.

"Goddamn it…how the hell…that's them," James said without pointing. "Don't do anything. Just keep going. Don't hide…just act like it's another fine sunny Ohio winter day."

James was doing everything to fight the feeling in his chest. The dog was in sight…and he was doing everything he could to ignore and be ignored.

James held his breath as they passed the car and time seemed to slow down. James watched out of the corner of his eye. The occupants of the other car were talking, and just as they passed, the cars hanging parallel for what seemed to be the longest of moments, he saw the passenger point. This dog wasn't going to be ignored.

Nicole, Kevin, and James turned simultaneously in their seats to look out the back window. They watched in horror as the car accelerated and made a pin-point sliding U-turn at the next intersection.

"Go," James said, "Go, go, go!"

"Chill, brother. He might have a '69 'Cuda, but I know this town like the back of my hand."

"Go!" Kevin added.

Doug took the next left and hammered the gas down the narrow street, lined with parked, snowed-in cars on both sides of the road. James felt the car's rear end shimmy, and he spoke over his shoulder.

"If you weren't buckled in, I'd do it now."

The answering seat-belt clicks were nearly simultaneous. They heard the car careen around the corner behind them. The Chrysler seemed to be plodding along. James imagined himself running through two feet of snow, the dog at his heels.

"I never understood car chases in movies," Doug said, clearly making small-talk.

He took another side-street with a hard right.

"What are they going to do when they catch up to us?"

"Ram us," Nicole said.

"Run us off the road," Kevin said.

"Shoot at us with guns," James said.

"Well, yeah…but…uhhh…huh…just like the movies, huh?" Doug said.

"Yep…unless somebody crashes," James said, cringing back in his seat, gripping the door handle and dash as Doug swerved nimbly to avoid a car backing out of a driveway.

"Whoa!"

"Hee-hee! Wet you panties, brother?" Doug said, thoroughly enjoying the moment.

"Maybe," Kevin whispered audibly.

They all heard as the black car laid on the horn, scaring the offending car back into its driveway.

"Dammit," Doug said.

They were hurtling down the side streets. James glanced over and the odometer belied a pace of approximately 60 miles per hour. The limit was no more than 25 in a rural area like this.

"Here comes the fun part," Doug said.

They watched as he deftly maneuvered a turn down a one-lane alley no one had seen until he made the turn.

"I hope this car is small enough...ooo!"

Nicole let out a squeal and covered her head. James flinched away from the door as the side view mirror collided with the corner of an alley fence. What remained was cracked glass and splintered plastic.

"Glad this isn't my car!" Doug exclaimed.

James noted the near giddiness in the guy. It was almost funny...if James hadn't been so close to vomiting. For a moment, he thought he could feel the ulcer developing. Nicole turned to look back out the rear window. Despite all the maneuvering, the black car was still in full pursuit.

"If *we* thought it was tight, he's in for a surprise," Doug said.

James turned in his seat just in time to see the same fence shear off the front right side of the classic's bumper. But, like a frenzied dog, the muscle car shrugged off the hit and charged through the alley after them.

"Oh shit..." Doug said.

James turned back just in time to see the empty aluminum garbage can roll out in front of them. They were on it before Doug could react and in a din of smashed metal, it was up over the windshield, flying behind them and into what was probably someone's yard. The end of the alley was upon them, when Doug started braking furiously. He had seen it before they had. The end of the alley and road beyond were poorly plowed and going straight would put them in someone's living room. He still slid as he navigated the turn, the 300M's tail end sliding this way and that, trying to find some traction. They made the turn, just avoiding another collision.

"Watch this one. He's coming way too fast. He'll never make it," Doug said.

They were halfway down the block when the Barracuda came barreling out of the alley sideways. The driver almost pulled it off, but the two extra feet he needed was taken up by a parked car that suffered a slamming sideswipe collision. The rabid dog only paused a moment before coming onward, unabated.

"Persistent bastard," Doug said. "Alright, we have ways of squashing persistence."

"Doug! Jeee…" James couldn't finish his sentence as Doug suddenly took a hard right, barely avoiding a car that had stopped to turn left. He gunned it down the short street. Blaring horns made the three turn to look behind. The black car had just avoided a potentially deadly collision with the stopped car. It came on with reckless abandon.

"Aren't there any cops in this town?" Kevin asked, voice raised.

"Oh, you *want* me to find the cops?" Doug said.

"No…on second thought. Doug…Doug? Good Lord…we're gonna die," Kevin whimpered.

Doug had barreled out the end of the road and pulled a hard left…into the oncoming traffic of a one-way road.

"Wheeee!" Doug yelled. "We only have two of these in all of town. Good thing they're two lanes! Whoa!"

"You're a fuckin' nut bar!" Kevin yelled from the back, as Doug swerved around another panicky on comer.

"Whee-hee!"

They maneuvered through a gap in traffic before making another right up a side street, finally going with the flow of traffic again. Doug let off the gas a little.

"No way he's going to follow that," Doug said.

"Go figure," Kevin said.

"Thank God," said Nicole.

"Maybe we lost him," James said.

"I'll believe it when I don't see him. Keep your eyes peeled. There are other ways around that street. He might just be smarter than we think," Doug said.

James deflated in his seat as they cruised down this new road.

"Nice driving. I couldn't have done it," he said.

"Thanks. I told you driving's sort of a treat for me," Doug said.

"Do this often, do you?" Kevin said.

"No, but boy have I been dying to. I've driven that route in my mind hundreds of times. Always thought it would be a great escape route," Doug said.

"How close are we to the highway?" James asked.

"About a half mile. I know a quick way to that hospital of yours. Know it well. A little too well, I guess. My gran...she...uhh...died there."

"Oh..." James said.

"Well...that was a great big silence grenade. It's ok...really. She was ninety-eight and went in her sleep. Guess if you gotta go, that's the way to do it," Doug said.

"Well, the quicker we can get there, the better...the hospital...not dead," James said. "This guy's got such a bead on us...What the...?"

Doug slammed on the brakes and the car skidded uncontrollably to the edge of the next intersection, where the black car was careening out. He jammed the shifter into reverse, and threw his arm around the back of James' seat, nearly knocking James' hat off.

"Hold on...reverse is not my specialty," he said.

James watched as the black car's wheels spun to gain traction on the roadway. The 300M weaved back and forth backward down the two-lane road.

"Stop, stop, stop!" Doug called out.

James glanced over his shoulder to see an oncoming car.

Nicole and Kevin were ducked down in the back, eyes wide.

"It's probably best that you can't see this," James said.

He turned back in time to see the bumper of the black car looming.

"He's gonna hit…uhhh!"

James barely got it out and the car lurched backward with the impact, but the collision sent the Barracuda's front end off at an angle and into the edge of a parked car. It was the opportunity Doug had needed.

"Hold on to your panties, lady and gents," Doug said.

With one swift motion, he spun the steering wheel around and shifted the car into drive. It coincided with an intersection and they slipped into the side street. That was when James heard it.

"Sirens. Those are definitely sirens," he said.

"Dammit," Doug said. "Let's hope he's more of an interesting target than we are."

"He's all tore up…that's gotta make a difference," James said.

"We're not exactly looking too pretty ourselves," Kevin said, pointing to what remained of the side-view mirror.

"Well, let's see if we can't make it a moot point," Doug said.

Doug looked in the rear view mirror and slowed the car accordingly.

"He must've heard the sirens too."

James looked back and it was like watching a lion tired out from a failed hunt. The black car was slowing.

"Now he's going to play the good citizen," James said.

"He won't get away with it in that car," Doug said.

"He's gotten away with a lot so far," Nicole said.

"He's got the right connections…that's the only explanation. Someone's tipping him off. Let's go," James said.

Chapter 30

"Mary Alice, unlike you, I'm no miracle worker," the man said.

He had a resigned look and shrugged his shoulders as he spoke. The toolbox he carried was worn and as grey as the coverall he wore. The cap on his head, which might have been white at one time, was the same shade of grey. He was facing a small, stocky, white-haired woman with a serious crease in her forehead.

"There's no excuse, John," she said, her arms folded across her chest. Despite her frown, John couldn't help but be somewhat amused by her pose; the happy, colorful, dancing bears peeking out from every part of the nurses smock she wore.

"It's unacceptable. I've sent half a dozen memos about it. It's just downright irresponsible."

"Mary…you know you're right, but the fact is they need to replace the entire door frame, not just the lock or the closing mechanism. This problem is rooted in the construction, and whoever approved it should have their license revoked. I mean, look at how uneven the jamb is. And the ceiling's not even level there."

She sighed deeply. It was a sound he was very familiar with.

"Now, if you don't mind. I've got a lav up on three that's working in reverse, so I'll be seeing you later, Mary."

"What did security say when you told them?" she asked.

"They told me they have a camera on the door and that you shouldn't worry," he said.

"I do worry. Have you seen them working, supposedly, in that video room? What a huge waste of money," she said.

"Exactly, Mary. So, if you could walk an elephant in through the front door and not be bothered, why address a back door that has a habit of blowing open in the wind?"

"It shouldn't be that way...and besides, it's not the elephants I'm worried about," she said.

"I'll be seeing you, Mary Alice," he said over his shoulder as he walked away

"John?"

Her voice had softened a bit, and she unfolded her arms. He stopped and turned to face her again.

"Mary Alice?" he said, rubbing his chin with a grubby finger.

"Did you hear about that shooting out Springfield way?" she asked.

"I did. Bad stuff. A shooting. Around here. And not exactly your accidental hunting type," he said.

"They said there was a man shot dead, who clear stood up and walked away. They still can't find him."

"Yeah? Hmm...well, I'll let you know if I spot him. That why you're so worried about this door?"

"You could say that," she said.

"Dead men don't just get up and walk away, Mary Alice," he said.

"No, I suppose they don't."

"I'll be seein' ya," he said, gave her a cheery wave, and walked away down the hall, his tool chest jangling away.

Mary Alice watched him go, then turned to look at the near-useless door. The door had been a common entrance for late shift workers. That was, until it stopped locking properly. Then they fitted it with an alarm and asked the employees to stop using that entrance. That worked until the door simply began coming open on its own. And, because this would set off the alarm, they removed the alarm. So, now they had a door with no alarm and no lock that occasionally flew open on its own. Employees had returned to using it as an entrance, despite Mary Alice's pleas. It just wasn't safe. It was frustrating and she tried to allow herself the freedom of being the one they couldn't blame, should something happen. But, she also didn't want to be the person who almost stopped trouble.

She made her way back to her station and sat down in the first chair. Julie, a young pretty blonde girl sat at the station, filling out a form. She had only been with the hospital for a couple of months, but seemed to fit in nicely with the other nurses. Mary Alice liked her especially because she was one of the few nurses who didn't smoke. It had never made sense to her why someone whose job it was to save lives would risk theirs so haphazardly. Julie spoke without looking up from the form.

"Still no luck with that door, Mary Alice?"

"The idiocy around here is mind-numbing sometimes...no offence," she said.

"Hopefully, you'll never have to say I told you so," Julie said, smiling.

"My father used to say, 'Hope in one hand and, well...shit in the other...and see which piles up first," Mary Alice said.

The word 'shit' had left her mouth with the air of someone who thought foul language left a bad taste in her mouth.

"Mary Alice!" Julie said, feigning horror. "You're a saucy old bird!"

"Old bird! You watch it there, you...young whippersnapper," Mary Alice said, winking at Julie.

"Have you checked on Mr. Cooper yet?" Julie asked.

"Was just heading that way," she said.

She stood and picked up a clipboard from the top of the desk.

"His levels were normal at dinner, but they've been peaking just before bedtime. They can't seem to get his dose right," Julie said.

"Mmmm...alright. I'll be back in a few," she said, turning, then paused and added, "If I'm not back in five, send out the posse."

"The what?" Julie asked. Mary Alice frowned.

"How old did you say you were?" she said.

"Twenty-four?" Julie said.

Mary Alice just rolled her eyes, sighed loudly, and walked down the hallway away from the nurses' station. It had been so slow in the maternity wing recently that they had accepted a low-risk case from the cardiac ward. There were only two babies on a ward that was capable of holding up to fifteen mothers. By the sounds of it, or lack thereof, the two babies were asleep. Good for the mothers, but it left a somewhat hollow feeling to the normally bustling hallway. The padding sound of Mary Alice's usually silent shoes actually echoed down the hall. She reached the far end of the hall and turned the corner. Mr. Cooper's room was far away enough so that neither he, nor the newborns, would bother the other. With atrial fibrillation, Mr. Cooper spent most of his time watching TV. He said that the irregular heartbeat made it difficult to focus on reading. Having had a quadruple bypass three weeks prior, his heart had never resumed a sinus rhythm and now his sugar levels were off as well. They had tried everything they knew, but it looked more than likely that Mr. Cooper would need a pacemaker. She stopped in front of his room and stared at the door. It was closed, despite the fact that he had requested it to be left open. She pushed on the door and found Mr. Cooper sitting up, watching *Jeopardy!* He smiled at her weakly, his eyes only half open.

"Evening, Mr. Cooper. I thought I told you not to get out of bed for anything," she said, chastising him.

"Miss Hampton, lovely to see you this evening," he said, somewhat dreamily.

"Mr. Cooper? The door. Why did you close the door?" she asked.

"This young man has won nearly twenty thousand dollars! He's brilliant!" he said, pointing to the TV.

Mary Alice scanned his clipboard and checked his drip line. She watched the heart monitor bounce up and down. Steady at sixty-five for a minute, then a sudden leap to the mid-nineties. This was usually associated with a pause as Mr. Cooper tried to catch his breath.

"It's been better today...I think," Mr. Cooper said faintly.

"Mmmm," Mary Alice said, reviewing the past weeks information.

"I thought how nice it would be to sleep in my own bed again...watch my own TV."

"Mmmm," she repeated.

"The doctor said I might be able to go home soon," Mr. Cooper said.

"Mmm...I'm sorry?"

"The doctor who stopped in just before. He was very nice. I don't think I've seen him before. He asked a lot of questions. Told me he'd seen worse...and that if I was worried about dying...well, then he asked me about my life...he was a bit strange...closed the door on his way out..." his voice trailed off.

"Mr. Cooper. Are you sure that was tonight? I don't..."

"You know I can't get out of bed without setting off that damn device you have me hooked up to."

"Mr. Cooper...what did this man look like? Did he have a badge."

"A badge? Not that I remember. He had a coat on…and a stethoscope. Otherwise…he was a bit tall…almost gaunt, very sunken eyes," he said, drawing in a deep breath at the end.

"Mr. Cooper…you'll have to excuse me. I need to check on another patient," she lied.

Mary Alice walked out of the room, a chill starting to work its way up her back. She looked up and down the hall, half expecting to see the man. She moved to a phone on the wall, picked up the receiver and punched in four digits.

"Hi Kenny, it's Mary Alice. Good. Who's on duty up there? Uh-huh. Has Dr. Stevens been in? On vacation. Right. Ok. You don't have anyone new up there, do you? No. Ok. Thank you, Kenny." She hung up with her finger and dialed another number.

"This is Mary Alice on three…" A long, bony arm reached around her head and hung up the line. Mary Alice let out a scream that was cut short by another hand wrapped around her mouth.

"Shut up…or you're a dead woman," the soft deadly voice came from over her shoulder.

The thin hands were surprisingly strong and with his free hand he grabbed her left arm and forced her against the wall.

"Tell me what I need to know and you live."

He reached up and pulled back on her hair with force.

"Understand?"

She nodded, still whimpering a little. He relaxed his grip a little, but still held his hand in position over her mouth, pressing her body against the wall.

"I'm looking for a man who shouldn't be here. A man who defied death recently. Do you know what I'm talking about?"

She nodded.

"Good. He's a dangerous man if he's still alive. You...haven't seen him...have you, Mary Alice?"

These last words were whispered in her ear and she shuddered as she thought his lips had brushed her ear. She shook her head.

"Are you sure? Are you sure you haven't thought that perhaps you saw him? Even if he wasn't there when you looked again? You see, Mary Alice, when you're a hunted fox, you learn to hide in plain sight. So, think hard. Think about anything odd that might have taken place in the last twelve hours. Anything at all," he released his hand from her mouth slowly, and added, "You know what happens if you cry out."

She stared into the whiteness of the wall in front of her, and shuddered again. She could feel him, perversely pressed against her back. She tried to focus on what he had asked.

"Yesterday...I thought I had seen a man...at the end of the hall...I didn't check right away...but ...when I went back."

"Footprints? Like he'd been walking in the snow recently?"

She nodded.

"And, did you follow them?"

"I followed them to this floor and they disappeared," she said.

"And?"

She shrugged.

"And...nothing...I didn't pursue it. I...contacted maintenance about fixing that back door."

"And, they obviously haven't been able to fix it...or I wouldn't be here."

"No..." she said.

"Now see, that wasn't so bad, now was it? You've been a good old girl and told me everything I need to know. Now, do us a favor and..."

But the man stopped and Mary Alice thought she heard him hold his breath. Footsteps were approaching. Someone was running down the hall. Mary Alice was suddenly thrown to the ground, the man running in the opposite direction of the approaching footsteps. She turned, just in time to see the man's white coat round the corner of the hallway she had come from. The exit to the stairwell nearest to her burst open and Charlie, the night shift watchman came puffing down the hall toward her, holding a stitch in his side. He was red faced and clearly out of breath as he stopped and bent near her.

"Are you...ok?" he sputtered.

"Don't mind me! He went that way!"

He looked reluctantly in the direction she was pointing. He lurched forward in more of a controlled fall than a sprint. Mary Alice stood up, rubbing the developing bruise on her arm. She walked back to Mr. Cooper's room and looked in on him. His eyes were closed and his mouth gaped open. She instinctively watched for a breath and glanced at the monitor. He was sleeping. The commotion had not disturbed him. She rounded the corner to find Charlie walking slowly back to him, still clutching his side. He held a white coat in his hand.

"He got away?"

He nodded without speaking, still huffing and puffing.

"Did you call the police?" she asked.

He shook his head.

"Do you want me to?"

"No. He was just a transient. Said he walked in the front door. By the time the police come, he'll be halfway to the interstate."

"But…" Charlie said.

"Maybe if you people did your job right the first time, something like this wouldn't happen," she said.

"I'll have to file a report," he said.

"You do what you need to and if that supervisor of yours needs me to answer any questions, you know where to find me," she said, realizing the pain in her wrist and rubbing it.

"Are you sure I can't call anyone?" Charlie asked.

"No, I'll be fine," Mary Alice said.

He looked at her furtively, then turned and headed back down the hall. She followed, watching him into the stairwell. She headed toward Mr. Cooper's room, but at the last moment, veered off into the neighboring room, without turning on the light. She closed the door and waited for a moment while her eyes adjusted.

"Did you hear that?" she asked to the darkness.

"You're my new best friend, Mary Alice," a man's voice came out from behind the bed.

"How's your chest?" she asked.

"Better, thank you," the man said.

"Is there anything I can get you?"

"No…you've really been more than helpful. You've already risked so much," he said.

"He might have killed me," she stated.

"Yes, he might have. I'm sorry for that," he said.

"Do you know who he was?" she asked.

"He's not the one who tried to kill me. I couldn't see anything without risking being seen. But his voice…there was something strangely familiar about it. I just can't place it though," he said.

"If he comes back…" she started.

"I plan on being long gone by then…and you can tell him the truth," he said.

"That's good…"

"Mary Alice…you've been a real saint. The kind of people I'm going to need if we're going to make it through all of this. I just hope you aren't the exception."

"You won't tell me your name?"

"It's better that way," he said. "This way you don't have to lie anymore. If I make it through all this, I'll come back and thank you in person."

"I hope you do that," she said.

"Yeah…me too," he said.

She opened the door slowly, looking up the hallway, and moved nonchalantly back through the doorway, ducking quickly into Mr. Cooper's room. She checked the chart of the now-sleeping man for the second time without really seeing what was written. She had to make a conscious effort to hold the chart still. Her heart beat so hard against the wall of her chest, she was afraid the sound might wake Mr. Cooper. She lowered the volume of the TV and left the room.

Chapter 31

Fred Taylor continued to dab at the still bleeding wound on his forehead. The pursuit of James with such reckless abandon had nearly cost the two men their lives. The Barracuda wasn't exactly designed with safety in mind, and though the car itself was still in working order, Taylor and the man in black weren't without a little damage themselves. Taylor turned to look at the man, his remaining good hand white-knuckled on the wheel. The other was pressed tight to his stomach, the tail of Taylor's shirt wrapped around his forearm in a makeshift tourniquet. It was already drenched in blood and the way the man gritted his teeth told Taylor everything about the pain he was in. He'd never felt more satisfied about someone else's misfortune.

The sudden departure from the main road startled Dr. Taylor. Over the roar of the engine, it was hard for him to distinguish anything, let alone the sound of a cell phone ringing. The man in black killed the engine before the car had come to a stop. He pulled the phone out of his jacket with his good hand, pressed a button and held it to his ear. He said nothing, but listened intently. Taylor turned his head to try and catch something, but either the volume was turned down, or the individual was speaking very softly. The sound of the rain hitting the roof didn't help either. The man in black coughed hoarsely once, then hung up the phone.

Without saying anything, he opened the door and went to the rear of the car, opening the trunk. When he came back he was holding a map. He shook the rain from his hat and took a long drag from a fresh cigarette. Taylor choked on the fresh cigarette smoke wafting through the car.

"That shit will kill you, y'know," Taylor said.

"Not soon enough for you, huh, Doc," said the man, ruffling the map in his hand and laughing harshly.

He examined the map for a moment, looked out through the rain-streaked window at a road sign across the highway, looked back at the map, and grunted. He tossed the map in the back seat, then examined the wound on his arm. In the accident, somehow his left arm had caught on the window handle. It had torn his jacket and dug a five inch gash in his forearm.

"Pretty bad, huh Doc?"

"I've seen worse," Taylor said.

"Won't heal on its own though."

"Not likely."

"At least it's not my shooting hand, right Doc?"

"Thank god for small wonders."

"Glad you haven't lost your sense of humor, Doc."

The engine of the car roared to life again and the man made an illegal U-turn as discreetly as he could on the quiet four-lane highway.

"Fucker's alive, Doc. Fucker's alive," he said.

"We knew that already…and besides, what difference does it make? All that matters is…" Taylor said.

"I don't remember asking your opinion on the subject."

"All I'm saying is Paynter can't do us any harm if he's out of the picture."

"You just don't get it, Doc, do you? There's more to this than that kid."

"He's not a kid."

"He's a fucking kid. What, twenty-three? Twenty-four? He's a fucking kid, and this'll all be that much simpler to deal with, with your buddy-pal out of the way. Besides, they won't let him just rot somewhere. They're like faithful dogs. Ready to jump off the bridge after their master."

"He's not my buddy-pal," Taylor said.

"Whatever, Doc."

Taylor sat silent for a while, watching the rain start to make a mess out of the snow-covered countryside. Fifteen minutes later, the black car slowed and exited the highway. Soon, they were passing the hospital. Taylor saw them before the man in black.

"Police, and lots of them," Taylor said.

"Motherfuckers," the man said.

"Maybe we should wait," Taylor said.

"We can't fucking well wait," the man said, a note of desperation in his voice. "We've already lost a lot of time."

"I thought I saw an office building on the opposite block. Probably backs up to the hospital," Taylor said.

"Well, at least one of us is thinking," the man said.

They turned the next corner and found the building with the parking lot adjacent to the rear of the hospital. The man parked in the first spot he could find and got out. Taylor was left to fumble with the door and chase after him as the man in black made quick strides across the lot. He stood for a moment, torrents of rain running off of his cap, assessing the rear of the hospital. They watched, just as a service entrance door closed.

"You don't go in the back when you're in your shape," Taylor said.

The man turned into Taylor so swiftly that he nearly fell down the embankment. His crooked face, inches from Taylor's, the rain from his cap, now pouring onto him. His smile was half cat-like.

"The union doesn't exactly provide me with health insurance," he said.

"They can't turn you away for that," Taylor said.

"Shut it, Doc. I need to find someone who'll fix this med-school 101 bullshit," he said.

"Then you kill Paynter," Taylor said, just able to ignore the rain streaming down his face.

"Are you really still surprised by that, Doc? Of course I'm going to kill him. That's my job! And if any of those brats show up, I'm going to kill them too. And, if they all happen to be in there, maybe I'll kill you too and move on. Ready, Doc? Let's go," and he half-slid down the muddy trough on the embankment to the parking lot below.

Taylor made to follow, but lost his footing near the bottom and landed, hands first, in a large puddle. What hadn't been wet before was now soaked.

"Great," he muttered and had to run in order to catch up to the man in black, who was reaching for the service door.

Expecting it to be locked, he was surprised when the door gave way. The man pulled it back slowly then, seeing no one, pulled it back the remainder. They stepped inside the entryway that appeared to be recessed at the end of the T-junction of perpendicular hallways. The man in black stepped to the edge of the hallway. Had anyone been in the hall ahead of them, it would have been impossible to hide. He edged his way into the hall, looking both ways. Seeing no one, he waved with his good hand and they stepped into the middle of the hall. As if alerted to their presence, a head popped out of a door halfway down the hall, a frown creasing the brow of a middle-aged man in blue scrubs.

"What the...? Excuse me? Can I help you? This isn't an entrance!" the male nurse said

The man in black didn't miss a beat. He pulled his arm in close to his side, cradling it against his jacket, but revealing enough of it so that the nurse could see the blood. He mewled horribly at the man.

"I need a doctor, bad," the man said in a simpering voice, and Taylor had to resist the strong urge to laugh.

The nurse glanced at the arm and his expression changed immediately.

"Oh my god. You should be in the emergency room. Let me get you a wheel chair," he said.

"No! You gotta look at it…you gotta fix it. Now!" the man in black cried, and the nurse looked from Taylor to the man in black and back again.

"I think he's in shock," Taylor deadpanned.

"Well…," the nurse said and he drew in close enough to see just how bad it was, and cringed. "I really need to get you to the ER a-sap, mister."

The man in black shuffled forward, drawing the nurse in closer to him. The humanity he had developed as a nurse was overriding any sense of danger and Taylor watched as the spider drew the fly into his parlor.

"I need…I need…," the man was saying, and he was bending over now, lower and lower and whispering the words softer and softer.

"Oh man," the nurse said and moved to comfort the man in black. It was what he'd been waiting for. "What do you need?"

"I need you to take me to a fucking doctor. Now!" The gun had come out quicker than Taylor had expected and the barrel was in the nurse's face, which had suddenly drained of all color.

"Je…Jesus Christ, mister. Jesus…what the…"

"Someone who can stitch…I don't care if they've got an MD at the end of their name…I just need someone who's good with a needle and thread."

"I…I don't know…"

The man in black pressed the barrel against the nurse's face. His badge said his name was Steven.

"Steven," the man in black said, "If you don't know, then I have no use for you. And, if I have no use for you, then I'm going to kill you. Got it?"

Steven nodded.

"Good. Now, where can we can we go for a little privacy and someone who can sew?"

"Third floor is quietest," Steven said, trying to back away from the barrel of the gun.

"Well, let's go then," the man in black said.

He waved toward the nearby stairwell and tucked the gun inside his coat.

"Run and I shoot you. Try and tell someone and I shoot you and them. Speak too loudly and I shoot you. Getting the picture, Steven?"

The nurse nodded and they went into the stairwell and up.

Chapter 32

James was glad for the rain. It gave him a sense of cover that he felt they had lacked. In broad daylight, he thought, it was easy to look someone straight in the eye and see them for who they really were. At least the rain would make them blurry and, hopefully, unnoticeable. As they arrived at the hospital, his heart sank.

"Good God," Doug said, continuing on past the hospital entrance. "What the hell is that all about?"

They all looked out the window as they passed; two police cars, three ambulances, and a fire truck, all lights flashing, lined up along the curb outside the emergency room entrance. Doug continued on to the next block before turning.

"It looked like there was a small office complex behind it. Maybe we can park there and come in the back," Kevin said.

"It's worth a try," James said.

"Why do you think they're all there?" Nicole said.

"It's a hospital, sweetie," Kevin said, "They tend to attract law enforcement and other uniform-wearing types."

"Ha ha," she said, "You know what I mean."

"You think they found your doctor?" Doug asked.

"I can't imagine they would need all that to take him in," James said.

"What if him calling us was a trap…like he was forced to call or something," Nicole said.

"I thought of that, but I didn't hear it in his voice," James said.

Doug pulled into the parking lot of the building that was adjacent to the rear of the hospital. He backed into the first space he could find.

"Just in case," he said and killed the engine.

They sat silent for a moment, listening to the sound of the rain on the roof of the car. Kevin broke the silence.

"Think he's got an umbrella in here?"

They all chuckled a little before actually determining that, no, there was no umbrella in the car. There was a map of the Gulf coast, a Burt Bacharach CD, and a box of tissues.

"Florida plates," Doug said, "Don't imagine he has much use for one."

"Yeah, cuz it never rains down there," Kevin said.

"I guess we're gonna get wet," Nicole said, and immediately regretted it. The boys all smirked at one another.

"That's what she said," Kevin muttered.

The brothers burst out laughing. Nicole blushed, rolling her eyes.

"Pigs to the end," she said. "Ok, very funny. What's the plan?"

"Plan?" James asked, still smiling broadly.

"Yes, you know. One of those things you come up with just before you do something stupid," she said, and the smile left his face.

"You think they're expecting us?" Doug said.

"Do you think they'll just let us walk into a hospital we have no right being in and just walk out with someone who might need their help more than ours?" Nicole said. "Do you think that perhaps that car stopped following us because they already knew where we were going, just like they seem to have known all along? That maybe they're watching this place right now, waiting for us to make a move. That we might not make it across the parking lot alive? Am I the only one who's dedicated any brain time to this?"

"No," Kevin said, "I've been thinking about that too."

"And?" she said.

"And, I'm having trouble getting us past the door, let alone finding Paynter," Kevin said.

"Yeah, me too," James said.

"Well, I don't think sitting here, agreeing that it's hopeless is going to help us any," Doug said.

James flinched and they all froze as someone raced across the parking lot toward them. A man, covering his head with a sodden brown paper bag was sprinting right for them.

"What...?" Nicole started, but James shushed her.

"Wait," he said.

The man ran past them, fumbling with some keys. They all heard the man cursing. He pulled the door to the car next to them open and started it. He probably hadn't even seen them.

"My heart's racing," Nicole said.

"That's ok," Kevin said, "I think I wet myself."

They all turned to look at him, Nicole moving away instinctively.

"It was a joke, people!" Kevin said.

They watched as the car pulled out, leaving an open space next to them. James stayed facing forward as the conversation resumed. He didn't want to be caught off guard again.

"Well, they're looking for four people, right?" Nicole said. "So, why not split up? Two and two."

"I don't like that idea," James said.

"Makes sense, though," Kevin said.

"Strength in numbers," James said.

"We're not storming a castle, Jimbo," Doug said.

James didn't look back at any of them. He just shrugged and continued to watch the parking lot.

"Well, I don't have a plan, so whatever you guys decide," he said.

"James, don't be like that," Nicole said.

"I just…I don't want to get split up…I don't want to lose anybody. Not now…not now that we're together," he said, shrugging again.

Kevin and Doug looked at one another and raised their eyebrows at one another, but Nicole shook them off. She leaned forward and touched his shoulder.

"We're going to get through this James, but we can't realistically do it all together. And, I really think this is one of those times that splitting up might actually give us an advantage."

He didn't say anything, but the tension seemed to drain from him a little. His hand met hers in an awkward sort of pat and his ears turned crimson.

"Well, whatever we're doing, we should go now…the rain is letting up a bit," he said, and they all looked out the front windshield.

Sure enough, the torrential downpour had subsided enough for them to see clearly across the parking lot. Though the buildings were adjacent, they could now see that this street was slightly elevated from the street on which the hospital was. There was a drop off of about ten feet difference from the back of this lot and the back of the hospital lot.

"I'll trade you my Ted's Towing cap for whatever you have," James said.

Kevin donned the other cap, pulled it tight on his head and said, "Sure about that?"

James looked around and laughed at the Brown cap with bright orange lettering perched upon Kevin's head. It read "Hooters."

"It fits," James said.

"Right," Kevin said, "Who's the best actor?"

The other three looked at one another nonplussed. Kevin had a wad of tissues in his hand. Nicole coughed a little.

"What about actress?" she said.

"I have a role planned for you already. One the boys can't play," Kevin said.

"I played the lead in our eighth grade musical," Doug said.

"You can sing too? A man of many talents," James said.

Doug looked a little taken aback by the surprise in James' voice.

"I don't think American Idol has anything to worry about, but yeah, I can carry a tune," Doug said.

"Think you can play sick?" Kevin asked. "You know, without overdoing it too much?"

"I'll give it a shot," Doug said, grabbing the tissues from him.

"Good. That actually makes sense," Kevin said.

"What do I do?" Nicole said.

"Hopefully, just look pretty, but you're his wife…errr…girlfriend," he said, pointing to Doug. It was Doug's turn to blush a little.

"I don't like the sounds of this," James said.

"Why? Because your girl is going to role-play with another guy? Jesus, James, get over it. With luck, they won't even have to do anything. We might need the distraction though, and Doug doesn't know what Paynter looks like, so he might be more useful this way. No offence, Doug," Kevin said.

"Ummm…none taken," Doug murmured.

"If we have to walk in the front door–" Kevin began.

"If we have to walk in the front door, we're as good as caught," James said.

"Which is why we'll need a distraction, James," Kevin implored. "Don't you see? If Doug causes enough hell…"

"He might just get himself arrested," James said.

"Doubtful," Kevin said. "But, he might just take enough eyes off of us to sneak through."

"This is insane," James said. "It's not going to work. I don't care how much fuss he makes…it's just not that easy to get in…"

"James…it's not a fortress we're talking about. It's a big office building full of doctors and a few sick people. Plus, we're in northwest Pennsylvania! What could a bunch of young people be up to out here?" Kevin said.

"James?" Nicole said.

"Yes?"

"Did you text Paynter like he asked?" she said.

In the excitement and anticipation, James had completely forgotten why exactly they were there. That there was a man on the inside of that building that needed their help had been totally lost to him and he hated himself for a moment. James pulled out the phone and typed a quick message. [Hello sunshine]. They sat, staring at the phone in James' lap, waiting for the response. A minute went by…then two.

"What if those cars *were* there for him?" Nicole asked.

"They weren't," James said, staring at the screen in an attempt to will a response from it. It was another moment before it buzzed to life.

[HELLO JERSEY. 3RD FLOOR. ROOM 346].

[Is there a back door?] James typed.

Again, there was a long delay for the response.

[SERVICE ENTRANCE, REAR PARKING LOT, DOESN'T LOCK. BE CAREFUL].

[Always], James replied.

[PS CRAWLING WITH COPS AND SPOOKS].

"What's a spook?"

"What do you mean," Kevin said.

"Paynter said it was crawling with cops and spooks," James said.

"I don't think he means ghosts," Nicole said.

"I think they used to call rogue agents spooks," Doug said.

"Like CIA?" Kevin asked.

"Yeah…I think so," Doug said.

"Great…whatever that means," James said.

"I think going in pairs makes the most sense…just in case," Kevin said.

"I can agree with that…so long as we're going in the same door," James said.

"We should stagger our arrival at least," Doug said.

"Just remember," Kevin said, "You should still play up the sick routine, just in case someone is watching."

"You just want to see if I can do it," Doug said, the hint of a smile at the corner of his mouth.

"Maybe," Kevin said smiling back.

"Let's go then," James said and he and Doug opened their doors at the same time.

They were soaked by the time they reached the back of the parking lot. The rain was still coming down heavily as they surveyed the rear of the hospital. From their vantage point, they could see the emergency room entrance at the side of the building was still crowded with emergency vehicles and police cars.

"Not as many as before," Doug said. "That's good."

"Look!" Kevin said, and pointed to a man hurrying across the parking lot with a sort of skip in his step. He had on a set of coveralls and they watched as he approached an entrance at the rear of the building. He simply pulled at the handle and the door came open.

"No keycard or anything," Nicole said.

"You can bet we're not the only ones who know about it," James said.

Kevin turned to Doug and Nicole. "You two go. If someone's inside, play it up. Tell 'em you were afraid to go in the emergency entrance for fear of getting in the way. If no one's there, try and head up to the third floor. We'll wait till you're in. Go."

James and Kevin watched as Nicole and Doug crossed the parking lot. She threw an arm around Doug's shoulder and James had to shrug off a mild sense of jealousy. It had been too long since he'd had a private moment with Nicole. He knew this was nothing, but it was strangely hard to watch. Doug was just a bigger version of himself. At that distance, it could've been him if he squinted his eyes.

The rain was pouring down James' face now, despite the efforts of the Ted's Towing cap. His jacket kept him warm, but as he looked at the sleeves, he wondered just how long it would keep him dry. He turned and looked at Kevin, who hadn't taken his eyes off the pair walking across the lot.

"A part of you is enjoying all of this," James said.

"What do you mean?" Kevin said, but James could tell he knew exactly what he meant.

"This sudden show of authority. A plan. Focus," James said.

"Guess you don't know me very well," Kevin said.

"I know enough," James said.

"Well, maybe I was sick of sitting on the sideline, watching you guys bungle things," he said, still not looking away from the door.

James saw them disappear from the corner of his eye.

"They're in," Kevin said.

"How long do we wait?" James asked.

"I think a sixty count should be plenty. I figure if they ran into someone, they'd either kick 'em right back out the way they came in, or sorta force them to where they're pretending to go."

"I'm glad one of us can think," James said.

"I think better in the rain," Kevin said, then he started down the slope without a word to James, who followed his brother, remaining a couple steps behind.

They crossed the parking lot and James' stomach lurched when a car rounded the corner of the building a bit too quickly. They stopped momentarily in the road, then Kevin broke out into a jog to the door. It took James a moment to overcome the urge to *not* run forward. Paynter's waiting for us, he thought, and his feet unlocked from the ground. Kevin had reached the door before looking back. He beckoned impatiently and James hurried his pace. Kevin pulled the door open and the two slipped inside. James had barely scanned their surroundings when a voice called out.

"Excuse me?"

A female nurse about halfway down the hall had spotted the pair. She made toward them.

"C'mon, this way…move!" Kevin said, and pulled at James' arm, half dragging him into a stairwell.

Kevin scaled the steps three at a time, and in wet shoes, it took every ounce of James' energy to keep up and stay on his feet. Kevin threw open the door on the second landing then continued up to the next landing, where he caught James and held him, motioning for him to be quiet. They heard the footsteps of the nurse come up the stairs and stop at the landing below. James looked down and saw the puddle forming at their feet. Kevin seemed to notice it at the same time, but shook his head. If the nurse was that observant, then they probably deserved to be caught. They listened as the door to the second floor was pulled open again and the nurse went through. No sooner had the door closed than Kevin moved up the stairs at a slower pace.

"I wonder if Nic and Doug had a hard time," James thought aloud.

"Doesn't matter," Kevin said, "That's why they're role-playing. Just in case."

"What was our 'just in case'?" James said.

"I don't know...I'da thoughta somethin'," Kevin said as they reached the third landing.

"Three forty-six," James said.

"Thank you," came a voice from the next floor, and both brothers jumped. They both moved to the edge of the stairs leading up to get a view of the speaker. There, at the base of the next landing, an elderly-looking man stood, a straw fedora with a red plaid band perched atop wispy white hair. His red jacket was a stark contrast to the white shirt and pants he wore. James noticed that the man wore no socks with his loafers. The sunken eyes had a sense of energy and madness in them.

"Jesus, mister. You scared us," Kevin said.

"I said, 'Thank you'," the man said.

As he approached the edge of the landing above, James took an involuntary step backward. The man was dressed for a summer stroll through a park in Florida. There was something oddly familiar about him, James thought.

"Why would you thank us," James said.

"Because, you see...dearest James, we're looking for the same person, you and I."

He spoke in such a creepy tone that James shuddered. He and Kevin turned to look at one another and were caught flat footed as the old man quickly reached the edge of the landing in two strides and threw himself down onto them from eight steps above. His open hand landed squarely in Kevin's chest, knocking the wind out of him and sending him flying across the floor, while his left fist caught James' nose and cheek, throwing him to the ground at the man's feet.

"What a couple of dumbass pussies," the man said, looming over the two, now withdrawing a long-barreled gun from an inside pocket of his red sport coat.

"I thought maybe you'd put up some kind of fight at least."

James made to get up, wiping and tasting the blood from his upper lip. The man quickly pointed the gun at Kevin, who lay clutching his chest and gasping for breath.

"Not if you want to watch your brother die," he said. "Now, back over here."

He waved the gun in James' face until he had moved across the landing.

"Who the fuck are you?" James said.

James looked at Kevin who seemed to have no sense of what was going on. His only concern was regaining the breath that had been knocked out of him. He made loud gulping sounds.

"If you've hurt him…," James began.

"You'll what," the man said, and a look of disgust crossed his misshapen face. James looked at the sunken eyes that belonged to a face that seemed to lack any muscle tissue at all. In fact, it seemed like the man before him had walked out of a concentration camp photo. He was taught skin on bone, every one of which should have broken in that jump. He looked 80, but there was something in the eyes. Something younger.

"You'll kill me?" the man asked. "You're standing on the wrong end of the gun to be saying that. Besides...you can't kill something that died a long time ago," he said.

"So what are you going to do?" James asked

"We're going to go visit your friend, the good Dr. Paynter."

"You think they'll just let you walk through the ward like that?"

The man drew closer to James, the barrel of the gun the only thing between them. James could smell agedness pouring out of him.

"You think they'll stop me?" he whispered, the beginnings of a wicked smile creeping up the corner of his mouth.

The man's head suddenly turned, but the door to James' left burst open so quickly, neither had a chance to move. It caught the old man full on the shoulder and the body that hurtled through the door took the old man with him. But, whoever it was had overestimated his speed and angle and James watched as the two plunged over the edge of the landing. The old man's face flickered fear for a moment and the two were gone, landing in a tumbling, bone wrenching heap at the bottom of the stairs. The trance broke and James bolted for Kevin and, helping him to his feet, he didn't look back as they went through the door onto the third floor ward.

Chapter 33

The door to Norris' motel room slammed closed behind him. He stood beneath the small awning, relishing what little cover it was providing from the downpour. He pulled up the collar on his coat and spoke into the cell phone.

"Say again?" Norris said.

"That Chrysler from last night," Dennis said.

"What of it?"

"Might have a connection to an incident over in New Jersey. Connected with a murder."

"Murder? Can't be the same."

"Elderly man found dead after the homeowner called and said someone had broken in. The owner beat feet, but left his car. Interesting side comment here. Says that someone had called 911 the *previous* night from the same house. When police showed up, the house was empty. Owner's car was still there. They waited around, but no one ever showed up. One witness described seeing a bunch of kids and an old man hop in a Chrysler. Some signs of forced entry at the rear of the house, but no signs of a struggle," Dennis said.

"Bunch of kids and an old man?" Norris asked.

"Coincidence?"

"Doubtful. Who was the old man?"

"Neighbor who lived alone. He wasn't exactly breaking in. I mean, the guy had on some PJs, slippers, and was carrying his newspaper," Dennis said.

"So, he walks in for a neighborly visit."

"And the kid shoots him."

"The 911 call makes it pretty clear that it's the owner, though. You can hear the old man call him by name. Voice is a bit scratchy for a young guy, but there you have it" Dennis said.

"But, then why does he still pull the trigger?"

"Don't know, but he says 'thank you' right before he does it."

"That ain't right," Norris said.

"Not at all. So, his name's already been out there. His photo has even been plastered all over as a person of interest. He's actually listed as armed and dangerous here."

"Somethin' ain't right, Den. They don't send ex-CIA assassins after kids with guns. What's the kid's name?"

"Masterson. James Masterson. Twenty-four..."

"Jesus..."

This time the cough that interrupted Norris came out in full and he hacked till the pain seared his chest and the urge to cough was abated by fear; he smacked his tongue on the fresh taste of blood in his mouth.

"Yeah...brown hair, green eyes, six one, medium build. I'll send a photo to your phone," Dennis said.

"Huh...hey, this didn't synch with the shells from the hotel, did it?" Norris asked.

"The Jersey shells were high caliber but there's nothing back on yours yet. You know how ballistics can be. There is something interesting on this. A file posted to this just two days before was given the highest security level," Dennis said.

"How do you know it's the highest?" Norris asked.

"Trade secret," Dennis said.

"On a kid? Can you find out anything?" Norris asked.

"I'm already on it. You know I like nothing better than a 'do not enter' sign," Dennis said.

"And, text me those specs. I've got a memory like a sieve lately."

"John...be careful. At this level, bad things can happen in a hurry."

"I read that. Thanks, Den."

Norris placed the phone securely in the pocket inside his coat. He coughed again, this time spitting a stream onto the stoop of his room, the rain washing it away. He jogged lightly over to his car and got in, cursing the wet and cold. His phone rang again.

"Norris," he said.

"Agent, this is Lieutenant Fields. You'd better get over to the hospital in Lewiston. Seems all hell has broken out. We've had calls coming in reporting security breaches. We've also had a sighting of the Barracuda..."

"Say no more...I'm on my way," Norris said and hung up the phone.

Norris propped the blue light on the roof and covered the seven miles in minutes. He pulled into the parking lot and found two marked cars with their lights on. Robinson and

Fields were standing on the curb wearing their full rain gear. Norris pulled in behind the first car and leaped out, his 9 mm Glock in hand.

"Agent…is that necessary?" Fields said looking warily at Norris' sidearm.

"Where's the Barracuda?" ignoring his question.

Fields pointed to the rear of the building.

"In a lot adjacent to the rear parking lot. Beat up pretty bad. Looks like it was in a wreck or two."

"He's here then," Norris said. "Lieutenant, I suggest all of your men take the safety off. This man will kill without a second thought."

"I've got two men up on the car," Fields said.

Norris looked the man in the eye.

"Can you spare more?" Norris asked.

"No sir, those are the only other men I've got. State said they're sending some of their own, but who knows how long that'll take…"

"Get those men back down here, Lieutenant. You'll just risk losing them if you don't," Norris said.

Fields nodded and Robinson radioed the two deputies to come back.

"Does this place have security?" Norris asked.

"A single guard who normally sits at a bank of monitors on the first floor," Fields said.

"Sounds efficient," Norris replied.

"Said he got spooked after a rear entrance suddenly became a high traffic area. Also said they've got a nurse who's missing from his post. When we arrived, the guard had left his post and now we can't find him either. There's been scattered reports coming into the front desk from around the building. Someone reported a fight. Someone else thought she saw a man with a gun. There seems to be several groups of people roaming around the building. We just can't seem to pin it down to one particular location."

"If there's only five of us, I don't want us split up. None of your officers is to go it alone. Trust me, bad things happen that way. Got me, Lieutenant?" Norris said.

"Yes…yes, sir."

"Who does that leave us?"

"Cruz and Jacobs," Fields said, and pointed to the two officers who had just rounded the corner of the building.

Norris strode towards them with Fields and Robinson close behind. Even in the downpour, he could tell neither was over the age of twenty-five.

"Jesus, Fields. You file your help wanted ads in the high school paper?" Norris asked, looking the two men up and down.

Cruz opened his mouth to respond, but Norris flashed him a quick look that the man was at least smart enough to read.

"There is a man inside this hospital whose job it is to kill people. He's good at what he does, but he might be getting sloppy. Things appear fairly out of control around here and

263

that's not like him. I want you to have your sidearm out with the safety off. If you have any qualms about going in there, let me know right now. I don't need someone getting spooked and setting off a bloodbath."

Both young deputies nodded grimly and removed their sidearm from their holsters.

"We're looking for a man who typically wears a black newsboy cap and jacket. Probably don't even know what a newsboy cap is…but never mind. He's got light hair, red once…might've faded a bit now, about five ten. Crooked face…only the left half works. We're also on the lookout for a young man by the name of James Masterson. He has dark hair and is approximately six one. I would show you his picture, but the one inch by one inch blurry photo on my cell phone is next to useless. He is a person of interest in two recent murders. He may be armed and dangerous. If you see the man in the newsboy cap, I will tell you it may be wise to shoot first and ask questions later. Hesitate and you might not leave this hospital alive. I kid you not. Any questions? No? Good. Follow me," Norris said, and he walked into the entrance and through the sliding glass doors, the three officers trailing behind him.

"Now who in the hell are you?" an elderly man stepped right up into Norris' face. The man, a volunteer named Frank judging by his name badge, was a wall of a man for his age and stood a head taller than Norris. Norris held up his badge for the man to peer at through thick-lensed glasses.

"It's about damn time. I was about to call the National Guard. The local police certainly don't seem to have the time…" but the rest of what the man said was drowned out by the commotion brought on by the clear sound of a gunshot within the building followed by several screams. Norris pushed past the man, making sure the four officers were still behind him and he entered the nearest stairwell.

Chapter 34

James found himself half-dragging Kevin down the hall. Kevin was still gulping in air and rubbing his chest.

"C'mon…just a little further," James said, and he pulled him the rest of the way around a corner, propping him up against the wall. His face was pale and his breathing was ragged.

"Jesus, in the middle of a fucking hospital and I can't even get you a…"

A shot rang out from the stairwell they had just left. There were several screams and people started running through the halls.

"Holy shit," whispered James.

"I'll be…ok. Just…need a breather. Paynter…gotta find Paynter before…," Kevin said.

James looked up and down the hall. It was chaos. There were nurses running everywhere, eyeing the two strangers as they passed, in a hurry to go where, he did not know. Above the din, James heard several babies crying and he realized where they were.

"Well, we can't stay *here*…c'mon…this way," he said.

He threw one of Kevin's arms around his shoulder. Kevin was slowly gaining his breath back and they rounded another corner. This part of the hallway was much quieter, but the occasional face still peeked quickly out at them with frightened eyes and quickly ducked back in.

By the time they approached room 346, the ward was deserted. It seemed to be a smart choice for Paynter. The rooms at this end of the hall appeared empty. They rounded one final corner and lurched into the doorway of 346. James blinked at the emptiness, Kevin's ragged breathing becoming less pronounced. They stared stupidly at one another.

"Did you get the right room number?" Kevin asked.

"He said 346," James said.

"Maybe Doug and Nic got him," Kevin said.

"Why the hell wouldn't they stay put?" James asked.

"Maybe tall, old and ugly snuck up on 'em...," Kevin said.

"No, he didn't know where they were, remember?"

"No, all I remember was his size tens flying at me and his arthritic fist knocking the shit out of me," Kevin said with little mirth in his voice.

"Sorry I didn't react..." James said, propping Kevin against a wall.

"Who the fuck...could've seen that coming? Like a geriatric...fucking superman," Kevin gasped.

"More like a flying elbow from Jim Superfly Snuka off the top ropes," James said.

Footsteps out in the hallway made them turn at once. There was nowhere to hide in this room. They listened, James holding his breath, as the footsteps approached, then continued on down the hall.

"Can I go home now, James?" Kevin said, and James wasn't sure if he was being serious or not.

"Only if I can come with you. C'mon," James said, and he pushed the door open again and moved quickly into the hallway.

Kevin no longer needed his help and he matched him stride for stride, though his fist still rubbed the spot of impact on his chest. James aimed for the next stairwell. A commotion they heard down the stairs prompted them to go up. A nurse burst through the door at the top of the stairs and nearly bowled them over. She looked more concerned about getting away from something than stopping to consider James and Kevin.

"Think she was scared?" Kevin said.

"That seems to be a running theme around here," James said.

They paused by the door and could clearly hear a man shouting.

"What do you mean you can't stitch it? Are you a doctor or not? Perhaps you just play one on TV? C'mon, *doctor*, do your stuff," a voice rang out through the floor.

The response was so low that James couldn't make it out. There was a distinct sound of metal hitting flesh and something hit the ground in the hallway. A third voice spoke just loud enough for James to hear.

"He won't do you any good unconscious."

"Shut up! Am I surrounded by idiots? You...Steven...find me another doctor. Now! Preferably one that hasn't forgotten the long lost art of the needle."

Footsteps moved away from them and James cautiously peered into the hallway. Several worried looking nurses were peeking out from behind a nearby station.

James and Kevin made their way to the counter. A young nurse, not much older than himself, James imagined, sat half-crouched behind the desk. Her colleague had a phone pressed to her ear and was relaying their location to someone on the other line. The girl, Julie according to her badge, looked at James with her mouth slightly agape.

"My friend here…he just got a pretty serious beat down by an old man…any chance one of you could look at him?" James pleaded.

"He wasn't that old," Kevin complained.

"You're not with them, are you?" she said.

James had to resist the urge to laugh in her face.

"No," James said.

"He was quick for an old man, y'know," Kevin said.

"You're cops?" the older nurse suddenly interjected.

"Ummm…no," Kevin said.

"Who is that?" James said, pointing his thumb down the hall.

"Crazy ass son of a bitch came in here with a gun, a nurse, and an old man in tow. Said if he didn't get a doctor to fix his arm, he was gonna start the killing with Steven, the nurse. He's a good nurse too," she said.

"Any chance you can look at my ribs? They feel like they're all bussed up," Kevin said, aiming his question directly to Julie.

James looked at him cockeyed, but walked him around the back of the station desk and dropped him into a chair.

"You'll be ok here?" James said, and suddenly Kevin seemed to remember why it was they were there.

"Where are *you* going?" he asked.

"To find out what the hell is going on," James said.

"James, dude, stay here. There's no reason…"

"No one else is going to die because of me, Kevin. Jesus…do you know how many it might be now? This whole thing is insane. Insane! It's gotta end somewhere, and maybe…maybe if it ends with me…well, that would be ok," James said.

"James…Jesus…man, don't do this," Kevin was lifting his arms, cringing, and trying not to cry out as the older nurse pulled his shirt off over his head. He was still soaked to his jockeys. The bruise and the red marks across his chest were already turning a variety of colors.

"Enough people have been hurt, Kev. Maybe…he'll be reasonable."

"Why the hell would you think that at this point?" Kevin said, stifling a humorless laugh.

The gunshot from down the hall made all of them hit the deck. Nurse Julie had pressed her body against Kevin as if to shield him and despite the circumstances, he couldn't hide his pleasure. She then went right back to examining his chest. James turned in the direction of the gunshot and started walking.

"James, get your ass back here," Kevin hissed at him, but James ignored him and kept walking.

James passed the unconscious body of an Asian doctor sprawled out on the floor. A small trickle of blood ran from his forehead and there was the distinct impression of the gun handle. As James made his way down the hallway, the man's voice grew louder. He stopped at the entrance to the stairwell.

"The next one doesn't miss, God dammit," came the voice.

James could feel his knees weaken. He balled his fists and forced the fear back, shouting out.

"Then aim the next one at me you cowardly motherfucker!"

His words carried down the sterile white walls. The silence that followed was only interrupted by the sounds of distant goings on. James thought he heard crying coming from somewhere. There was a monitor beeping down the hall, probably indicating a kink in the line. The all too familiar hospital smell was mixed with what must have been gunpowder. His mother suddenly flashed into his mind and he felt guilty for having kept her out of his thoughts for so long. He'd been a bit busy. All of this had become second hat to him after her cancer diagnosis. The hospital. The sights and sounds. The emotions. He pressed against the fear trying to well up through his chest. No, damn you, he thought. The voice that broke the quiet was cool and methodical.

"Hey Doc, I believe there's a large set of balls in the hallway. Could you check for me? Now."

The familiar head of a small balding man peeked around the corner, the tops of his glasses just coming into view. His eyes met James' for a moment, then disappeared.

"Dr. Taylor?" James called out, but there was no response.

Instead, a man in an old-style cap rounded the corner, a crooked smile that might have actually been a grimace graced half his mouth. He held a bloodied left hand loosely against his black jacket. The gun was held haphazardly in his right and he waved it as he spoke, as if it were an extension of his arm.

"Oh, don't bother Dr. Taylor right now, James. He's busy trying to find me a real doctor. Amazing what they'll call a doctor nowadays. Nobody around here seems to remember how to stitch. Maybe they're afraid of making a mistake. I can't understand why everyone is afraid of me. I'm only…"

"Why are you talking?" James interrupted, throwing the man completely off, wiping away any semblance of a smile from his contorted face. The man hesitated.

"I…you're a brazen little fuck, aren't you?"

"I don't need you boring me with some diatribe about how scary you are and how you're going to kill me. Do they teach you that at bad guy school or is that just something you picked up from watching too many movies?"

"You've been watching too many movies, James."

"We're not exactly on a first name basis. You can call me Mr. Masterson. Or, is this an ice-breaker or something? Hi, my name's James and I like baseball and going to the beach...so, what's your name?" James said, half-shouting, not knowing where it was coming from.

He just knew that if he kept talking, it meant he wasn't dying. At least not yet.

"Jesus, shut the hell up, kid," and the man lifted the gun at a slightly more imposing level, though not quite aiming it at James.

"Are you and Dr. Taylor good friends now? Share knitting patterns and the like? Hmmm? Maybe know one another's favorite Dunkin Donuts coffee flavor? Get one another little surprises? Share your innermost thoughts and dreams in the car ride? Planned a little road trip for next year?"

James was shouting now, his voice reaching a crescendo.

"Maybe go hunt down some more innocents? Run, rabbit, run! See how they run? Oh what fun! Here comes the sun! There can be only one!"

"Jesus, kid, you forget your fucking meds or…" there was a resounding crack and the last thing out of the man's mouth was a guttural exhalation of breath as he collapsed beneath the blow that had just been applied to the back of his head. James' mouth fell open as the man crashed to the floor, eyes rolling to the whites, his gun spinning to James' feet. Behind him stood Dr. Taylor, his own gun held backward in his hands. He stared at the man at his feet, then back at James.

"I'm so sorry, James. I'm really…I didn't know it would lead to…this."

He gestured at the man in black who was slowly reaching up to the back of his head with his good hand, his eyes moving wildly about, seeing nothing. He coughed and gasped and curled into the fetal position on the ground.

"Is Paynter alive?" Taylor asked.

The question sounded so odd to James. It was coming from the wrong person.

"I…I don't know. I think so," James said, keeping his attention fixed on the man at his feet. The eyes blinked slowly and a constant moan was filling the air.

"I didn't mean for this…I…I never wanted any of this…I just wanted the world to know…"

"What?" James asked.

"…that what we did was good and there were brilliant, thoughtful people behind it. Not monsters. I'm not a monster, James. We're not monsters…"

He was pleading to James now, looking ever smaller, his hands wringing in front of him. He dropped his own gun at his feet.

"Dr. Taylor, I don't understand," James said.

"We were the best…that's why they came to us…they got the best…and then," and the small man's face suddenly twisted in anguish, "they ruined us. All of them…killed…wiped from the earth to clean up their mess. We'd performed miracles and they rewarded us with hell."

James's focus had been diverted just long enough. He glanced back and flinched. Two things happened simultaneously. James dropped to the floor to grab the man's gun and the man spun on the floor, reaching for Taylor's gun. He brought it up quickly and fired a round so close that James' was sure Taylor was dead before he crumpled into a pile on the floor, motionless. Then they were staring at one another, guns raised inches apart, the man in black crouching on one knee, still trying to blink the pain away with gritted teeth.

"Stupid...so stupid...must be from the lack of sleep. I mean, really, I could hear him coming. Put the gun down, James. We both know you won't use it," the man growled.

James focused on the trigger that lay beneath his finger. He'd never even held a gun before. A part of him wondered if he'd ever hold one again. This man was a professional. Sure, the man was injured, and probably sporting a concussion now, or perhaps even some trauma, but he'd just laid out Taylor without a thought. He'd done it on instinct. A survival instinct that James was fairly sure still lay dormant within him if it existed at all. There was something in this man's makeup that made him able to do what he did. It wasn't in James and a part of him hoped it never would be. He began to lower his gun. Then he noticed the movement.

"James, I said drop the gun," the man said, looking like he was tired of arguing and he might just shoot James to not be bothered with him anymore.

"I think I'll take my chances," James said. "I mean…you didn't even kill Taylor."

The man looked into James' face, the wicked smile creasing one corner of his mouth, but it faded when he saw James smiling back, a glint of malice in his eye. Taylor, who had slumped into the corner of the wall, was pushing himself to a sitting position and beginning to mutter at the top of his lungs.

"Stupid asshole…they're blanks. You think I wouldn't have killed you a long time ago if they were anything different?" he said, speaking so loudly, that they probably heard him on the next floor.

The man in black looked stupidly at the gun in his hand, which he then tossed to the ground.

"Goddamn prick," the man said.

He stopped and stared up at James who was now lording over him. James could feel the anger welling up inside him and the arm that held the gun level with the man's head was shaking.

"This is over. It's over, you…you son-of-a-bitch. You hear me? Or is it? If they don't arrest you, I get this strange feeling that you're just going to pick right up where you left off tomorrow morning. Well, maybe it's time the shoe was on the other foot. Maybe you don't need to see another tomorrow, you baby-killing sack of shit."

"I never killed…" the man stuttered, fear sneaking into his eyes.

"Shut up, dammit! You have no right to speak right now. No right. You…you lousy, no good motherfucker! How dare you! How fucking dare you. I've never been so fucking scared in all my life, and for what? Can you tell me that, motherfucker? Can you tell me why you've put the fear of death into me? Why I should deserve such treatment? Why? Why?! Answer me, God dammit!"

The man stared at the end of the gun that seemed to waver back and forth across his face. He shrugged a little.

"Someone wants you dead," he said.

"It's that simple," James said, not really asking, and the anger had left his voice.

It was that simple and somewhere inside he knew it. This wasn't a personal vendetta. It was a job that one man had paid another to do. It wasn't supposed to be face-to-face. That wasn't the original plan.

"Yeah, I guess," the man said.

"James." Kevin's voice was soft but firm. "Let him go."

"Why? Why should I let this bag of shit go? The rabbit's got the fox by the tail and you're telling me to let him go."

The door to their right opened, much to everyone's surprise. A smallish man, with salt-and-pepper hair, and a long tan trench over a wrinkled gray suit walked in slowly through the door. James could see four police officers crowding the stairwell behind him, pistols in hand, staring at the gun in James' hand. The door closed behind the man who held up a badge in his right hand. He held up his empty left. James only glanced briefly at the man, quickly returning his gaze to the man on the floor at his feet.

"Because you're no fox, son, and you don't really want to be one," the man said.

"Who the hell are you?" James said.

"That's just a rusty old piece of sorry FBI garbage," the man in black said. "Better known as Special Agent John Norris."

"But you are right about one thing, James. He is a bag of shit," Norris retorted.

"How the fuck does everyone know my name?" James said.

"You're big news, James," Norris said.

"Excuse me?" James said.

"Why don't you put the gun away first. I think you're making the rookies back there nervous," Norris said, and pulled his own piece out of his pocket in a manner that showed he had no intention of pointing it at James.

James lowered the gun, but kept a wary eye on the man at his feet.

"Go on," James said.

"You're a ways from home, aren't you James?" Norris said.

"When you're running, you don't tend to care how far, or which direction you head in," James said.

"And why are you running?" Norris asked.

"Because of these two assholes, I guess," he said, pointing to the two men on the floor.

He glanced at Norris, who was now staring fixedly at Kevin.

"You guys come in pairs?" Norris said.

"He doesn't know," the man in black said with a knowing chuckle.

"What?" Taylor suddenly shouted.

He was daubing the blood that appeared to be emanating from his ear.

"Shut the hell up, Doc!" the man in black shouted back.

"So, it wouldn't have anything to do with the old man in Jersey…your neighbor," Norris said, and this made James turn his head again.

"Doesn't know what?" Kevin said from behind.

"I didn't kill Mr. Isaacson, if that's what you're implying. I wasn't even in the state at the time," James said and raised a hand to silence Kevin.

"Then who did?" Norris asked.

James gestured to the man at his feet with the gun.

"Who do you think?" James asked.

* *

"I'm so sorry for all this," Paynter said again.

"Stop apologizing," Nicole said.

"You couldn't have known...," Doug started, but Paynter cut him off.

"No...that's the problem. I had thought of this. I just...I guess I just hoped that it wouldn't be this bad. And now...it seems like it's worse than I could have imagined," Paynter said.

"But, now we're all here and that's good, right?" Nicole said.

Paynter stared at her.

"You're a sweet girl, Nicole, but this is just the beginning. If we make it out of here..."

"*When* we make it out of here," she interrupted.

"Yes, when we make it out of here, we still have a lot of work to do," he said.

"Someone's coming," Doug hissed. They froze and listened to the sound of footsteps run past. They all jumped as a loud popping sound echoed through the hall.

"That was a gunshot," Paynter said.

"That can't be good," Doug said.

"James," Nicole whimpered.

"Is fine," Paynter said, squeezing her shoulder and patting her on the back.

"Still, where there's fire..." Doug said.

"Yes, let's see if we can't head that way. It didn't sound like it was on this ward," Paynter said.

"I'll check the hall," Nicole said, and cracked the door to look up the hall. It was clear and she opened it further, leaning out the doorway to look down the hall. Paynter heard a little scream, then she was lifted off her feet and pulled the remainder of the way out. Doug pushed Paynter aside and lunged into the hallway.

"Doug, no!"

* *

"Old man probably deserved it," the man in black said.

"What!?" Dr. Taylor shouted out again.

James moved without thinking, grabbing the man in black by the collar and pressing the barrel of the gun against his cheek. He could feel the man's teeth scrape the barrel.

"You motherfucker, I oughta kill you," and the look reflected in the man's face told James he was beginning to believe that James just might be capable of it if pushed hard enough. Rage pierced his thoughts and he could only focus on the movement of the trigger beneath his right finger. He was aware of the movement to his right. The door opening and several shouts to halt and freeze. It would be so easy, he thought. Norris was shouting something and then the spell was broken with a cry from the other end of the hall. It was his name, and it was a voice he recognized. It took everyone's attention. The rage faded and his grasp slackened on the man's bloodied shirt. He threw him back to the floor and stepped away, still staring him down. The edge of the man's lips curled a bit, or maybe James imagined the smile. But, the wink was clear. His left eyelid had definitely batted momentarily and James looked away in disgust. He had heard Nicole. Then there was another scream.

He turned to look down the hall and his knees nearly buckled. Even from the other end of the hall, he could see how ashen she was, her normally neat locks still plastered to her face from her run through the rain. He'd never seen her so scared. She stood awkwardly, as if on her tip toes, her head tilted as if…then he saw him. The barrel of the gun was propped just over her right shoulder. The old man from the stairwell was leading her roughly by the ponytail on the back of her head. Tears streamed down her face. Two of the officers raised their weapons and started moving toward her. A shot rang out, pitting the floor at the first officer's feet. He jumped wildly and dodged into an office doorway. The others all fell back, but James continued forward.

"Don't, Fields, at this range you're more likely to hit the girl!" Norris barked.

"Nic…Nicole!" James said.

The gun in his own hand felt heavy, leaden with the doubt of his ability to use it if necessary. He dropped it, the metal clanging against the linoleum floor.

"James!" Norris called, but James had no reason to stop now.

"James…no…don't. Please. I'm so sorry," she said, flinching a little as the old man behind her pushed her a little further.

"It's ok. Are you ok?"

"Nnn...no?" she said and cracked a frightened smile.

"Awe, how sweet. Take a good look lover boy. You won't be seeing this one for a while," the old man said.

"You...who the hell are you?"

"Still haven't figured it out, huh James? I'm you, plain and simple. Come back from the future. You see, I hated myself so much that I came back to kick myself in the ass," he said.

"You're insane," James said.

"Possibly," he said, shrugging.

"Let her go. She's got nothing to do with this," James said.

"Put the gun down," Norris called out from behind him. "We've got the hospital surrounded."

James glanced back and saw that Norris had his piece raised.

"Back off," James hissed. "You worry about that one."

"Don't be a hero, kid."

"Heroes don't die, remember?"

"Your friend is a horrible liar, James," the old man said.

James took another step forward and the old man matched it with a step back toward the stairwell behind him.

"Why are you doing this?" James asked.

"Oh, do you really want to know, James? Or, are you just stalling for time?"

"I'm stalling," James said.

"A moment of honesty in a world of lies...I like that. But really, that's the best you could come up with?"

284

"Wanna tell me about your childhood instead? Nicole there is into psychology. Maybe she could help you work through some of the obvious issues you've got going on," James said, spreading his hands before him as he moved continuously forward.

The man looked at his watch, then back at James.

"You're a cynical little prick," he said.

"I'm sorry, but until a few days ago, my world wasn't quite the intricate stack of lies it is now," James said.

The old man stopped moving backward, looked around Nicole's head, and straight into James' eyes.

"You have no idea," he said.

"What do you know about me?" James asked.

"Stalling, James."

"No. I really want to know. I'm asking you what the hell do *you*...know about *me*? Who are you?"

"I told you, James. I am you..."

"Bullshit," James said, cutting him off.

"Maybe so...but probably closer to the truth than you could ever imagine," the old man said.

"How's that?" James asked.

The man paused in the doorway to the stairwell.

"Did you ever ask your uncle what he did...does for a living? Hmmm?"

"Ted? What's he got to do with this? He's a carpenter. Always has been...I don't get it."

"Awe, poor James. Just another lie to throw on the pile. And such a noble choice…carpenter. Yes, indeed. So noble…like he could build a fucking ark if he wanted to and just float away with the flood when it comes. Like it never happened. Well, James…the flood is coming…and Uncle Ted never quite finished his ark."

The old man laughed dismally and tugged on Nicole's hair, making her flinch in pain. James' brow furrowed, but the man quickly dragged Nicole the rest of the way towards the top of the stairs.

"Find your Uncle, James, and let's see how deep the layers go," the old man said, then he deftly swept Nicole up over his shoulder with one arm like she was a sack of flowers and bolted down the steps.

James plunged into the stairwell after the old man.

Chapter 35

There were yells and shouts behind him, but James wasn't hearing anything but the sound of his wet sneakers squeaking on the linoleum as he rounded each landing. Reaching the first floor, he burst out the first exit he saw into what appeared to be a fresh cloudburst. The dark sky made day seem like night. He scanned the parking lot. Halfway across, he could see the old man's head bobbing along at what appeared to be a jogging pace. He was headed toward a large white car that seemed to be running, waiting for him. Kevin came right after and grabbed James' arm, but James flinched hard and turned as if to fight. Kevin held up his hands.

"Whoa, brother," he said, looking scared at what he saw in James.

More footsteps came down behind them and Doug and Dr. Paynter came out the door into the rain. They were barely stopped, when James lunged at Paynter, a finger pointed accusingly.

"You have a lot of goddamn explaining to do," James yelled.

Doug moved slightly between James and Paynter, raising his cane slightly. His larger girth was enough to keep James from poking Paynter right in the face. James pulled the Ted's Towing cap off his head and tossed it in Paynter's general direction.

"I…" Paynter stammered, "It's good to see you too, James."

"Has everyone lost their minds? What the fuck is going on around here?" James shouted.

"I...we'd...better go after her," Paynter said.

"The cops won't be far behind us," Kevin said.

"I'm not through with you," James said, and he turned and broke out into a run back to their car.

"I didn't think it would be that easy," Paynter said, and they all fell in behind James, who was almost across the parking lot and up the embankment.

Kevin and Paynter helped Doug up the muddy slope. They all turned to watch as the old man's car pulled out of the parking lot. The white Grand Marquis disappeared quickly around a corner. Two officers popped out of the door they had just left.

"He made a right," Doug called out.

"Let's go!" James said, and they piled into the very beaten looking sedan.

"Glad to see you boys have been treating my ride with care," Paynter said.

"You should see the other guy," Doug said as he started the car.

"Hello? Cops right behind us, bad guys getting away...let's go!" Kevin said.

Doug punched the pedal to the floor and raced out of the parking lot, ignoring the stop sign. He bypassed all means of caution and took corners at much higher rates of speed than James could have imagined possible considering the conditions. And yet every move of the car was controlled. Doug's hands seemed to glide effortlessly across the wheel, moving precisely, never overreacting. His eyes scanned the road ahead.

"Everyone check the side streets," James said.

"Rain isn't helping any," Kevin said.

"Hang a right!" Paynter shouted.

Doug threw the car into a controlled slide and took the next right. James braced for the impact with a parked car, then unhooked his clenched hand from the door when it didn't happen. They were barreling down a narrow side street. The white car passed at a cross street, moving just as quickly.

"Where'd you find all-season radials in Florida, doc?" Doug said, conversationally.

He rolled through the stop sign at the end of the road, then pulled out where James saw no room. Horns blared, but they managed to slip through. James didn't want to know by how much.

"I figured his breaks worked," Doug said.

"Bought 'em online," Paynter said. "You're Doug, right?"

"That's me, but you already know all about us, from what I can gather," Doug said, and they could see the taillights of the white Grand Marquis three blocks ahead of them.

James turned in his seat slightly.

"Yeah, I guess I do," Paynter said, his voice just audible above the sounds of cars being passed and rain on the windshield. The buildings had thinned as they approached the outskirts of the small town.

"You better get that story straight, Paynter," James said.

Kevin pointed and shouted at the same time, "He turned!"

"I see him…hold on," Doug said.

They passed an abandoned gas station and turned at a white clapboard fence. The road quickly turned to dirt. They watched as the big luxury car bounced into potholes without slowing down.

"Jesus," James said, bracing for the impact, as the wheels bottomed out.

"Sorry," Doug said, sounding more angry at himself than with the conditions.

"Where the hell…" Kevin began.

"It's the local airport," Paynter said. "There was a sign at the end of the road."

"What's he going to do? Fly away?" Asked James, the hint of a laugh in his voice.

"Nothing would surprise me at this point," Paynter said.

"No way," said James.

"This guy's been one step ahead of us every time," Paynter said.

"Well, there's no way…not this time…," James said.

The Grand Marquis hung a sharp left and plowed through a loosely padlocked metal gate.

"I guess he doesn't have an appointment," Doug said. They were thundering after the white car, which had turned onto the runway. If James hadn't known better, he might have thought the man was trying to take off.

James watched as their speedometer reached 80 and they were still losing ground to the white car. They were almost at the end of the paved surface when the car spun sideways and came to a halt at the edge of the tarmac. Doug followed suit and the cars could have been parked next to one another. The doors flew open almost simultaneously. The old man came out, holding the gun at James, and slowly alternating it between the three boys. They watched as he opened the back door and pulled Nicole out from the back seat. Her hands were somehow bound behind her and the way she limped, James thought that perhaps her feet were bound as well.

"Let her go," James said, rounding the front of the car.

Then a second old man got out of the car. He turned to James. He was identical to the first. They were even dressed the same.

"Oh no, you've caught me," the second old man simpered, a Cheshire smile across his face. "Whatever shall I do?"

"No fucking way," Kevin said.

James held his hands out to his sides imploringly. "What the hell is this about? Who are you? Why are you doing this?"

"Did we miss the multiples convention?" Doug asked.

"Shoot the fat one if he speaks again," the second old man said.

"More stalling tactics, James," the first old man said.

"Just wondering why I'm standing in the middle of an old abandoned airfield, soaked to the core, asking some loopy fucks what the hell it is they think they're doing."

"Waiting, James. Just waiting," he said.

"Waiting? For what?" James looked around mockingly. "I think you're going to have to shoot us after all."

"James…nooo," Nicole cried softly.

The smile washed off the first old man's face. "Don't tempt me."

"Well then what? What the hell–"

His words were cut by the sudden rush of wind and rain that spiraled around all of them. The sound of the blades beating the air above them made all of them duck except for the old man. James went prone into the slushy muddy grass as the red and gold helicopter came down ten feet above their heads and landed deftly behind the old man on a patch of solid snow.

"Waitings over, I guess," the second old man shouted and he turned to run to the chopper, the side door having been opened for his arrival. James running after them before any of the others could hold him back. He saw the first old man swat at the hand of the pilot who appeared to be lifting a gun toward James.

"No!" he cried, then, reaching the door, they tossed Nicole into the back without ceremony. Someone inside was pulling her in further. Someone was shouting "Go" when James leapt. The last old man on the chopper had not yet closed the door.

James felt the chopper lunge beneath his weight. He had caught both the old man's leg and a part of the landing runner in his grasp and it wavered momentarily. The old man cried out, then began kicking fiercely.

"Get off you fool!"

He leaned down and slowly began to pry James' hand away from his leg. There was tremendous strength in the thin fingers. A strength that made no sense for his age. Their eyes met, and for a moment James might have mistook a look of compassion in the man's eyes.

"Let...go...," he said.

When James didn't comply, the old man lashed out fiercely, striking James across the face. The chopper lurched off the ground again and this time, James' feet left the earth. He heard Nicole scream. A second pair of hands was pushing on him and he looked up to find the second old man smiling at James as he put a hand on his face and pushed. His one hand slipped away from the old man's leg and he shouted a curse that no one heard over the din of the chopper blades. They were ten feet off the ground and moving higher. James hated himself as his other hand slipped away from the chopper's landing runner. He just avoided a final blow from the second old man as he fell away. They all seemed to be floating together in space for a moment and James had just enough time to register that even the pilot had looked the same. He fell back to Earth and braced himself for the crunch of his bones against the ground, but it never came. The pool of sod, slush, and mud that he landed in must have been about two feet deep. He found his feet quickly, not feeling any pain from the fall. He threw a handful of whatever he could grab at the chopper that was already well out of reach. He ran, or tried to, through the snow and mud after the chopper.

"No! No…you bastards. Come back. Damn you, no! Come back and fight…come back. Just bring her back. She's got nothing to do with this…damn you…whatever it is…it's not her fault."

He stood in the middle of the half-frozen mud puddle, the water well over his sneakers. The chopper rounded back the way it had come, and disappeared quickly into the rain and clouds. It could have gone in any direction for all James knew and a pain welled in his chest as he watched it go. He had just let Nicole die…or worse…he had killed her. Which possibility was worse was not yet clear to him. He had agreed to bring her along and now it was going to get her killed. But they don't really want her…they want him…they want all of them. He heard the footfalls behind him and a new energy entered him.

He turned, his anger surging into his fists. The three came across the field towards him. He ran toward them, then screamed maniacally and lunged at Paynter, taking the old man down into the mud.

Chapter 36

"Jesus…James!" Kevin cried.

James lifted Paynter by the collar and shook him, his face half-covered in muddy filth.

"What the fuck is happening? What the hell have you brought on me and my…Nicole…what the hell have you done…"

Doug and Kevin were forcibly pulling him off and his burst of energy was fading. He rolled over into a heap, his face brushing a patch of snow.

"How could you do this…why couldn't you have left well enough alone."

Kevin helped Paynter out of the mud, repeatedly apologizing to him. Doug half-carried James back to the cars, where he slumped into the back seat, a heap of sodden mud. They all got back into the car. The silence was broken by Kevin.

"Well, the helicopter was a complete surprise," he said, shaking his head. "Yep, didn't see that one comin' *at all*."

"I--," Paynter began.

"You need to start explaining," James said abruptly, sitting up and jabbing a finger into the air that threw some more mud around the already disgusting interior. He looked around him and lowered his head.

"I need to get out of this car, and you need to start talking like there's no tomorrow…I feel like I can't breathe. Doug…take us over to that old hangar. Please."

"Sure," Doug said.

He started the car and they drove the two hundred yards to the empty hangar.

They all got out and Paynter leaned against the hood. He sighed deeply and rubbed his chest without thinking. James stared hard at Paynter, half trying to see something in his eyes, half trying to inflict some sort of telekinetic pain. Paynter offered neither a sign of understanding or pain. He simply looked away.

"Whenever you're ready," James said.

"James, please, I'm–" Paynter said.

"Don't!…start apologizing again. I can't take another hollow apology," James yelled, jamming his fists into his coat pockets.

"I'm…" Paynter began, realizing that his instinct had become to start each sentence with an apology.

Paynter stopped and ran a hand through his muddy hair and James wondered if he had always looked that old. James turned and walked a pace. Despite the cavernous space provided by the empty hangar, he couldn't escape the creeping sense of claustrophobia.

"I can't take anymore lies. I'm wallowing in a cesspool of lies that just seems to be sucking me down. I seem to remember you promising some sort of truth out of all of this, but you forgot to tell me that you'd be heaping on a couple more layers of deception in order to get me there," James said.

"James, please…just take a breather for a minute and let me explain," Paynter said.

"A breather? A bunch of crazy old dudes just made off with my girlfriend and there was nothing I could do to stop them! I don't need a breather. I feel like I've been taking a breather all my life and when it came time to step up, I didn't have it in me. Let your guard down and you never know when someone might show up to kill you or steal a loved one. I don't think I'll ever take a breather again, to tell the truth. You know what I've learned? I really hate surprises, and you know what else? I really don't like guns, and come to think of it, I don't really like feeling like my life will never see the better side of normal ever again."

Paynter stood up straight, and moved away from the car, his hands outstretched.

"Are you going to give me a chance?" Paynter said.

Kevin and Doug watched like spectators at a tennis match, knowing that to interject with even a cough might bring James' wrath onto them instead of Paynter. They said nothing.

"A chance," James said, stopping and turning in mid-pace. "A chance? How many do you want? I haven't been keeping track, so I'm not sure if you've really got any left."

Paynter took a step towards James and held his hands up in a gesture of acquiescence.

"Please," he said.

James stopped his pacing and stood facing Paynter, his arms folded across his chest, his eyes on the ground at his feet.

Now it was Paynter's turn to pace. He walked from the front of the car to the back, his hand resting momentarily on the trunk of the car. He rubbed some mud between his fingers thoughtfully.

"What I am going to tell you is the complete truth," he began quietly.

"Well, it's about t--," began James.

"Shut…up," Paynter said turning on him and pointing his finger at James.

His face coiled in an angry scowl that frightened all three of them.

"Just shut up for two seconds. You don't understand any of this…any of it. You've been dealing with this for…a couple of days…I've lived with it for nearly twenty-five years."

Paynter paused, wiped something from each sleeve as if it mattered, then grabbed each lapel of his coat, as if he were a British barrister about to plead his case. "Twenty-five years…good God. Now listen, and keep your mouth shut. Hold your questions till the end. It's not going to make sense if I have to jump back and forth and…I want to get it right the first time," Paynter said.

"Fair enough," James said.

"What I told you before was only partly true…in a sense. You see…Doug and Kevin…they aren't really your brothers…per se. At least, not in the way that makes the most sense. They're…copies. You're all copies. All six of you were…are copies of…someone else. A man that may or may not still be alive."

James arms unfolded. He jammed them back into his pockets and bit his lip. Kevin and Doug instantly became more attentive. Paynter held up a hand, pleadingly.

"Please, this is hard enough. There is much more to tell, and I promise I will answer every question you have. Just let me get through this."

"Let me give you a little history lesson…a brief history lesson. In 1979, a man by the name of Karl Illmensee stepped into the public eye and claimed to have developed a means of cloning frog embryos by simply removing the nuclei of an existing cell and transplanting it into a fertilized…err…enucleated egg. It was huge scientific news. This was a huge breakthrough in genetic research and truly represented a huge leap for what man could accomplish. But, the American government was caught off guard a little. Their genetic research was poorly funded at the time and worlds behind if what he claimed was true."

"What--," James started, but Paynter ignored him and plowed ahead.

"Like the space race, or the nuclear race, there was now a gap in what American scientists knew, and what the Europeans knew. And, at the height of the Cold War, this was extremely significant. The Branches Project was started in the summer of 1980. I was a budding physicist. Fresh out of MIT. Cloning sounded like a great place to make a name. It was unchartered territory and I was going to be on the forefront. Fred Taylor and I worked in a small facility in Iowa with a handful of assistants. At first, we tried following what little we had heard about Illmensee's method, but found it nearly impossible. And, for good reason. Illmensee turned out to be a fraud. None of his experiments could be reproduced. But, by the time we had found that out, we had already taken a step off of that path onto the right course. It was Fred Taylor's work that pushed us in the right direction. Without him, Dolly might have truly been the first cloned mammal."

Paynter stopped his pacing for a moment and looked out into the field, where the rain had picked up. He took a couple more steps, the sounds of his heels against the hangar cement echoing against the aluminum walls. James resisted the urge to raise one of the many questions this conversation had sparked in his mind. He rubbed his mouth with his hand and spat out the mud he'd forgotten about.

"And, there it was. In two years, we had done what it had taken a liar to do in three. Only we'd actually done it. We had a method for transferring the nucleus of an existing life form into the cell of an unfertilized egg and creating a near duplicate copy of the existing life form. We started small, of course. Mice, and small rodents, and worked our way up to larger mammals. It was a feverish pace. I don't remember much of that time, because all we did was eat and work, sleeping when we could sneak in an hour or two. Like I said, there were only a handful of us, but Taylor and I were the only ones who knew the whole story."

Again he paused and said, more to himself, "We were too young, or too ignorant, to consider the consequences of what they were asking us to do. Or maybe both. They had given us a challenge and we felt like we were heading toward something great. Something we could be proud of. It was a stressful time too. No one was sure of the results, but the money kept coming down the line to move things forward. We had no limits."

"By the Fall of '82, they had already made the decision to clone a human. Or, they had at least made the decision to make the attempt. It was still all extremely quiet, so they needed people who would be willing to cooperate for as little as possible. It was decided that the clones would be male. A suitable donor was found. A young military man by the name of Sebastian Walters was chosen. He had no idea what he was being asked to do, nor was he ever told. Or, at least he wasn't supposed to be told. I think someone thought twice about having him around after the fact. He somehow found out. Ran around trying to tell anyone who would listen that he had been cloned by the government. It wasn't hard to lock him away."

"You said you didn't know if he was still alive," James said, forgetting his vow of silence.

"He may well still be alive, but I never bothered to find out. I was more concerned with you boys. He'd already been 'taken care of'," Paynter said, raising his hands to make air quotes.

James watched as Paynter again walked to the other side of the car. He leaned over to look at some of the damage, but James didn't think he was actually seeing it. He was somewhere else.

"We impregnated forty women in the first round of testing. They were housed in the most high tech prenatal care facility the world had ever seen. By the end of the first two weeks, seventy-five percent of our mothers had self-aborted...miscarried. We had actually calculated a total failure, so we were actually sort of hopeful at that point. There were only nine viable fetuses at the end of the second month. Taylor and I celebrated every additional day. To us, it was a miracle we had gotten as far as we had. We had already beaten ridiculous odds at that point. Who was to say that we couldn't keep it up? At six months, we had seven; he died in the seventh month. Twenty years later and we might have been able to save him. As it was, on September 3rd of 1982, the first cloned baby boy was born in a laboratory in Iowa. He was in excellent health, and we drank ourselves stupid that night celebrating. Five others followed him, just as healthy, and all showing the same genetic traits as the donor they had been bred from."

Paynter paused, pressing his fingers together at the tips and bringing his hand to his mouth.

"Are you fucking kidding me?" James whispered.

"The last baby boy was born at 9:17 AM on September 19, 1984. I kid you not, James. You wanted the truth. There it is."

"I'm a clone?" James said.

"If that's the truth, then I'd like you to start lying to me again," Kevin said under his breath, turning his head away from Paynter.

"I was the last one. Huh," Doug said softly.

"That isn't the end of it, James, please listen."

James folded his arms again, his mouth taut.

"Two weeks after you were born, the project was terminated. The hard way. It seems that the experiment was kept under much tighter wraps than we had been led to believe. And, when it got out, someone decided that it was too risky to have something that controversial come out in public. Ilmensee was a sham, and as far as anyone could tell, the Russians had never even considered starting their own cloning project. It was money lost in a war that didn't exist. And, by then, they had decided that the idea of cloning was really against everything the country had started to define itself as. It was all a bunch of bullshit. Bureaucratic bullshit that coincided with a reelection. So, they sent some professionals in to terminate the project. The women, who had given birth to the six of you, were quietly assassinated in ways so as not to arouse suspicion. Accidents happen, I guess. The facility where we had done so much good work was destroyed in a fire conveniently attributed to a gas leak. Phase two was completely wiped out. Amazingly, all members of the staff were also in the building at the time of the fire, and no one managed to escape."

"Phase two?" he said.

"I'll get to that," Paynter said, then walked back to see the three dumbfounded young men looking at him in various states of disbelief. Paynter folded his arms and stared at the floor.

"To my own credit, if you can call it that…maybe paranoia is a better term, I had seen it coming…some of it. I had developed a contingency plan. Something had told me that when I stopped receiving contact from my usual internal sources, there was something wrong. I selected the few people I could trust and created a plan B. It was ambitious, and it could have failed if any of the pieces had not been in place at the time, but somehow we managed or…more likely, we were allowed to manage. You and the other five were allowed to survive. I hid you away the best way I knew how. I tried to scatter you into the wind, leaving you with a small piece of information that might lead you to one another…with some help. We placed you all in childless families, where your origins wouldn't necessarily be called into question. There were only a handful of us who survived it all. Fred Taylor, my secretary, and myself as far as I know. We all had to go into hiding. Now, it's just Fred and I. They killed Agnes a couple days before I arrived."

Paynter's words hung in the air. He looked afraid to add anything else. Afraid that it might create enough weight to collapse the building.

"So…we're clones," James said.

Paynter nodded as if James had just stated the sky was blue. Kevin chuckled and leaned against the car.

"Wow...I thought I had it bad getting dates before," he said, shaking his head.

"What the heck am I going to tell my Mom?" Doug asked.

"Tell her you're a miracle of modern science. Tell her you're proof that science doesn't create monsters. Or, tell her nothing. Look at you three! You're all...exactly how you should be..." He turned away from them and rubbed his eyes. "It took a lot for me to not seek you out a long time ago. But, that was when I was still running..."

"Or, Doug, how 'bout this," James said, and he couldn't hold back the cynicism in his voice. "You could tell her that you're proof that God doesn't really exist. Because how could he exist if man can create *and* destroy life. I mean, who needs God? Jesus, it makes me want to crawl in a hole. If Taylor was trying to expose this, then maybe these other guys are right. Maybe we should all just take a bullet. I'd rather do that than stand up in front of the world and become a magnet for every religious freak who wants to make me into a scientific martyr."

"I think that's what they're afraid of. I think they're afraid of the global repercussions that would come along with such a revelation," Paynter said.

"Then why let us survive in the first place?" James said.

"That I'm not so sure of. If they really wanted to kill you or me, they could have done it years ago, and much more quietly. And, I don't know why Taylor decided to stir the nest...twenty-four years of running maybe...but now it's going to take a lot more than smoke to calm them down. They're afraid. He must've sent information somewhere."

"They're afraid? Huh…go figure," James said.

"What about the tall, old, and creepies?" Kevin said.

Paynter pressed a finger against his mouth thoughtfully.

"I…I actually don't know—"

"You said you had the answers," James said.

"Yes, and I might, but I actually don't know the truth about him…them," Paynter said, and he looked at James.

"Try me," James said.

"You see, there was rumor…about a third phase. One that had been covered in so many layers that it became buried to those who were working on it. They…they were attempting to…modify the subjects," Paynter said.

"Modify?" Doug said.

"Boost hormones. Faster, stronger, smarter, more easily adaptable," Paynter said.

"Super clones," Kevin said.

"In a way, yes," Paynter said.

"And why would you do that?" James asked, not needing to hear the answer.

"To build an army," Doug replied. "Just like in the movies."

"An army of assassins. That was what they had planned for you. You would have the perfect alibi if no one suspected you had an identical twin…or twins…who could prove your innocence."

"Except something went wrong," James said.

"You mean, other than hitting every branch of the ugly tree on the way down?" Kevin said.

"Apparently," Paynter said. "Did you ever read about Dolly and what happened to her?"

The boys shook their heads collectively in the negative.

"They cloned her from an adult, which meant that the DNA they used was already developing anomalies and mutations. We used stem cells before anyone in the public had heard the term."

"That's what he meant," James said.

"That's what who meant?" Doug said.

"The old man. He said he was me..."

"He's not old, James," Paynter said. If my calculations are correct, and the rumors are true...which they appear to be, then he...they...are approximately six months younger than you three."

"That's insane," Doug said.

"That sort of explains why he was so strong...built like a straw man, tough as stone though," James said.

"And who raised them?"

"There's the kicker," Paynter said. "I have no idea. For all I know, they were raised by the government."

"That would make sense, especially if they were planning on using them as...an army," James said.

"Can you imagine an army of old men jumping out at you…throwing their teeth as a last ditch effort…creepy bastards," Kevin said.

They all chuckled nervously.

"I don't think that was the plan. They might have appeared normal for a while…until things started to break down. They probably had very difficult childhoods. I imagine they must be on some serious enhanced substances to be jumping around like they do."

"Steroids?" Doug asked.

"Among other things," Paynter said.

He moved to the rear of the car, leaned against it, and gazed out of the hangar doors into the field beyond. The three young men joined him.

"I also imagine…that they're on borrowed time," Paynter said.

"Jesus, don't make me feel bad for them. The assholes just took Nicole!"

"Why do you think they're after us?" Kevin asked.

"Revenge!" Doug said before Paynter could speak. "I'd be pretty pissed off…more so than I already am. And, for them…Jesus…if I looked like that and could blame a handful of people…well, I don't want to make it sound like they're behavior is justified, but--"

"You're pissed?" Kevin said.

"Of course I'm pissed," Doug said. "I'm as pissed as James is. Maybe I just don't yell and scream like him."

James blushed.

"This all sucks...on many levels. You never dreamed of having a brother or sister growing up? I did. All the time. Somebody I could play football with in the back yard. I never understood why my parents never had another kid. I begged my mom on a regular basis. Sometimes she'd just say no as if it was something I was being silly about. Other times she'd cry and I'd walk away feeling ashamed. I learned to stop asking. So, yeah, I'm pissed."

"But, you were making bagels in a shop in the middle of fucking Ohio. And, you," Kevin said, pointing to James, "You were doing what? Pushing a pencil in a dead end job for the past three years, hating life?"

"And, now we're running for our lives, hoping against hope that our loved ones don't come to any harm, and trying to assess what a shortened life would really mean at this point," James said.

"Isn't it great?" Kevin asked.

They stared at him in disbelief.

"I mean...I haven't felt this alive...in my entire life. This...this is living. I feel like I've been slapped out of a stupor. James, you said it yourself. We've been given a big wakeup call to life."

"This isn't life," James said.

"No. You're right, but it ain't sitting at a desk having your brains sucked out by a computer monitor day after day. This is how change comes about. You think we'll evolve by sitting at a desk, or behind a counter, or on a curb?"

"So, now we're the pinnacle of evolution?" Doug said.

"Can't you feel it? I should be exhausted, but you know what? I'm alive with energy. I feel like I could go another day without sleep."

James turned to Doug and said, straight faced, "I'll have whatever he's having."

Doug shook his head, smiling a bit.

"Screw you guys..." Kevin said, fighting off a smile of his own.

"I guess we owe you some thanks, Dr. Paynter," Doug said without looking at him.

"My thanks was seeing each of you again. I dreamed of this day for years. You were...you were sort of like the sons I never had. Sort of tough to get married when you're on the run. I think Taylor felt...feels the same way."

"Funny way of showing it," James said.

"He did save your life back there," Kevin said.

"He also pointed a gun at me in my own home. Sorry if the warm fuzzies haven't quite kicked in for him yet," James said.

"I'm really sorry this hasn't gone quite according to plan. I really didn't--," Paynter said.

"What about my uncle?" James asked.

Paynter blew out a breath that hung in the air before them. "Well, I was hoping to avoid this, but–," he said.

"...but you promised the truth," James said.

310

"–I promised the truth…the whole truth. So here it is," Paynter said.

"James…your uncle and I go way back. We served briefly in the Navy together. We were good friends, Teddy and I. He's a good man, your uncle. Has a head for what's right and wrong in the world. Well…he disappeared for a few years after the Navy. I went to MIT and heard from him maybe once a year. He'd write a note busting my chops about something or wishing me a happy belated birthday six months after the day. Then, about a year into this project he called me. Seemed nervous at the time. Told me some things I thought only Taylor and I knew. He seemed to know that it was going to be terminated. He's the one who gave me the heads up about 'changes' and that's when we decided to act. He asked me to do him a favor. He wanted to keep an eye on one of you. Somehow felt responsible. Said his brother…your father, James…couldn't have any kids of his own. And could we please give him one of the boys."

"Ted knew all along," James said.

"Yes. He kept me up to date with you," Paynter said.

"So, he's not a carpenter," James said, now very distant.

"Not professionally. I think he picked it up as a hobby, but as it turned out, he was a Navy SEAL. Could have probably gone up the ranks, but showmanship was never his thing."

"No…no it wasn't."

James looked down at himself. He was a walking mud puddle.

"We'd better get going," he said.

"Where?" Doug asked.

"My uncle's place up in Michigan. He said that's where he was going," James said.

"I think that would be unwise…that's what they want. That's the only reason they took Nicole," Paynter said.

"Are you saying we should split up?" Kevin asked.

"We've only got one car," James said.

"Not anymore," Doug said, dangling the keys on the end of his finger. "I got myself a shiny new Grand Marquis."

"Well, wherever we're going, I need to get out of these clothes. I'm soaked," James said.

"Yeah, join the club" Kevin said.

"We could go to my house," Doug said.

"No," Paynter and James said it together.

"They might be watching your parents place now," Paynter said, then added when Doug frowned, "I don't think they have anything to worry about. It's not them anyone is concerned with."

"The less they know the better. All we need is for another loved one to get in the way," James said.

"They won't kill her, James," Paynter said.

"I don't…need to hear that," James said. "I need to hear a plan…I need a next step before I go out of my mind from standing still."

"I have an old friend in Ohio. Not more than four hours from here. She…she might not be happy to see me, but--"

312

"This sounds promising already," James said.

"We don't exactly have a menu to choose from, James," Kevin said.

"Can we trust her?" Doug asked.

"You can. Me on the other hand…well…," Paynter scratched his chin and shrugged.

"Great," James said.

"Why do I get the feeling that we might be better off not visiting this woman," Kevin said.

"Sounds like we have more to worry about visiting her than staying put," Doug said.

"Listen, she and I go way back…and we were really good friends, but men and women sometimes…I…you know…things happen," Paynter said.

"You old heartbreaker, you," Kevin said.

"Yeah, except…she thinks I'm dead," Paynter Saud.

"What? Good Lord. I've heard enough. Explain in the car," James said.

"Who's going in the Marquis?" Doug asked.

"Doug, do you want to go in the Marquis?" Kevin asked mockingly. Doug nodded his head like a little kid being offered chocolate.

"I'll go with Doug," James said.

"Oh," Paynter said, but he let it go when James started to walk away. "Do you want a ride to the car?" he called out after him.

"Naw…maybe the rain will wash some of this shit off," James shouted without turning.

They were on the road minutes later, the white Grand Marquis following the beat up Chrysler. James slumped in the passenger's seat, warding off any sort of conversation Doug attempted to start with him. He told him to wake him if someone started shooting at them, but only if they would survive. Otherwise, let him sleep. Sleep came quickly, but he stirred frequently with the same image in his mind when he woke; the glimpse of Nicole's face as the helicopter pulled away. He knew she must've been scared, but there was something in her countenance that told him she was more afraid for him than for herself. He hoped that she had seen the same. At last, sleep took him and he dreamed no more.

Chapter 37

"Hello, John," the man in black said.

"Don't you speak to me," Norris said.

"After all these years, John, still no kind words for your old friend?"

"You're going away this time...*friend*...even if it's in a body bag," he said, his hand clenched around the grip of his gun. He could feel the cough coming on, but pushed back on it hard.

"You think so?" the man asked. "Do you really think so, John?"

"You're a scumbag," Norris said.

"I'm just man with a job, John. Just like you. Paid by the same people even," the man said

"Bullshit," Norris said.

"Oh c'mon, John. Think about it. Think about the last time you saw me," the man said and now he slowly got to his feet, hands spread before him.

"Remember? Can you remember that day, John? I can. You know why? Because you cost me big time that day."

"All I know is you killed innocent people that day," Norris said.

"Innocent maybe, but the government wanted them dead. That's why they had you to protect them. You stuck your nose where it didn't belong. You know that. You knew what was going down, and yet you still jumped in, trying to be some sort of hero. Fucked my job up big time. I had to leave the country

315

because of you. Had to live in a dozen South American shit holes for ten years because of you. Meanwhile, you freaked out…lost a couple partners, lost your wife, nearly lost your job…on more than one occasion. Oh, I know all about it, John. Now look at you…twenty some odd years later and you're still trying to wear that little cape and leap from tall buildings. Still jumping in head first and hoping for a soft landing. The only thing you seem to have learned is to leave the partner at home…"

"Ahhhhh!"

Norris grabbed the man by his jacket collar and slammed him against the opposite wall, the gun pressed against the man's temple. They were nose to nose.

"Agent Norris!" Fields called out behind him.

"I should have killed you when I had the chance…"

"When was that, John? College? After one of our drunken bouts? After I fucked Lizzie what's-her-name? A girl you didn't give two shits about until you found out I'd nailed her. You're not still bitter about that, are you? That isn't what this is all about, is it? No…I can see that it isn't. It's something else. Something you've had brewing for a long time now."

"Shut up," Norris said, shaking him by the collar again.

"You see, John, you've spent way too many years thinking about me. I, on the other hand, couldn't give a rat's hairy ass about you to be quite honest. Oh sure, I got my updates, just out of curiosity, but you…you seem to have been holding a grudge. A bit obsessive perhaps? Yeah, I'd say so. What say you, Dr. Taylor?"

"Someone say my name?" Taylor said, when he noticed the man in black had turned to speak to him. He could hear nothing in his right ear and the left seemed to be stuffed with cotton. He shrugged and pretended to ignore the situation again.

"Oh, he's going to be fun in the car," the man said.

"What makes you think you're going to be driving again anytime soon?" Norris asked through clenched teeth.

"John, I told you…we're working for the same people. I expect you'll be getting a call any moment now," the man said, looking over Norris' shoulder.

"Bullshit," Norris said, relaxing his grip and moving a step back.

"The hell it is," the man said, lowering his voice. "You think I'd have let you slam me against the wall like that? You could be dead by now, John. You and I both know that. Sure, you're a tough old cock, but you've been filling out paperwork at a desk too much recently. And, that cough. You should really get that looked at."

"Fuck you," Norris said, trying to hold it back, but the pent up cough released as if summoned and Norris turned choking and sputtering bloody mucus into his hand. He doubled over from the body-racking coughs. The man stood behind him, saying something, but Norris could only cough. The urge eased finally and he stood up, rooting into his pocket for his handkerchief.

"What did you say, asshole?"

"Check your phone," the man said.

Norris looked perplexed until he heard the beep. He pulled the cell from his inside his coat and flipped it open. One missed call.

"Better call 'em back. Might be important," the man said, smiling.

Norris held the phone up, as if it were strange to him, and pushed a button. It only rang once.

"Norris?"

"Who's this?

"This is Deputy Director Williams."

"Jesus Christ," Norris whispered.

"Why aren't you in Cleveland yet?" Williams asked.

"I...I've become involved in a local matter," Norris said.

"So I've heard. Listen, Norris, just drop it and report to Cleveland," Williams said.

"Why are you suddenly being nice to me?" Norris asked.

"I'm trying to save your ass...one last time. You're meddling in something we shouldn't be touching. It isn't our business, John."

"What the hell is going on here," Norris said, the inflection gone from his voice.

"John..."

"You never call me John...what the hell is this?"

Norris turned and assessed his location in the hallway. He might be able to outrun them. If Robinson wanted to catch him, there was nothing he could do but shoot him. He'd aim low if he had to.

"Walk away from it, John. It's for your own good," Williams said.

"Yeah, maybe so," Norris said, "Maybe you're right."

"I'm glad you agree, John…"

"Yeah, maybe I should just roll over when told. Like a good ol' dog. Just like you say," Norris said.

"John…that's not what I meant. You've got to believe me. Listen, if you won't go quietly…"

"What have you told Fields?" Norris said.

Fields and Robinson both started to move at the same time.

"Lieutenant Fields and I have been in communication," Williams said, and now Norris was slowly backing away from all of them.

"What have you told them, Williams?" Norris said, and he turned and began walking away quickly.

"Agent Norris?" Robinson called.

"He's been told to make sure you drop all of your activities immediately. You are to report…"

"Cleveland can kiss my ass and so can you," Norris said, then turned and threw the cell phone at Robinson, who had broken into a trot behind him.

"Don't do it, Robinson," Norris called over his shoulder as he turned to run, his lungs burning. "Don't you do it! Go back to your quiet little neck of the woods and live the life of a towny cop!"

Norris made it to the end of the hall and plowed into the stairwell doorway ahead of him. One flight down, he hurdled the crouched figure of a paramedic, three men looked up. They were placing a heavy set man in a white shirt and black pants into a body bag. The zipper moved over the name badge on his blood soaked chest. It read "Charlie."

Epilogue

On the northern edge of Lake Michigan, up past the great Green Bay, a spit of land juts out into the lake, just south of the Hiawatha National Forest. If you follow route 483 down the peninsula, a mere 8 miles across at its widest, you'll eventually come to a bend in the road called Devil's Corner. It was here that Ted Masterson had staked his claim. The country was exactly what he was looking for; rugged, intimidating, but also full of the kind of people you could trust. The kind of people who did as they were done in return. His thirty-five acres allowed him the type of privacy he liked. His nearest neighbor was a five minute drive on roads they didn't even bother naming.

Here, he had tucked himself away, half hoping to forget the world; half hoping the world would forget him. But, despite his seclusion and the hours spent immersed in manual labor around the farm, he couldn't allow himself to forget. Once a year, he would start preparing, sometimes unbeknownst to himself, to leave his retreat. He would visit his brother in New Jersey. He would visit the boy. Make sure all was well. Make sure that his mistake had not cost his brother any more than it already had. Then his brother had died unexpectedly. It wasn't supposed to happen that way. Little brothers were supposed to bury you, not the other way around. He had remained stoic through the service. A hardened face of courage for Maggie, only a few years from death herself, and the boy. A lie revealed only the week following his burial, when he spent three straight

321

days weeping alone in the darkness of his cabin. When the sorrow finally abated, he plunged himself into the farm, pushing himself to his own physical limits and beyond. It was only later that he could admit that he'd been trying to kill himself. Trying to break the heart in his body as his brother's had been broken.

He was soon confronted by a new sorrow. Maggie was dying. There would be no merciful quickness to her death. He watched from afar as she withered under the chemotherapy. James rose to the occasion, becoming the kind of young man Ted had hoped he would become. He wasn't blood, and Ted couldn't see him as a military man, but he always felt that the boy had something in him. Something that lay just beneath the surface, waiting to be scratched out. His mother's death had made him bleed, but he would be ok. He was going to be ok…with some help.

Ted looked down at his hand, which was still on the phone's receiver. Dan Johnson up at the airport had just called in. He knew Ted well. Knew enough of Ted's history to understand his desire for secrecy. Knew that someone who asked where Ted Masterson lived was probably looking for trouble. Knew that someone looking for him after dark was really looking for trouble. There were at least two of them, perhaps a third in the car, but he couldn't quite see. Came in on an unregistered chopper. No flight plan needed for a chopper in that region.

They were about a half hour away. Even if they didn't know where they were going, they could still be there within forty-five minutes. It wasn't a large place.

Ted changed into his fatigues and pulled the rifle out from under his bed. The black cap was snug on his head, and the uniform was a little tighter in places it hadn't been before, but it would do. For a moment, he considered taking the boat out into the lake. From there, he could watch at a safe, unapproachable distance. Instead, he made his way out into the woods about a hundred and fifty yards from the house. He could easily see the house and the driveway. He glanced at his watch once and began to count down in his head. He glanced in his binoculars at sixty second intervals and checked his surroundings every two minutes. He closed his eyes and focused on the sounds of the woods around him. He heard the car approach from about a mile off. Saw as the headlights turned into his driveway. Watched intently as the car moved brazenly towards the house. Whoever it was, wasn't concerned with how much noise they made, which worried him. He glanced over his shoulder trying to decide if the sound he had heard was an echo from the car in the driveway, or whether his instinct was correct. The car hadn't stopped though. He raised the rifle, placed the sight to his eye and steadied his breathing. He watched as a man got out of the car. An odd looking man in a red coat, white pants, and a straw fedora. The man must be freezing, Ted thought. Then he heard it again and turned his head. The butt end of a gun came down upon his temple and he saw no more. As the darkness came, he heard a man's voice.

"Hello, Uncle."

About the Author

Raised in the "wilds" of northwestern NJ, Andy admittedly led a bit of a sheltered life. Books and a vivid imagination were a large part of his childhood. After an ill-fated and thankfully brief college career as a Chemistry student, he discovered a love of writing. He studied Literature and Creative Writing at The Richard Stockton College of NJ, where he first got the idea for *Multiples of Six*.

He now lives in the not-so-wilds of NJ, with his wife, son, two cats, two chinchillas, a salamander named Fred, and an ever-changing number of fish that may...just may...have cannibalistic tendencies. He looks forward to telling stories that people like to read.

If you liked this book, Andy hopes you'll take the time to let him know! If you didn't like it, he hopes you use kind words to tell him so. He can be found all over the internet in various forms:

http://www.andyrane.com

http://andyrane.blogspot.com

http://facebook.com/AndyRaneAuthor

Twitter: @andyraneauthor

Look for the second book of the *Six* trilogy, *Divisible by Six*, in late 2011/early 2012!

www.ingramcontent.com/pod-product-compliance
Lightning Source LLC
Chambersburg PA
CBHW062028170626
46813CB00001B/326